FORGET OR FORGIVE? NEVER!

SUSPENSE, DARK SECRETS, AND REVENGE WITH A TWIST

CHARLOTTE STUART

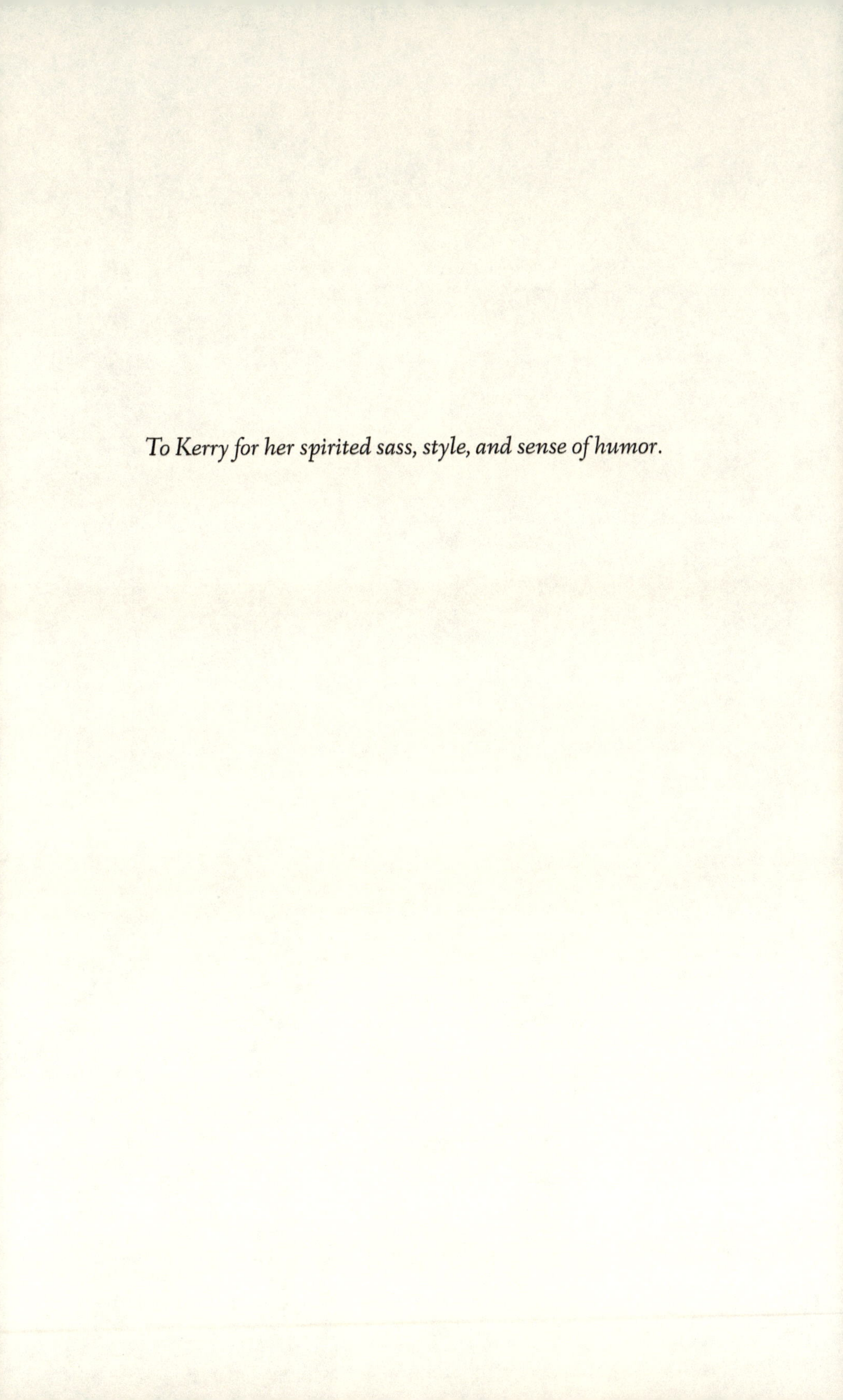

To Kerry for her spirited sass, style, and sense of humor.

*"I tell you everything that is really nothing,
and nothing of what is everything . . ."*
—Charles C. Finn, American poet

*"I can be changed by what happens to me.
But I refuse to be reduced by it."*
—Maya Angelou

"The world spins. We stumble on. It is enough."
—Colum McCann

EYE OF THE BEHOLDER

Being unattractive has been central to everything I am and everything I've done. I realize that doesn't excuse me in the eyes of the law. Nor will it earn me God's forgiveness, because I don't regret what I did. I'm not even a little bit sorry. If you've ever felt terribly wronged by someone, maybe you will sympathize with my journey of retribution.

My name is Callista. It means "most beautiful" in Greek. Unfortunately, my face is composed of mismatched and exaggerated features. Even as a baby my features were more gargoyle than Gerber's. In grade school someone nicknamed me "fugly," and it stuck. I think they liked the way the word rolled off the tongue, like a train gathering speed for an upcoming hill.

For some reason, people seem to assume that my appearance is somehow *my fault*. After all, it's who *I am*. But only on the outside. Inside I'm just like most people—a bit insecure, vulnerable, and desperate to be loved.

After finishing my PhD in math, I landed a great job. For once my intelligence seemed to be more important than my looks. It felt like a new beginning, a chance to be part of a team, an opportunity to prove my worth. I poured myself into my work. I was there earlier than anyone else and stayed after everyone had gone home. If someone needed assistance on something, I was there for them. I became the "go to" person when there was a glitch or a problem that needed solving.

At long last I felt like I was coming into my own. I was hardworking. I was smart. I was creative. Most important, no one contributed more to the bottom line of the company than I did. It was all there in black and white for my powerful and handsome boss Dane Weaver to see. I was convinced that someday soon, everyone would "see" me differently, my accomplishments would overshadow my unattractiveness, and I would get the recognition and acceptance I longed for.

Based on my life to that point, I should perhaps have kept my optimism in check. If I'd dampened my enthusiasm with a splash of reality, I might not have been leveled by the wave of disappointment I was about to experience. But I let my desire for acceptance and recognition drown out the inner voice that was urging caution.

When the huge and profitable Landberg project reached its conclusion and a meeting was scheduled to celebrate our success, I bought a new suit and got myself psychologically ready to accept the kudos that were about to come my way.

Then there was the incident.

2

THE INCIDENT

You may be wondering if I resemble either of my parents. The answer is "no." They are average in every way, from their looks to their lives, to their brain power. But as soon as I was able to understand verbal and nonverbal communication, I knew they were embarrassed by me. When I was a junior in high school, they decided I should get braces to straighten my crooked teeth. The braces weren't all that bad, but the kids started calling me Jaws, the character from the 007 movies. Anything for a laugh. After a very long year, my braces came off. My teeth were perfect. But my face hadn't changed. My parents seemed disappointed.

The only thing I had going for me was that I was smart. I completed my BS in under three years and got a full scholarship to go straight into a PhD program. Although I was sharper than most of my peers, I couldn't help but notice that students with lesser abilities got more kudos for their efforts than I did. More office time with professors. And more job offers after graduation. But in spite of these slights, as soon as I completed my degree, I landed my dream job at Keller and Eaves, a large prestigious company. And now I was about to be rewarded for my business acumen.

. . .

Everything about me isn't unattractive. My shoulder length, straight auburn hair is my best feature. On occasion in the past, I've draped it over the edges of my face, like a femme fatale from a movie classic. But I know it doesn't really hide what's underneath, so I usually settle for comfort and tuck it behind my ears. But because of the celebratory nature of the meeting I was about to attend, I fussed with my appearance more than usual. I used a curling iron on my hair to create loose, outward waves before deciding the fashion wasn't right for me. I put on lipstick, took off the lipstick, penciled on eyeliner, took one look, and wiped it off. I also attempted to camouflage a mole with some liquid concealer but found it only served to draw attention to the dark lump. I finally gave up. What I had accomplished on the project was far more important than my physical appearance.

My new suit was lovely though. It was dark green with a tradiional cut that suggested my curves without overstatement. I chose a light green blouse with subtle yellowish flowers to complement and brighten the forest green theme. The jade in my gold ring was the perfect final touch. From the neck down and from the back, I looked terrific.

I was ready.

Adriana, another project member, was coming out of the 3rd floor bathroom as I started down the hall to the conference room. She was wearing a short pencil skirt that clung like a second skin and a V-necked blouse that left nothing to the imagination, her round breasts elevated by a very efficient push-up bra. Appealing eye candy but not a particularly valuable project member. She'd performed liaison duties with management, busywork that the hardcore worker bees hadn't wanted to deal with. She'd also ordered our lunches and brought us coffee. Chatty and flirty, she was popular with everyone. Unfortunately, I seemed to always be the last person she served and had to force myself to refrain from complaining when my coffee was invariably cold. Still, it wasn't hard to warm up coffee in our microwave.

I didn't try to catch up to Adriana but trailed her down the hall to the conference room. My boss was standing next to the entrance and started smiling when he caught sight of her. He opened the conference room door, his hand on her back as they disappeared inside. I told myself he hadn't seen me and that was why the door practically shut in my face.

Fifteen team members had worked on the project full time for almost eight months. I had quickly become the unofficial leader because I was the one who came up with the plan to accomplish the ambitious but initially vague goals. I was also the troubleshooter for the problems that arose. Without me the project would not have met the desired parameters nor been implemented on schedule and on budget. This was my moment to shine, my chance to be recognized for all my business prowess and management abilities.

It was a large room, surrounded on three sides by beige walls, with tall windows overlooking the city across what was considered the front of the room. For this kind of meeting, they always pulled the vertical shades to provide a backdrop for whoever was speaking and to keep people focused on what was happening *in* the room instead of staring at the skyline. The shades were beige like the walls, and most of the men were wearing neutral or dark bland colors. Only the trendy attire of the women present provided a touch of brightness to the otherwise vanilla scene. Including Adriana's hot pink blouse.

The room was bursting with animated voices and wall-to-wall people. I saw a few of the Landberg executives talking to my boss near the front of the room. Adriana was still at his side, looking very pleased with herself. At the back there was a long table filled with pastries, fruit plates, and drinks. As I glanced around, I noted various Landberg team members chatting with each other or with other company elites. They all looked happy, pleased to be in the spotlight for a successful project. One of the leads looked over and waved at me. I smiled back and headed for the food table to get a cup of coffee.

There was a silver urn labeled "coffee" next to another silver urn labeled "decaf." There was also hot water and a selection of teas in a fancy wood box with a brass clasp, each section labeled so you didn't have to sort through to find what you wanted. After putting some cream in my coffee, I eyed the pastries. My stomach said "go for it," but I didn't want to get caught with my mouth full if someone came over to talk with me, so I resisted.

I might as well have filled my plate. No one approached me. The chatter level had increased in volume, and people were smiling and laughing as if the coffee was liquor and they were at a party. After taking a few sips of my coffee, I joined a small group of colleagues and stood near a tiny gap in their tight circle. They were fully engaged in conversation, and I felt like I was hearing the punchline without knowing what the joke was about. Although I had worked closely with them on the project, they weren't personal friends, so I felt out of my comfort zone with casual conversation. I was relieved when there was a squeal from a microphone and everyone turned toward the front of the room.

"Please take your seats," my boss announced.

After dropping my coffee cup in a waste basket, I found a spot at the end of a row about two-thirds of the way back, straightened my jacket and smoothed my skirt as I sat, then tucked my feet with their low-heeled shoes under the folding chair. I wondered if my boss would ask me to stand when he acknowledged our success. Maybe he would have all of the team members stand. Then my heart almost stopped beating as I saw him looking around, his eyes settling on me as he waved me forward. I was so excited I almost tripped over my own feet as I hurried to the front of the room.

Dane met me at the end of the front row of seats and said, "Ah . . ." Then he hesitated as if . . . as if he couldn't remember my name. "I forgot to bring the chart with the timeline projections. Could you run to my office and get it?" He turned and headed toward the microphone before I could ask any questions.

As I left the conference room and made my way to his office, two competing thoughts fought for attention. Maybe he wanted me out of the room so he could say something about me before I returned. Or maybe he had simply forgotten the chart and needed someone to fetch it. The latter seemed the more likely. If only he had referred to me by name. And said "thanks" or "I'd appreciate it" before dismissing me like an errand boy.

I took the stairs to the sixth floor rather than wait for the elevator. The chart was on the table along the north wall of his office. I rolled it up and headed back to the conference room. When I arrived, I noted that the team members had apparently been standing and were just taking their seats. Adriana was at the front of the room with Dane. He saw me and urged me forward. I half expected him to ask me to stay when I handed him the chart, but he didn't. Confused and uncomfortable, I headed back to my seat, but someone had taken it in my absence. Not wanting to disrupt anyone by trying to slip past them to get to an empty chair, I went to the back of the room and stood next to a table filled with company brochures. I was the only one standing.

"Now that you've met the team," Dane said. What? His statement felt like a physical blow. I put my hand on the table to steady myself as he continued. "Let me remind you how quickly this incredible project was completed. Adriana, since you were instrumental in making it happen, why don't you summarize for us."

Adriana stepped over to the chart and began her summary. I heard her voice but was having a hard time listening to what she was saying. All I could think of was Dane saying "now that you've met the team" and then referring to Adriana as being "instrumental in making it happen." Was this some kind of joke? Did he honestly not understand the inner workings of the project? My mind darted back to the few conversations we'd had in the past. Shouldn't he have realized I was the only one on the team with the knowledge to turn unclear goals into reality? Did he really think Adriana was smart enough to have performed a vital function? And why were my colleagues sitting there grinning and applauding as if what Dane had said was true?

They all knew that I had been the unofficial person in charge and that Adriana had been little more than a flunky.

I continued standing at the back of the room, my mind awash with contradictory thoughts. I wanted to protest the injustice of the situation while at the same time I wanted to run away, to leave behind the smiling toadies and the unworthy Adriana. This wasn't the first time I'd been ignored or overlooked, but I still hadn't seen it coming. I couldn't bear to listen to what Adriana was saying. Nor was I able to pay attention after the applause for her ended and Dane began giving his closing remarks. Instead, all my mental energy was focused on trying to corral my chaotic thoughts and decide what I should do after the presentation when everyone started milling about, eating, chatting, and congratulating themselves for a job well done. Should I pretend the slight was nothing and attempt to blend in? Given the blow to my bruised ego, was that even a possibility? How could I remain silent about the injustice I'd experienced? How could I overlook Adriana's betrayal and my boss's arbitrary dismissal? How could I look colleagues in the eye knowing they had supported this charade?

When the final applause died down, I slipped out the door and went back to my cubicle.

It wasn't unusual for me to be the only one at my desk in our designated team area, but everything now felt different. I had assumed all of my hard work would eventually pay off; but I'd been duped. Deceived. Still, I was uncertain what my response to being overlooked and disrespected should be. I couldn't think of anything I could say or do that could make me feel okay about what had taken place.

When I heard someone coming, I panicked. I wasn't ready to talk to anyone yet. But it was too late to leave, so I looked down and pretended to be studying some papers on my desk. James, one of the people who had sometimes stayed late to work on the project, stopped at my desk and waited for me to look up. When I didn't, he said, "I didn't see you in there when Dane introduced us."

I glanced at him and struggled to keep my voice neutral. "He sent me to get the timeline chart."

"Oh, that's too bad." James paused, shifting his weight from one foot to the other, like he wanted to say more but didn't know how to say it.

I wanted him to go away, but I couldn't resist asking, "Were you surprised he gave so much credit to Adriana?"

He hesitated for a moment. "Yes and no. She *was* the liaison and she's, well, she's very pretty." A pink tinge flooded his pale complexion as he added, "Maybe he's sleeping with her." He said it quickly, as if he was embarrassed for even thinking it. Then he gave me a weak smile and went to his desk.

Perhaps I should have accepted his explanation and moved on. But after that conversation I began having dark moments filled with black thoughts. Past slights mingled with inner rants about unfairness. When other team members returned and stopped by to say they were sorry I'd missed being thanked for my role in the project's success, my anger was fueled rather than mollified. I appreciated that they were trying to be kind, that they were acknowledging that I should have been recognized for my work. But no one had stepped up to name my contributions in public. Even though realistically I couldn't imagine how that would have been possible, I found myself wallowing in self-pity and felt my heart grow cold, slowly contracting into ice.

Then Adriana returned to the hail of "well done" and "kudos" and "way to go," even though everyone knew she hadn't made any real contributions to the success of the project. Nevertheless, if she had said something kind to me instead of walking past without so much as a glance in my direction, what happened next might never have happened. But she chose to ignore me. And that was the point at which self-pity turned into an overwhelming desire for revenge. Dane would pay for the wound he had inflicted. And so would Adriana.

3

DANE

A plan began to form in my mind, one that would even the score, at least in this one tiny part of my life. But first, I decided to give Dane a second chance. I'm not sure why, although it was partly in the hope that he would say something that would keep me from going down the path I was about to travel. Once committed, I knew I would follow through. I always do. That's one of my strengths. Although in this instance, it could also be my downfall.

Dane's office was two floors directly above our project cubicles. He didn't have a corner office, but he did have an outstanding view of the city through a glass wall that ran the length of his space. The glass wall along the hallway had blinds for privacy and a regular door. The blinds were pulled when I arrived unannounced. I knew that if I tried to make an appointment, it could take a while. He was a busy man. And I wasn't prepared to wait.

I knocked on his door, a bit timidly, I admit, but he heard it. "Come in," he called.

When he saw me enter, he looked surprised. "Oh," he said. "I thought it was the coffee I'd asked for." He glanced at his computer screen. "I don't see an appointment."

"I'm sorry; I don't have an appointment," I said, my voice apologetic, my head bowed slightly forward as if I was asking for forgiveness. In spite of my business accomplishments, I still felt socially inadequate when dealing with others.

He quickly regained his composure. Using his official voice, he said: "You can make an appointment with Connie." He was dismissing me. It was awkward not to take the hint, but I'd come this far and didn't want to leave without getting some answers. Answers that would take me on a journey from which there was no turning back.

"This will just take a few minutes," I said, managing to sound more confident than I felt.

He hesitated then waved his hand, like a lord granting a peasant an audience. "Get on with it, then."

"You *do* know who I am, don't you?" This was his first test.

"Yes, you worked on the Landberg project with Adriana."

I refrained from asking if he knew my name; it was obvious he didn't.

"Do you know what her role was?"

"Of course."

"So, you understand she had nothing to do with the development and implementation of the actual project?" This was his second test.

"Don't be ridiculous."

Ridiculous? I wasn't the one besotted with someone because of their perky cleavage and suck-up demeanor.

"Do you know what role I played?" Be careful how you answer, I silently warned. Three strikes and you're . . . dead.

"As I'm sure you know, I wasn't involved in the details of the project. It's my job to manage. And that's what I did. Now if you're through, I have an appointment coming up."

I stood there a moment, staring at the handsome face that was scowling at me, obviously wishing I would go away. Was it just yesterday that I'd thought he was smart enough to see beyond my appearance, to appreciate my ingenuity and competence based on what

I'd done for the company? I'd even fantasized about becoming romantically involved with him, although realistically I'd known that was never going to happen. For the first time I questioned my own reasons for looking up to this man. Sure, he was an executive, but had I assumed that he was good at his job primarily because he was attractive?

He raised his eyebrows dismissively. "I believe our conversation is over." The unstated command was "so get the hell out of my office."

How had I thought this rude, shit-for-brains manager was worth working sixty hours a week for so he and his bimbo could revel in the glory of success? *My* success.

"Yes," I agreed. "Our conversation is over." It was time for action.

Since I'd given my boss a second chance, I decided to extend the same opportunity for a reprieve to Adriana. I was curious what she would say if it was just the two of us. Perhaps she had been so flattered by all of the attention showered on her by her boss that she couldn't bring herself to speak up and admit that she hadn't been at the helm during the project. The praise and admiration might have been irresistible. Even though she knew they were undeserved. If so, that was something I could understand, although perhaps not completely forgive.

I caught up with her in the breakroom. She was chatting animatedly with two other admins, ones who had never been elevated to serve on a project team like she had. They started giggling about something, then one of them signaled the other two that they should keep it down because someone—me—had come in. I walked over, caught Adriana's eye, and asked if I could have a few minutes. She didn't look pleased by the interruption, but the two admins quickly retreated, leaving us alone in the room.

"I wanted to congratulate you," I began. Adriana gave me a closed-mouth smile and seemed to relax. Had she anticipated that I was going to challenge her right to recognition for the project? "I assume you were supposed to bring the chart with you." I don't know where the thought came from, but it suddenly all made sense.

"I forgot it," she said, sounding ever-so-slightly defensive.

"And I assume you suggested to Dane that he send me to fetch it."

Now she was starting to look uncomfortable—as well she should be if I was right.

"Someone had to get it. We needed it for the presentation." The reference to "we" rankled. Also, she didn't lie very well, a definite tell with the way she glanced up to the left and avoided looking me in the eyes.

"Here's what I don't understand," I said. "What difference would it have made if I'd stood up as part of the team, since you already knew you were going to be given credit for the success of the project?"

"Well, I wouldn't put it like that."

"How would you put it then?" I wasn't about to let her off the hook. There was too much at stake. For both of us.

"I was the liaison." She sounded so proud.

"Do you know who came up with the plan, who did all the troubleshooting and shepherded it through to completion?"

"There were fifteen *equal* team members. No one was no designated leader," she said, citing our original mission. The approach had been an experiment suggested by a consultant who didn't stay around to see how it worked out. If I hadn't stepped in, it would have been an unmitigated failure.

A manager from another team came in and smiled warmly at Adriana before going over to get some coffee. She smiled back, a toothy smile to let him know she was available.

"Sorry, I have to go," Adriana said, pushing her chair away from the table.

Before she could leave, I said, "Remember the proverb: you reap what you sow."

She stood up and after a moment's hesitation, glared at me. "Is that a threat?"

"No, it's a proverb."

She looked confused, then said. "Well, if that's all—"

I didn't bother with a reply. She'd flunked her test.

4

THE PLAN

I excel at creating and implementing corporate plans, but what I needed to do next was unlike anything I'd ever done before. The goal was easy to articulate: eliminate Dane Weaver without getting caught. He had become for me the symbol of all the bullying and putdowns I'd endured over the years. Although he may have acted out of ignorance, I'd given him the opportunity to reconsider what he'd done. Instead, he had committed the ultimate betrayal by ignoring the facts and continuing to let himself be blinded by Adriana's charms. Perhaps this didn't justify a death sentence, but once the idea took hold, I became obsessed with figuring out whether I could make it happen.

Statistically, less than half of the murders in the United States are solved. But that meant that half are, and I didn't want to go to jail. Putting together a plan to rid the world of Dane Weaver was not only new territory for me but tricky to research. Anything you do online is traceable, crime novels aren't necessarily specific or trustworthy, and true crime books are about criminals who were caught. It's helpful to know what to avoid, but I was looking for a creative approach that fit my particular situation and skill set. I not only needed to come up with a detailed plan, I had to do a careful risk assessment by analyzing and tweaking each step in the process to ensure I could get away with it.

The first task was determining what method to use. This was complicated by my personal feelings about whether it was necessary for Dane to understand why he was about to die. Was the message as important as the final act? Or was taking away Dane's life enough to satisfy my desire for retribution, my overwhelming need to get payback for all the pain I'd suffered at the hands of others over the years.

If I wanted to confront him to let him know why he was about to meet his maker, I would have to use a threat, probably a weapon of some sort, to keep him from simply walking away. Since he was undoubtedly stronger than me, a gun was the most obvious choice for that purpose. But guns are both traceable and difficult to dispose of efficiently. There was also the possibility that he would call my bluff, and I end up shooting him before I had a chance to explain why he was being targeted. Even if I could think of some way to lure him to a remote location, I would still have to deal with the same issues: how to keep him there while we talked, and how to cope with the aftermath.

Sneaking up on him from behind and hitting him with a heavy object so I could tie him up and take him somewhere for a private talk seemed plausible on the surface. But I had no idea the amount of force needed to render someone helpless, and I didn't want to get into a physical fight that I might not win. Besides, transporting a body, even a live one, posed all sorts of challenges.

As I ticked through the list, every approach I could think of that would give me time to castigate him verbally before I ended his time on this earth appeared to involve unpleasant or high-risk behaviors. I finally concluded it was best to gloat on my own after the deed was done.

Having ruled out face-to-face elimination methods, I considered other approaches favored by crime fiction. A car accident due to faulty equipment was a popular ploy. I wasn't against a cliché approach, but anything involving manual manipulation of a vehicle seemed unnecessarily complicated, as well as too unpredictable. A push down the stairs—again, too unpredictable. Staging a suicide— from what I've read, faking them can be tricky. Nor did Dane seem like the suicidal type. An overdose was a possibility. But unless I could somehow con him into taking something on his own, coming up with a way to force him to do so took me back to square one.

After much deliberation, I settled on poison. I realize it's known as a female murderer's weapon of choice, but it had the advantage of being something I could accomplish at work where there were plenty of suspects. Nor would I have to be present when it took effect, thereby reducing the risk of being caught.

Task One decided, I turned to Task Two. It involved researching his eating and drinking habits while at the office. If he had a routine, planning his demise would be challenging but doable. If not, being prepared to take advantage of a situation when it arose was a possibility, but not a very practical one. My cubicle wasn't even on the same floor as his office, and I couldn't come up with a viable way to administer poison in a public meeting.

After considerable back-and-forth deliberation, I decided that if he didn't have predictable patterns for eating or drinking at work, I would have to come up with a Plan B. But first, I would investigate whether Plan A was an option.

Assuming for the moment that he was a man of habit, Task Three was deciding on the "what" and involved a series of sub points for consideration. Whatever poison I chose would have to be something I could get hold of in a way that couldn't be traced to me. That automatically eliminated a fair number of options. I also wanted something that required only one dose; otherwise, I would have to take risks on multiple occasions. Ideally it would be something not usually tested for. And finally, it had to be fast acting. If it didn't work fast enough, I didn't want him taken to a hospital emergency room where some hotshot intern might earn his chops by figuring it out and saving

Dane's life at the last minute. Like in some TV medical drama. If he was forewarned that someone was trying to harm him, it might be impossible to get a second chance.

When I got started on Task Two, I quickly discovered that tracking Dane's habits and schedule was even more problematic than I'd imagined. I could hardly spook around his office without a reason. I didn't even have an excuse for being on that floor in the building. Nor did I have access to his calendar. I could identify meetings he was likely to attend, but that didn't do me any good. I needed to find a time when he was eating or drinking alone in his office. Employees ate at their desks all the time, surely even executives did that upon occasion.

Then, merely by accident, one day in the break room I overheard Connie, Dane's admin, complaining about him expecting coffee midmorning at 10:00 sharp and again at 3:00 on the dot. French press, one cup made from his own special beans.

Gotcha, I said to myself.

The only question was whether there was something I could mix with his coffee that would get the job done. On to Task Three, the poison of choice. That turned out to be easier than anticipated.

The library is a wonderful resource. There are cameras, but they are mostly visible, intended as a deterrent as much as for crime detection. I often went to the library to browse books, so it wasn't an unusual activity for me. And I'd looked up mushrooms before several years earlier when I'd gone mushroom picking on my own, using pictures from a book I'd perused as a guide. I'd ended up being too uncertain about whether the ones I'd gathered were safe to eat and thrown the lot out. But this time, after studying pictures in a number of books, I felt fairly confident about what to look for and where to find them. And this time I wouldn't have to toss any; the more poisonous the better. Once in hand, I could grind them up, sneak into where he kept his supply of coffee, and mix them in with his expensive special blend.

I had a hard time deciding between Death Caps and Destroying

Angels, both from the Amanita family. Like their names suggest, they are toxic and produce painful symptoms that can kill. Within 6-24 hours after ingesting as little as one-half of a mushroom, the person suffers from sharp abdominal pains, vomiting, and diarrhea. After about 24 hours, the symptoms ease, and there is a period of false recovery for several days. Then the symptoms return and may follow with heart and kidney failure that can require an immediate organ transplant or result in death. From ingestion to death in less than two weeks. A pretty miserable two weeks followed by oblivion.

The Death Cap is the cause of the majority of deaths from mushrooms. Probably because it closely resembles a number of edible species. It is characterized by a large 2-to-6-inch cap which is mostly white but may have greenish to olive-brown tones. Death Caps may also have a faint, sweet aroma, or no odor at all. Not a helpful distinguishing characteristic for the amateur mushroom hunter.

The Destroying Angels has a white stalk and gills with a cap that is either white or white around the edges with a yellowish or tan center. Like the Death Cap, they are easily mistaken for a number of other edible mushrooms.

Both mushrooms are found singly or in groups in parks, wooded areas and even in back yards. Neither have known antidotes, but if treated immediately, a few people survive. That assumes the source of the illness can be readily identified. In Dane's case, I doubted there would be a quick diagnosis. In fact, I was counting on it.

The time I'd thrown out the mushrooms I'd picked, I was so concerned they could be toxic that I'd even tossed the basket I'd used, thankful I'd worn gloves when I was harvesting them. Now I hoped that when I returned to the same area that my fears had been justified. That I really had stumbled upon an area where there were a fair number of deadly fungi.

A weekend hike in the same area was all it took to find and verify. I had my choice of either Death Caps or Destroying Angels. Although I leaned toward the Destroying Angel because of its name, I finally chose the Death Cap for its reputation as a killer.

Consuming as little as half a mushroom was supposedly sufficient for my purpose, and boiling mushrooms wasn't supposed to diminish their toxicity. There was, however, one question that remained: would drinking the liquid from the mushroom/coffee mixture as opposed to actually eating the mushroom do the trick? After doing some calculations, I decided to put four mushrooms in 12-ounces of coffee beans. To put in more might call attention to the difference in texture and color.

I felt a bit guilty about doctoring a well-known brand of coffee that I also personally favored—in case it was discovered as the source of his illness or death. It would be unfortunate if my actions resulted in a nation-wide recall that hurt coffee sales; my complaint was with Dane, not the coffee company. On the other hand, I thought it likely that the company had insurance to cover things like that if officials identified the source and falsely assumed it had been added to the coffee *before* time of purchase. My hope, of course, was that the poison wouldn't be identified in any normal bloodwork that was run during the course of his illness, at least not until it was too late.

Once I'd decided on the means, I focused on delivery details. I'd managed a reconnaissance of the area around his office one night when I'd worked late, assiduously avoiding cameras and late-night cleaners. There was a tiny room adjacent to Connie's office where she kept the coffee and brewing equipment. It wasn't locked. While checking it out, I noted two encouraging things. First, Connie obviously didn't wait until the last minute to grind his coffee. She kept the ground coffee in a glass container next to the coffee maker on a side table. Second, the glass container appeared to be identical to the one in the break room downstairs. I could borrow the break room's container, put in the concoction I prepared, then switch it with Connie's container. An in-and-out operation. Of course, I could still get caught making the switch. But no crime worth committing is entirely without risk.

With means and delivery decided, I turned to the mixture preparation stage. Unfortunately, the Death Cap was too light to blend with dark brown coffee beans, but I remembered reading an article I'd stumbled across about an activity for kids—tie-dyeing mushrooms by applying food coloring with a spray bottle. At the time, I'd only looked at the article because I found the idea bizarre but amusing; now I was glad I'd read it. It took some experimenting to achieve the right shade of brown, and if Connie paid close attention, she might notice some color variations or realize the texture for the ground beans was off. But I was counting on the fact that Connie disliked making the coffee in the first place, irritation hopefully clouding concentration.

My only other concerns were the brewing aroma, taste, and ensuring no one else drank the mixture. For obvious reasons I couldn't taste test the outcome. I only hoped the coffee smell dominated the slight mushroom scent and that the flavor wouldn't be altered enough for him to reject the coffee. Afterwards, I needed to remove whatever coffee remained of his private, doctored reserve, just in case someone decided to poach some of the expensive beans. Stealing a few beans from the boss shouldn't result in a death sentence.

The night of the exchange, everything went exactly as planned. And if it hadn't been for a last-minute change in Dane's 10:00 coffee routine, it would have been the perfect crime.

5

PRIME SUSPECT

When Detective Peters introduced himself, flashed his credentials, and said that he had a few questions for me about Dane's death, I was barely able to control my panic. My "of course" came out weak and a bit husky, and I had to force myself to look him in the eyes, but I didn't think my inner turmoil was obvious.

"I'm set up in the conference room down the hall," he said. As we headed together to the conference room, I caught a slight whiff of a musky aftershave. Was Detective Peters concerned with his masculine image? Unlike me, he had a forgettable face, a standard set of features with dirt brown hair and matching eyes. Average height and build. Nothing to stand out. Nothing to make people stop and stare. I envied him that.

On the short walk to the conference room, I concentrated on steadying my breathing. I didn't sense that Detective Peters was a coiled snake waiting to strike, but I couldn't afford to let my guard down. I had to be careful about what I said and how I behaved and avoid giving off a single guilty vibe.

Dane's death had been in the local newspaper the past week, as filler between more important stories. He was, after all, not a celebrity, just one of many executives in a large company. It was billed as the *mysterious death of a high-ranking executive at Keller and Eaves.* You had to read most of the article to get to his actual name. What the reporter found fascinating took the lead—the sudden death of an otherwise healthy, middle-aged male. According to the article, he'd become ill at the end of a work day. Later that same evening, he was rushed to the emergency room with stomach problems and returned home after his condition stabilized. They assumed it was food poisoning. For several days after that, he had what appeared to be a full recovery. Then four days later he unexpectedly died from kidney failure. The cause was being investigated. The reporter's message: death can strike anyone when they least expect it.

That was the only news story I'd found, although his death may have been mentioned on some local TV news channel. It seemed to me that if officials considered it a possible homicide, it would have merited more news coverage. Although maybe the police suspected foul play but were sitting on the evidence to gain leverage when questioning suspects. I doubted Detective Peters would volunteer any additional information about cause of death during my interview with him, but it seemed to me that it would not be inappropriate to ask.

There was a long table in the conference room with enough chairs to seat ten people comfortably. At the far end of the table there was a carafe of coffee, a stack of paper cups, and a row of plastic cups filled with sugar packets, artificial creamer, and swizzle sticks. Were the cups' contents supplied by the company, or had they been lifted from a Starbucks or a MacDonalds, I wondered? Would a police officer do that, or were they a gift for a man in uniform? Did that kind of thing really happen?

Most of the chairs had been folded up and were leaning against the back wall. There were two chairs placed on opposite sides of the table at the far end near the coffee. He motioned for me to have a seat.

"Coffee?" he asked. I nodded yes. I didn't really want any, but it would give me something to do if I needed time to think. "Sugar?"

"No thanks." I was pleased to hear my voice come out steady and confident.

He poured two cups of coffee, put a packet of sugar in one and handed me the other. I didn't say anything, waiting for him to make the first move.

"Dane Weaver was your boss," he said.

He had a tablet with what looked like a list of names in front of him, but the print was too sloppy and too small for me to read upside-down at a glance. I noted there appeared to be checkmarks by most of the names though. If it was a list of interviewees, I was apparently one of the last people he was interviewing. I must have been away from my desk when he approached my officemates.

"Yes, he was." I added, "Tragic to die so young. Do they know cause of death yet?"

"They're working on it." He picked up another tablet and placed it on top of the list of names and took a quick look at it before asking, "How long had you worked for him?"

"Just over two years."

"Was he a good boss?"

"The best," I said without hesitation. "Very supportive."

He glanced down, moving his finger down the tablet page. "Do you like your job?" His eyes met mine with a penetrating stare.

I wasn't expecting that one. "It's a good company, and I've been engaged in a series of interesting projects. So, yes, I like my job."

"No problems with anyone?"

Oh, oh. Tread lightly. "No. I'm focused on work. I don't socialize much." That was a lie—I don't socialize at all.

"What about with Adriana Lane?"

I quickly decided to be straight about what had happened. "Do you mean was I upset because she got public credit for a project that I was largely responsible for?"

From the way he tapped a finger on his coffee cup, I guessed he already knew about that. "Why don't you tell me about the project and your relationship with Ms. Lane."

"Well, she was the liaison for the project, and I was a member of the implementation team. No one was officially named as 'leader,' but because of my expertise I often took the lead. She didn't have much to do with the actual planning and day-to-day operations. But she is a very attractive and articulate woman, and as liaison, she was the face of the project. That's why she stood alongside Dane at the project completion celebration. Personally, I thought she got too much credit based on her limited role in the project and said as much to her." I took a sip of coffee to consider what else I wanted to say. "But I understand that's how things work in large corporations. And," I added, "in life generally." I took another sip. "Does that answer your question?"

"What was her relationship with Dane Weaver?"

"He was her boss."

"Do you think there was any more to it than that?"

"I suspected as much, but I don't really know." Where was this going?

"Did you ever observe any dissention between them?"

I took another sip. If I didn't watch out, I soon wouldn't have any coffee to sip as a diversion tactic. "I don't know how to answer that."

"Did you ever hear them arguing?"

"Not really."

"That's vague."

"Why are you asking me these questions?" It was beginning to sound like they had picked up on something unusual about Dane's death. It also sounded like Adriana was a possible suspect. Unless this was some elaborate strategy to get me to implicate myself.

Detective Peters leaned back and studied me. He didn't look put off by what he saw, just thoughtful, like he was trying to read my mind to gauge the best interrogation approach. Finally, he said, "Your colleagues describe you as brilliant and hard working. You are apparently the go-to person on projects. Always patient. Never critical. A problem solver rather than a finger pointer. That's high praise."

"It pleases me that anyone on the team would say those things." It also surprised me that they would describe me that way to a detective.

"They said that if anyone in the group was a neutral observer, it was you. That you are only interested in the work."

"I try to stay focused on the job at hand and not get distracted by gossip or petty arguments."

"My guess is that you are also attuned to any problems with working relationships that could impact output."

"I do my best to create a collaborative climate."

He laughed. "You are also very careful with your words."

"I like sticking to facts."

"And you didn't actually witness any problems between Adriana and Dane, but . . ." he paused. "Somewhere deep down did you suspect all wasn't perfect in paradise? Would that be fair to say, even without facts to back up your suspicions?"

"You probably know that I have every reason to resent Adriana, so I wouldn't want that to cloud what I might say about her. If you have any specific questions . . .?"

He reached out and picked up his coffee. Was he, too, using his coffee as a way to bide for time to think? "Let's say there's something suspicious about Weaver's death. Given that, who do you think I should talk to?"

I paused and pretended to consider his question. "He was a good manager, but he managed from a distance. I'm sure you've already talked to people who knew him much better than I did. And I know nothing about his personal life. But Connie, his admin, would be at the top of my list. She kept his schedule and acted as gatekeeper. And she's a smart, observant woman."

"Did you know she makes coffee for him, orders his lunches and even organizes snacks?"

"No, but that doesn't surprise me. He was a busy man." I paused. "Is that somehow significant?" My heart had skipped a beat at the word "coffee."

"We're not sure yet."

"Waiting on facts before you point fingers?"

He blinked, then said, "No one credited you with dry humor."

"It's in my Meyers Briggs profile though."

Detective Peters smiled. "Well, Callista Jones, you are an interesting woman." He stood up. "That's all I have for now. But if you think of anything, here's my card." He handed me a small white rectangular card with an official looking insignia and his name and contact information. Then he reached out to shake my hand. His hand was warm, his handshake firm but not too firm. I found myself smiling back at him, warning myself not to let down my guard. He might not be a snake, but he was still undoubtedly a very dangerous man under the circumstances.

Several team members were huddled in conversation when I returned. Under most circumstances I would have passed by without making eye contact, but I was curious. I stopped next to them, and they quickly made space for me. "Did you just get interviewed by Detective Peters?" someone asked.

"Yes, any idea what's going on?"

"It's about Adriana," someone else said.

"What about her?" I asked.

"We heard that she wanted Dane to divorce his wife, but he refused."

That was a showstopper for me. "Really?" I asked. I wasn't sure exactly what I was questioning, but I wanted to keep the conversation going.

"Of course he wouldn't leave his wife," another team member said. "He had kids and a comfortable life. As well as wealthy in-laws. Adriana should have known he was stringing her along."

"Why is a possible affair relevant?" I asked. "What am I missing?"

"There are rumors that he was poisoned." Everyone nodded in agreement.

"Poisoned?" Damn. They knew. "But I thought he was sick from something he ate and recovered. Was that related to his death?"

"Well, according to one of the admins, Dane skipped lunch the day he became ill. All he had was his usual morning coffee, which Adriana took to him. Connie usually does that, but Adriana apparently insisted. Connie was upset but couldn't stop her. In addition, Adriana told her not to put through any calls while she was in the office with him."

"But even if she put something in his coffee, he'd recovered, right?" I said.

"If she was angry enough to do it once, who's to say that she didn't try again?" There were murmurs of agreement.

"Where did the rumor of poison come from?" I asked.

"Why else would the police be paying so much attention to the fact that Adriana served him his coffee on the day he got ill?"

"I'm not sure that actually proves anything," I said, secretly pleased that Adriana had picked that particular day to take Dane his coffee. If they tracked the poison but couldn't actually find evidence that she was the one who had put it in his drink, she would at least go through hell trying to prove her innocence. It would be an added bonus if they found her guilty. If they did, I wouldn't need to come up with any way to embarrass or retaliate against her.

"Well, they wouldn't be investigating Weaver's death if the circumstances weren't suspicious," someone said. "And they've asked everyone about Adriana's relationship with him."

"I think it's too soon to jump to conclusions," I said, hiding the smile that had formed in my head. I left the group to continue their gossip session and returned to my desk. What a delightful development.

Later that day I ran into Adriana in the breakroom. She glanced at me as if to check whether I was friend or foe, even though we had never been on friendly terms. I decided to be supportive; it was the least I could do.

"No one really believes you poisoned Dane," I said, getting right to the point.

As if on cue, she started to cry. "Thank you for saying that, but I'm afraid they do."

"It's too bad he died right after the two of you had a disagreement. That's an unfortunate coincidence." Although I would have planned it that way if I had known.

She wiped her eyes with a Kleenex and took a deep breath. "It was all my fault. I shouldn't have given him an ultimatum."

"No, it wasn't your fault. He wasn't being honest with you." She apparently needed to talk to someone so much that she was willing to overlook the fact that the only other time we'd engaged in conversation was after the Landberg fiasco.

"I . . . I thought he loved me." The tears returned, streaming down her face, and she started making little snuffling noises. Her mascara joined the tears to turn the rivulets into dark, squiggly lines.

"It's possible to love more than one person," I said, as if I would know. "What you need to do is remain calm and let the police complete their investigation. I'm sure they will figure out that you weren't responsible for what happened to Dane."

"I would never have hurt him," she said before breaking down completely. She collapsed on a chair and put her hands up to her face to cover her roiling tears and muffle the sobs.

Two people from another team came in, looked in my direction and raised their eyebrows in question. I put a hand on Adriana's shoulder and said, "It will be all right. The police will find out who did this to Dane. You're not going to be arrested for his death."

Upon hearing my sympathetic comments, the two people quickly departed without getting whatever they had come in for. I patted her shoulder a few more times and left her alone to regroup.

Adriana might not be arrested for Dane's death. They couldn't prove her guilt . . . since she wasn't guilty. But circumstantial evidence might be sufficient to keep her in the prime suspect spotlight. And, as long as she remained the focus of their investigation, they wouldn't be spending time looking elsewhere. Like at me, for instance. Thank you, Adriana.

6

____

A LITTLE LIST

Most people have felt put down by someone. Or ghosted without knowing why. Or bullied. Or had their feelings hurt. Or been ridiculed or embarrassed by someone in front of others. I've heard people say that a single such event marked them for life. For me, however, it was a lifetime of mistreatment and mockery, death by a thousand cuts. A thousand acts of abuse that sucked the joy out of my life one cut at a time.

Of course, there have been people who have been kind to me too. But often times I've sensed that they felt sorry for me rather than harboring true affection for the ugly duckling that I was. It's possible that the hard shell I erected to deflect rejection had made it impossible to recognize sincere overtures of friendship. It was easier and less painful to isolate myself than to keep hoping for acceptance. However, when I started having some success at work, I let my defenses down. In retrospect, that was a mistake. And now that I've had a sweet sip of the nectar of retaliation, I've started thinking about specific people in my past who deserved to be held accountable for their behaviors.

In retrospect, I realize that poisoning Dane may have been an overreaction. He became symbolic of past wrongs for me and was sacrificed for the collective behaviors of bullies and mean-spirited people I'd encountered over the years. Not that I regret what I did, but I wasn't going to become a serial killer. In the future I would make the punishment fit the crime.

Unlike Gilbert and Sullivan's "Little List" of irritating people, the list I've started compiling consists of anyone who in some way caused me some level of pain in the past. My initial brainstorming session filled several pages with names of my personal tormentors. I added a few more as unpleasant memories came back to me in dribs and drabs, sharp reminders of how unkindness had shaped my psyche. Next, I set about prioritizing the names on my list based on the egregiousness of their behavior. Finally, I considered potential opportunities for getting even balanced against risk levels.

Putting together action plans for revenge required both creativity and caution. For instance, I had to make sure there were no patterns that would lead back to me. Like targeting too many individuals from the same time period or group. Or re-using the same retaliation strategies. I also had to be inventive and mindful when researching people and topics. Any investigation I did had to be done discreetly, without calling attention to myself. I'd been lucky with my first target, but only with very careful planning would I be able to work my way through my list without tripping up somewhere.

The very day after I started compiling my list, an opportunity appeared as bright as the sun coming out from behind a cloud—an invitation to my high school class reunion. Quite a few of my former classmates had made my list, but only two were in the top five: Taylor Finn and Hugh Graham.

Taylor had been the yell queen and the driving force behind a group of girls who paraded their popularity in part by putting down those less fortunate. I wasn't the only person whose life they made miserable, but somehow none of us victims had banded together to either commiserate or defend ourselves. Looking back, that seemed a shame. But at the time, my misery was personal. They mocked me in public every chance they got, calling out my flaws, making up jokes about my appearance, time and again reducing me to tears and destroying my self-esteem. One time, Taylor cornered me at my locker and asked how I was able to live with the face I saw when I looked in a mirror. She almost sounded like she truly wanted to know what it felt like to be ugly. But why she bothered to confront me like that, I don't know. Perhaps she reported the conversation back to her buddies, and they all had a good laugh.

Hugh and Taylor were an item for senior year. He was the stereotypical dumb jock. Good at football and attracting girls, but without any brain cells to spare. If he'd applied himself to his studies, he might have done okay, but instead he cheated on tests and conned people into writing his papers for him. I admit to being one of those conned, and I might have continued helping him if I hadn't heard Taylor making a comment to a group of her friends about Hugh sweet-talking "lovesick Fugly" into doing his homework. Everyone laughed, of course. The truth of her remark pierced the fog of my self-deception with a quick and painful jab. He'd taken advantage of my vulnerability while apparently making fun of me behind my back.

The next time he asked for my assistance, I refused. That not only surprised him but ticked him off. And he wasn't about to let me off the hook without letting me know what a loser I was. So, he encouraged his male friends to harass me whenever the opportunity presented itself. They offered me their cocks, asked me if I wanted to suck them, and engaged in vagina-penis banter when I was within earshot. They also made comments about my looks: "*She is sooo ugly the frog ran away when she tried to kiss it.*" Stupid things. Anything they could think of to get me to react. One time someone came up behind me and reached around to grab my breasts. Then he loudly proclaimed how great I was from behind. For the most part, I tried to ignore their taunts, but this physical attack was too much. I went limp long enough for him to loosen his grip. Then I turned quickly and kicked him in the balls before running off. It was the only time I fought back.

Eventually they got tired of making the effort to get a rise out of me. But their insults clung to me like tattoos.

Given the nature of Hugh's offenses, he was the frontrunner on my "little list." But Taylor was a close second, and she was an easier target. Hugh could wait. He wasn't about to fall off my list.

The reunion was in an old theatre that no longer showed movies but was used for a variety of events. It wasn't the showcase it used to be, but even with the seats removed and the floor leveled, it still had an appealing gothic feel with its high, ornate ceiling, its peeling gilded pillars, and the burgundy velvet curtain at the back of the narrow stage. I had spent many happy afternoons as a youngster watching movies while eating popcorn and drinking cola. Alone, of course. But still happy memories. It had been an escape into other worlds, places where people struggled and suffered, but whose stories more often than not had happy endings. Back then, that gave me hope for my own life.

Just inside the entrance was a long table with nameplates lined up in uneven rows, showing gaps where people had already claimed theirs. The two women seated behind the table were engaged in lively conversations with several classmates. I didn't recognize anyone and had no interest in trying to join in, so I found my name, peeled the paper off the back of the label, and pressed it next to the V neck of the expensive dress I'd purchased for the event. My face may not have improved, but my station in life had. My expensive clothes would let everyone know that.

It crossed my mind that someone might look at my outfit and think "lipstick on a pig," but I didn't anticipate anyone maligning me to my face. After all, we were adults, conditioned by a world that favored behind-the-back insults. Besides, a lot of my former class-mates still lived in the tiny town I'd grown up in, their lives insulated from the larger world, and their incomes limited by location and education. Whereas I was a success story by local standards.

And I was confident my parents boasted about my job, if not about me.

I heard Taylor's laugh before I saw her. It was loud, like the hot pink dress she was wearing. She looked as though she'd been shrink wrapped in it, but then, she had the figure to pull that off. Her blond hair had artificial highlights and was puffed to perfection. Surrounded by adoring former classmates, she was obviously still popular.

"Hi, Callista," a soft female voice said. I turned and immediately recognized another of the bullied victims from high school.

"Karen," I said. "It's good to see you." Did I mean it? I wasn't sure. We were never friends, but we certainly had a lot in common. I knew what I was doing there, but why was she attending the reunion?

"Nice dress," Karen said.

Karen was wearing a navy-blue skirt and a beige cardigan sweater over a nondescript blouse, an old-fashioned school librarian stereotype from an outdated YA book. She still had the same whipped dog look about her, shoulders slightly bent forward, eyes downcast, her voice an apology for being.

"What are you doing these days?" I asked, making polite conversation while I glanced around to see who else was there.

"I teach 8th grade, history and social studies."

"Where?"

"Here, at Hunter Middle School." I didn't know what to say. She had apparently gone to college and earned a degree and then chose to return to a place where she had been miserable. Why?

"I see Taylor still has an entourage," I said, changing the subject.

"Yes, she's a successful realtor."

"Is she married?"

"Yes. She and her husband have three children, a boy and two girls."

"The boy is the youngest, right?" Taylor was the type to keep trying until she had a boy.

"Yes."

The room was becoming crowded. It was time to wander around and get a feel for who was there. I told Karen that I was going to get something to drink, and she looked so stricken at being left alone, that I asked if she wanted to join me. She did. If I hadn't been focused on what was about to happen, I would have tried harder to connect with her.

We were half way to the drinks table when I spotted Hugh. No longer the football star, he was balding and had a sagging belly that hung down over his belt. Seeing that he hadn't aged well was satisfying, but that didn't make up for past wrongs. Sagging belly or not, I would see to it that he paid for his sins.

But first, it was time for Taylor to learn what it's like to be ridiculed in public. A tit for tat act of revenge consolidated into one knock-out punch.

The timing was perfect. A few phone-addicted people quickly got the ball rolling.

Finding a hacker to post porn pictures of Taylor on social media had been a bit complicated, but the guy I found hadn't asked many questions. He seemed satisfied to make a few bucks in cash for taking on the challenge of putting together the pictures and setting up an untraceable path so no one could link them to him and, therefore, not to me either.

I'd approached him in a coffee shop where I always saw him on his laptop, eyes riveted to the screen, earphones isolating him from the rest of the world. I knew I was taking a big chance sitting down across from him out of the blue and basically asking if was willing to do something illegal. But he hadn't looked surprised and apparently had no ethical qualms about doing what I asked him to do. It was a simple financial transaction. He didn't even ask my name. Of course, I had no doubt he could find me online if he tried. I wasn't worried—as long as he wasn't caught, he had no reason to point a finger at me. I paid him handsomely—in cash—for his work and quit going to that coffee shop.

Some of the pictures he used were hacked from Taylor's phone, but others were fake. The fact that she had been foolish enough to take photos of her private anatomy to send to a lover had been fortuitous. Otherwise, she could have claimed that she was the victim of a photoshopping hoax. However, since some of them were real, it would be more difficult for her to protest her innocence. I wondered if her lover would defend what she'd done or if he would remain anonymous. I'd asked the hacker to avoid showing any close-ups of his face; I had nothing against him and saw no reason why he should suffer for Taylor's indiscretions. I was just sorry I couldn't thank him.

Although I had some sympathy for Taylor's husband and children, I accepted that they were collateral damage. Her punishment was to be humiliated in public, like I had been so many times. I wanted to see the shock on her face and to watch her squirm when she realized what was happening. I wanted to gloat.

What actually occurred was even better than I'd anticipated.

When I first noticed people taking out their cell phones and staring in shock and awe at what they were seeing, I knew my plan was working. But it was an enterprising and tech savvy classmate that took my spiteful prank to the next level. Someone who had little regard for Taylor's privacy and the know-how to live-stream from their cell phone to the laptop on stage connected to a large screen for a presentation later in the event. The screen suddenly came to life, flooding the room with images of flesh that everyone immediately recognized as belonging to Taylor.

After a moment of stunned silence, there was a collective gasp that resonated off the theater walls as Taylor's voluptuous anatomy writhed in ecstasy. The volume was barely turned up, but low moans and a few whispered words chased themselves around the room. I had to fight back a smirk.

Karen was standing beside me, eyes wide as she stared transfixed at the screen. "Oh my," she said under her breath. "Oh, my." Then a faint smile appeared. I couldn't tell if she liked what she saw because she was attracted to female bodies or because she suddenly grasped that this was not going to be good for Taylor. Not for her professional image. Nor possibly for her marriage. Perhaps Karen was remembering what Taylor had been like in the "good old days" of high school, and the thought that Taylor was getting some bad publicity, some very bad publicity, pleased her.

"Not the slideshow anyone was expecting," I commented.

Karen glanced around at our former classmates who were staring at the screen in wonder and disbelief. Then she turned to me, "It's hard to feel sympathy, isn't it?"

The people around Taylor started moving away from her as it registered on them exactly what they were seeing. Taylor's back had been to the stage, but she whipped around to see what everyone was staring at. For an instant, she remained frozen in place. Then she screamed.

7

LEAST FAVORITE TEACHERS

Next on my list was my least favorite teacher from my freshman year in high school—Mr. Wilson. He was a fussy little man with wisps of gray hair subject to movement in the slightest breeze. The boys made fun of him because he taught English lit with sensitivity and passion. He was articulate, well organized, and well-read. I wanted to like him. But he had an eye for the pretty girls in class, giving them higher grades than I felt they deserved, and ogling their budding breasts in snug-fitting sweaters.

Based on his eye for the good-looking girls, I wasn't surprised that he looked right through me, as if I was a shadow and not a person. I was used to that. But he was indifferent to me at a time when I desperately needed encouragement from some quarter. And he was in a position to see me as an intelligent and promising student and not just a homely young girl.

At first, I tried very hard to please him. I'm sure I was one of the few students in his class who read all of the assignments and completed papers on time. I got good grades on tests and papers, but he never called on me when I raised my hand in class, even when mine was the first in the air. After it finally hit me that he would listen to banal comments from the attractive girls and seldom correct them for their superficial or just plain wrong responses to his questions, I gave up trying.

His other failing was that he was intimidated by the male bullies. Most of the time he let them do what they wanted in class. Unfortunately, what they wanted was to flaunt their maleness and cheat their way through. The pretty girls giggled at their jokes, while a cadre of unattractive girls helped the male bullies on tests and wrote papers for them. It apparently never occurred to Mr. Wilson how similar some of their essays were. He didn't even notice when one of the male students broke into his desk and changed some of the grades on his computer.

When the end of the class came and grades were posted, Mr. Wilson seemed surprised that my name was the only one with a 4-point. I'd achieved the distinction one test and one assignment at a time, in spite of being ignored. It wasn't the first nor the last time my intellect couldn't save me from discrimination. But it stands out for me because, at that point in my life, I still nurtured a scintilla of hope that being smart might be a lifeline. Mr. Wilson managed to compress what little optimism I'd clung to over the years into a tiny hard lump of bitter cynicism. That's why he was in the top five on my little list.

When I looked him up, I discovered he had recently retired. A little more research on social media revealed that he lived alone with his dog, Gertie. I drove by his house once and saw him walking a sad looking roly-poly dog with pudgy short legs. As I passed by, he stopped to let Gertie sniff a post. I caught a glimpse of the look of pride on his face as he watched his dog mark her territory, leaving her wet claim of ownership in the same way most intact male dogs do. Well, Gertie, I said to myself. You may be queen of your neighborhood, but I'm afraid you are going to be kidnapped and turned over to a shelter in another city. Sorry about that.

Mr. Wilson had destroyed my hope, leaving me feeling isolated and alone. Taking away Gertie seemed a fitting message, although he would never know who sent it.

. . .

It turned out to be amazingly easy to snatch Gertie when he let her out for her evening constitutional. She didn't even let out a single yelp as I lured her with pepperoni and baloney to the gate in the back fence. She was still chewing when I reached down, grabbed her, and shoved her in a bag. Then I ran like Santa Claus on steroids back to my car where I deposited her in the trunk with the remaining pepperoni and baloney. She seemed content.

Three hours later I left her on a leash tied to a bush next to the sidewalk at a neighborhood shelter over 200 miles away from Mr. Wilson's tidy home. I'd removed her collar with her name and address on it and replaced it with a cheap one I'd bought in a pet store. If she was chipped, he would probably get her back fairly soon; if not, I wasn't sure what her life would be like going forward, but I hoped she ended up in a happy place.

Although it wasn't terribly cold, I wrapped a blanket around her, said a few words of comfort, and patted her on the head before leaving her stranded. It saddened me that she was collateral damage, but it really was the perfect punishment for Mr. Wilson.

As I drove away, I pushed back the hood on my sweatshirt. I planned on ditching it at a rest stop in case there had been cameras in front of the shelter. Another precaution I'd taken was to park my car several blocks away from the shelter on a side street where I hadn't been able to spot any cameras. It was a chance I'd been willing to take. After all, I couldn't imagine police taking much time to track down someone who dropped off a stray dog.

Next on my list was teacher number two, this one a college professor. Sam Davies.

Things did get better for me in college. There was more diversity for one thing, and varying standards of beauty for different cultures. But I was still an unattractive white woman in the eyes of my classmates and professors. Tolerated and seldom publicly belittled because intelligence was valued more than it had been in high school. Although if I'd been both attractive and smart, I would have achieved more. People weren't drawn to me as a leader or influencer when participating in small groups sessions or study groups, even when it was clear I excelled at retaining what I read and coming up with ideas for group presentations. Little did I know at the time that this "failing" would follow me into corporate America.

Enter Sam Davies, twice awarded "teacher of the year," and quoted in the college newspaper whenever he expressed an opinion on teaching trends, student politics, or anything related to his current research. He was working on a book that he was very proud of and obviously believed it would guarantee his reputation as a scholar and serve as a stepping stone in the academic hierarchy.

Professor Davies wasn't particularly attractive, but he was youngish, dressed the part of a liberal academic, and wasn't too demanding with homework or reading assignments. His specialty was using mathematics to model real-word phenomena. For instance, he'd partnered with another scientist to develop strategies to encourage consumers to invest in alternative energy. And he'd worked on ways to prevent deaths in mining operations. Real practical kinds of things. But like many mathematicians, he dreamed of becoming famous by winning a million dollars for solving one of the six remaining "unsolvable" math problems listed by the Clay Mathematics Institute.

When I first asked him to be on my thesis committee, he tried to brush me off. But I persisted, providing him with some theories I was working on that I felt were consistent with his modeling research. He was particularly taken by one of my ideas and eventually agreed to be on my committee. What I didn't realize at the time was that he was more interested in using me to expand his own work than in helping me get my PhD.

Admittedly, it's not unheard of for professors to adapt, borrow or even steal their students' work without giving credit. After all, mentors and teachers can easily rationalize that it was their tutelage that enabled their students to accomplish what they did. From inventions to literary ideas to breakthrough formulas or new theories. It may be true that ideas are cheap when you lack a platform, and professors can use their positions to get products and ideas into the public arena. But shouldn't they at least acknowledge young students who contribute to their success? How much would it diminish their standing to admit they had a little help along the way? Even if from a lowly student.

Unfortunately, students impressed by their professors' standing in the academic community are generally slow to catch on. They are too busy seeking approval to have their BS antenna up and running at full capacity. I know mine wasn't. And once a professor has announced *their* discovery publicly, it's hard to dispute their claim.

I got my PhD in spite of Professor Davies. He steered me away from pursuing one of my most original and creative ideas for my thesis, and encouraged me instead to do something "safe." He acted as though he was doing it for my benefit, to make sure I didn't get delayed by the need for excessive research or stymied by unprovable facts. Still, when he kept coming back to my original idea in our one-on-one sessions, mining my brain for more details, I should have been suspicious. But I honestly didn't see it coming.

My theory became the basis for a book he got published while I was finishing my thesis. When it came out, I scoured the book for some indication that he realized it was *my* idea, not his, but there wasn't the tiniest indication that anything in the book had come from anyplace other than his exceptional brainpower and ingenuity. I doubt the book earned him big bucks, but it was good enough for fifteen minutes of fame in the world of mathematicians. If he'd mentioned me in an afterword, I would probably have felt somewhat mollified, grateful even, while at the same time aggrieved and cheated. But getting zero mention made me angry.

When I got up the nerve to confront him about it, he at first denied he'd relied on any of my ideas or analysis for his conclusions. And when I pressed him, he got defensive. He said it was the way things worked in academia, and I needed to get over myself. Furthermore, given his previous work and stature within the university community, no one would believe me if I challenged him. He implicitly threatened to interfere with the completion of my degree if I made a fuss. Although I was furious, I realized it was a no-win situation for me. So, I decided to suck it up and move on. But I never forgot what I considered his betrayal and theft.

Now it was my turn.

It took a lot of time and persistence to find half a dozen graduate students who admitted to being victimized by Professor Davies. But he'd apparently always been short on original ideas. At first no one wanted to be named in the article I said I was going to publish. To be honest, I was going to use their names whether they gave me permission or not, but my preference was for them to cooperate. Nor did I have a publisher for the article. I was planning on sending it anonymously to a reporter I was fairly certain would be happy to run with it. That way it would get to a larger audience faster. I engaged in one final deception when seeking victims—I didn't use my real name and had no intention of making my involvement public.

As anticipated, the reporter I approached was instantly all over the story. And before she ran the piece on professors stealing ideas from students, she found even more students to add to her series of articles. Not realizing I was her original source, she even contacted me. But I refused to talk with her. Nevertheless, based on what a fellow student told her, she speculated about whether anything in the book that *made* Professor Davies' career was his own and referred to a graduate student at the time of publication that had talked with other students about similar ideas. I was surprised and pleased that they remembered.

Universities tend to be tight-lipped about their failings, so I don't know what happened behind the curtain. But when Professor Davies moved to another, less prestigious college, I could make some fairly sound guesses.

Strike two for bad teachers.

. . .

The third teacher on my list was my Sunday school teacher, Mr. Whatley. He hadn't done anything as glaring as the other two teachers on my list, but because in my child's eye he embodied the church, his small sins seemed significant. Granted, you can't expect volunteers of a local church to be saints, but when I was in the sixth grade, I didn't understand how difficult it was to find good volunteers. And I considered my Sunday school teacher as an integral part of the church experience. It didn't cross my mind that he might simply be someone who donated time because he liked to have an audience.

When I started going to church, I eagerly accepted at face value our minister's promise that we were all equal and precious in the eyes of God. The sermons seemed tailormade for me. If I followed the path of righteousness and atoned for my sins, I would be welcomed into the community and find peace and salvation. Being a virtuous person in exchange for acceptance seemed like a pretty good deal to me.

And at first, I loved Mr. Whatley's weekly classes on religions around the world. He talked about tolerance and cultural differences and pointed out similarities between what at first glance seemed like totally dissimilar approaches to spirituality. We learned about Islam, Hinduism, Buddhism, Sikhism, Judaism, and a number of what he referred to as "folk religions." He also discussed Christian denominations, never once suggesting that one was better than another.

I was, of course, his star pupil, the front row student who was always able to answer whatever question was asked. I didn't talk while Mr. Whatley was speaking, giggle when he stumbled over a name, or ask questions to challenge his authority as some of the other kids did. I was the perfect, engaged follower.

Then one Sunday after a bad week at school where the other kids had been particularly vicious in their teasing, I decided to seek advice and solace from Mr. Whatley. Surely this kind Christian man would buoy my spirits by providing sage advice and comforting reassurance that I was a beloved child of God.

I waylaid him after Sunday school and asked if he had a few minutes. I can still picture him looking at his watch before saying, "Maybe another time." He hurried off before I had a chance to respond. At first, I was crushed, but I was willing to give him the benefit of the doubt. Maybe he'd rushed off because of some family crisis or an appointment that couldn't wait. He probably had no idea about how rude he had come across or how desperate I'd been to talk to someone sympathetic to my situation.

The next Sunday, I approached him just before class was about to start and asked if I could talk to him for a few minutes afterwards. Again, he looked at his watch, and I could tell he wanted to say "no." Instead he agreed to give me a few minutes. Although when class was over, he almost left before I reminded him that I had something I wanted to talk to him about. He quickly sat down on the edge of his desk as though preparing for a quick exit.

My gut told me I was making a mistake, but I'd gone to so much trouble to get a meeting with him, that I went ahead and explained my problem and asked what he thought I should do. His insensitive response devastated me.

"We all have our crosses to bear. Yours is that you are unattractive. When I was young, I wasn't athletic. So, I had to find other outlets for my talents. Accept who you are. God loves you." He stood up. His demeanor suggested he thought he had solved my problem with his cliches and was ready to move on. I had no choice but to thank him and let him leave.

It was the last time I attended Sunday school. I also quit going to church.

The two other teachers I'd targeted—Mr. Wilson and Professor Davies—were ones with which I'd had considerable interaction. But my brief exchange with Mr. Whatley was like surviving being struck by lightning; it's over in a flash, but it leaves its mark. How could he have been so unkind as to compare not being athletic with being unattractive? He didn't have "not athletic" printed on his forehead. Did he have any idea how badly he'd hurt me with his dismissive attitude? Would he care if he did? If I'd been a pretty girl with problems, would he have found more time for me?

It didn't take long to find Mr. Whatley. Unfortunately—for him and for me—he had passed away. Not only had he delivered a resounding blow to my psyche and deprived me of the solace of religion, he had cheated me out of seeking revenge.

His obituary said that he died "before his time" and would be missed by his loving wife, two children and his sister. I hoped he'd been a better husband, father, and brother than he was a Sunday school teacher. But since obituaries were to celebrate rather than criticize, that's something I would never know. The story didn't say how he died, but I fantasized that it was by the hands of someone whom he had wronged. There was also a rather lengthy summary of his life, including where he had worked, his hobbies, and one thing that stood out for me: *he would be remembered for the years he'd devoted to his church as a Sunday school teacher*. I definitely agreed with that.

Strike three for bad teachers. Only in this instance, he'd been struck down by God. If there was any justice in the world, he wasn't spending eternity in heaven.

8

THE DETECTIVE

It was the one-year anniversary of Dane's death. The sword of Damocles still swayed over Adriana's head, but she hadn't yet been charged with murder. Rumors of an impending arrest swirled about daily, but she was still free. At least in the sense that she wasn't in prison. The public had tried and convicted her shortly after she was labeled as a prime suspect. Her life had been on hold since then. She'd lost her job, her friends, her reputation, and the self-image that had fueled her confidence. I was one of the few people from her past who kept in touch. She often told me how grateful she was for my belief in her.

I confess that my main reason for staying in touch was to hear about the status of the case against her, although I'd also come to feel sorry for her. Even her long-time, fallback lover from the office, Marcus Manning, was only there for her when it suited him, probably for sex. She misguidedly interpreted that as caring. They'd had an off-and-on romance since college, and one day she told me that she'd always assumed that eventually they would end up together. I could have told her that would only happen if he thought it was in his best interest. He was the poster child for narcissism. And, as far as I knew, he'd made no public declaration of her innocence. The kindest thing I could say about him was that he had a face and body that would be good modeling outdoor wear—square jaw, windswept hair, and athletic build.

I had my own bone to pick with Marcus. He'd been a thorn in my side from the moment I joined the ranks of Keller and Eaves. He was ambitious in a cutthroat sort of way that made you feel he was someone who really would "sell his own mother" if the price was right. Especially if it would advance his career. He'd been part of the Landberg team and had been more roadblock than contributor. He apparently wasn't someone who considered hard work the path to success.

When Detective Peters called and asked me to meet him for coffee at the corner Starbucks, I didn't know whether to be concerned or not. After all this time, surely there wasn't anything new linking me to Dane's death. Or was there? Had I become complacent and let some damning piece of evidence slip by?

For once I left the office right at quitting time and nervously wended my way through the throngs of workers hurriedly departing for the day. What were they rushing off to do? Did they have hobbies they were passionate about or families they couldn't wait to embrace? Maybe they had kids to pick up from school. Or a lover to meet before going home to a family that used to mean everything to them but now drained their energy with their day-to-day demands and complaints. Or maybe they were hurrying to shop for groceries for a dinner they were preparing for family, friends or just for themselves. Or hoping to arrive home in time to watch an addictive TV program. Or to take their dog for a walk. Or maybe they disliked their jobs so much that they were physically and symbolically running away. The possibilities were endless. For others, but not for me. My work was my life.

When I walked into the Starbucks, I immediately saw Detective

Peters. His nondescript appearance seemed both comforting and a bit scary. I had to remind myself not to underestimate him. He'd been watching the door and waved me over. There was a coffee next to the seat across from him. "I hope you still like it black," he said. I noticed there were two empty packets of sugar and a wet swizzle stick next to his cup.

"Yes, thanks," I said as I sat. "How are you?" I asked, immediately chiding myself for sounding like I thought it was a social meeting.

"I'm doing well. And you?" He knew his lines.

I took the lid off the coffee cup to make it easier to drink, and the bittersweet chocolate aroma of the dark roasted coffee tickled my nose. "I don't like to drink through those tiny slots unless I have to," I explained. It was an inane thing to say, and it made me realize just how nervous I was.

"Me neither, but it's an occupational hazard. I'm always drinking coffee on the run."

What was my next move? Sip and wait? Ask him how the investigation into Dane's death was going? It had been a long time since there was anything in the news. "Good coffee," I said.

He immediately bridged the awkwardness of the moment with an acknowledgement that our meeting for coffee was not the norm. "You're probably wondering why I called."

"You caught me on camera doing a California stop at a stop sign," I said.

"If I had coffee with everyone who did a rolling stop . . ." He laughed.

"Is it a coincidence that you called on the one-year anniversary of Dane's death?"

"No, it isn't."

"And . . .?

"The investigation is still on-going."

I felt a catch in my throat. "After all this time. With no arrest made that I've heard about."

"At this point I think there may be a manslaughter or involuntary manslaughter charge soon."

"Why has it taken so long?"

"It's a complicated case. Some of us think the charge should be 'murder,' but that takes more evidence than we've been able to gather . . . so far."

"You're still investigating then." I hoped my hands didn't shake when I reached for my coffee.

"Yes, in fact I talked with Adriana yesterday. That's why I called you."

I sipped the hot coffee and waited for him to continue.

"You're not a very chatty individual," he said.

"Is that against the law?"

"A welcome relief, actually." He gave me a small, warm smile. It was hard to believe he was acting human and kind as part of his job. I had learned not to trust manipulators. And as a detective, he was probably adept at manipulation. So I remained silent. "Well," he said. "She mentioned that *you* are the only one from the company who stays in touch. I wanted to ask you why?"

"What can I say? If she had been charged with Dane's death, I don't think I would have visited her in prison. But until she's charged with something, I've assumed that maybe she isn't guilty. And if she's not guilty, she got a bum rap."

"You feel sorry for her?"

"A bit. It's not as if we were ever close. But I know what it's like not to have friends. Adriana was always surrounded by people. It must be hard to have all of those alleged friends abandon you so quickly."

"So, you *do* feel sorry for her."

"I wouldn't characterize it quite like that. I did work with her for almost a year on the Landberg project. It seems like a small thing to check in with her occasionally."

"If she's charged with manslaughter, will you continue your conversations?"

"Do you believe she murdered Dane?" I tried to sound incredulous without overdoing it. Adriana had suffered a lot this past year, perhaps even more than she deserved for what she had done to me. And if she was charged with manslaughter, I would suffer some guilt, but I would be safe. I had to remind myself that she would still be the dishonest, self-centered, conniving woman she was when she took credit for my work if she hadn't insisted on taking Dane his coffee that fateful day. To a large extent, she brought this on herself.

"Tell me what *you* think."

I pretended to give it some thought. "I know she was a 'woman scorned' and all that, but isn't it a leap from there to murderess?"

"That's why the charge will probably not be 'murder,' but 'manslaughter.'"

"Oh." That was in some ways a relief.

"The reason I called was to see if there was anything you've been chewing on lately to make you think she's innocent . . . or guilty."

I shook my head. "Not really."

"But you're still leaning toward 'innocent'?"

"I think she was truly in love with him."

"Even if she was, that doesn't mean she didn't get angry enough to kill him. I've known that to happen before."

"You've seen a lot more of this kind of thing than I have. I assume it hones your senses."

"Oh, my senses are finely honed." He looked me in the eyes. "But you worked with her. You saw them together. I trust your instincts."

The conversation was getting sticky. Nothing would please me more than having Adriana blamed for an act I committed. But I could hardly appear too eager to see her convicted. Especially since she'd labeled my calls as "supportive."

"Adriana doesn't strike me as the murdering type. But then she hasn't confided in me about the details of her relationship with Dane."

"How would you characterize your conversations with her?"

"Brief. Complaints about the justice system and how badly she's been treated by Keller and Eaves. Repeated protestations of innocence. Occasional questions about how team members are doing. That's about it. Not enough for a book, I'm afraid."

He paused. "And not enough to support a conviction."

"Sorry. Is there something you want me to ask her?"

"You'd be willing to ask something that might incriminate her?"

"We aren't friends. And if she killed Dane, I would like to know."

"I'll give that some thought."

"One thing I still don't know . . ." I hesitated, then spit it out. "What was the cause of death?"

"I can't say."

"But it was something in his coffee?"

He raised his eyebrows and put one hand up as if indicating "who knows?"

"Well, I assume whatever killed him was something Adriana had access to. But if you were able to link it to her, wouldn't that mean you could charge her with murder?" I paused briefly. "I know, you can't say. But it's that kind of thing that makes me think she could be innocent."

"You'd make a good detective."

"I do like solving puzzles."

"One of these days maybe we can have a more specific conversation about the facts in this case."

"I'd like that." I put the lid on my coffee. "If that's all . . .?"

"I appreciate your willingness to cooperate."

"Well, thanks for the coffee. I have a few things to do back at the office before calling it a night."

"You're a hard worker."

"I can't imagine that it's the end of the work day for you either."

"There are one or two more things I need to do in the name of justice." He smiled, stood, and walked me to the door. "Take care of yourself, Callista."

As I headed back to the office, I considered the "willingness to cooperate" comment. That seemed like something a police officer would say to a witness. Would the police call me to testify if Adriana was charged and the case went to trial? If so, I would have to be very careful not to sound anxious for her conviction. But I couldn't defend her too vigorously either. I would have to find the right balance between defending and damning Adriana for a crime I'd committed.

9

REVENGE PRANKS

Now that I've had some experience with revenge, I realize how many forms it can take. It's like a buffet of punishments. You can choose an hors d oeuvre that does little more than annoy the recipient. Or a side dish to irritate. A main course to exasperate. Or a full meal to infuriate. So many choices. Suffering is suffering, it's just a matter of deciding where you want to aim on the continuum of pain. Unfortunately, in Adriana's case, I'd quickly lost control of the situation, and she was in danger of having her life destroyed by being sentenced for a crime she didn't commit. In the future I intended to be more alert to how my actions could result in unintentional harm.

There was also the issue of risk to consider. Although I'd hoped that the cause of Dane's death would be attributed to a mysterious illness, the fact that it was identified as murder could have caused trouble for me. I thought I'd done a good job of covering my tracks, but you can never be 100 percent certain. Furthermore, murder investigations tend to drag on, drawing a lot of attention from both the media and the police. If I had been a serious suspect, that would have prevented me from working on my list for fear of exposure. Even so, under the circumstances it seemed wise for now to focus on small acts of retribution for minor offenses— hors d oeuvre and side dishes that were less likely to be pursued vigorously, if at all, by officials.

In the spirit of staying under the radar, I've taken one other action —I've done away with the physical list I made initially, my matrix of people and potential punishments. I put it through the shredder and then burned the confetti-like strips in my fireplace. For good measure, I scooped up and scattered the ashes in a funeral-like gesture over a small pond in a nearby park. It disturbed the resident ducks who thought I was feeding them something, but they were the only witnesses. The act ensured that my list would never be used as evidence against me. Instead, I carry around the details in my head, ticking off tasks related to individual punishments.

There was, however, one major disadvantage to tiptoeing through retribution—it was hard to know if the scales of justice had been evened out. Partly because it's difficult to follow up on what you've done without exposing oneself. The thought that I could put a lot of effort into an act of revenge and then never know for sure if it actually had an impact was like reading a whodunit that was missing the final chapter.

At least I got to be there in person for Taylor's fall from grace. And Karen has kept me apprised of what has happened to her since then. Apparently, the porn pictures have taken on a life of their own. Each time Taylor removes pictures from one social media site, they pop up somewhere else. Like whack-a-mole, they just keep coming back again and again. All this without my hacker or me lifting a finger. Even if she eventually manages to take all of them down, at this point the damage to her reputation has been done. As well as the damage to her marriage. Karen told me that her husband filed for divorce and that they are in a bitter court fight over custody of their three children. I regret the ripple effect my actions had on her family, but, as I've said before, she provided the catalyst for her own demise.

It's been harder for me to move on from what I did to Mr. Wilson and his dog Gertie. Losing a dog doesn't make the news, and I didn't want to search on social media to follow up for fear of leaving an online footprint. I did a swing through his neighborhood after work one evening and saw Gertie's face on "missing" posters pinned to light poles in the area as well as in store windows in a strip mall near his house. I considered going to the shelter where I'd left her, pretending to look for a dog, to see if she was still there. But going that far away to look for a pet might raise a red flag. I had to settle for imagining the denouement. Given that Mr. Wilson had been fond of Gertie, it was likely he had suffered feelings of deep personal loss when she went missing. And based on the signs he'd posted, it was unlikely she'd been chipped. I could assume a happy reunion was unlikely, unless by some fluke someone make the connection between the missing dog and the one in the shelter. It was just unfortunate that Gertie had to suffer in order to pay her owner's moral debt.

Then there was Sam Davies. There was no way I could know for sure whether he was happy in his new job, although I had serious doubts that he was. He'd lied and cheated to gain prestige, and his new position was definitely a step down. In addition, his ethical lapses were undoubtedly known by his current colleagues and students as well as by those from his former college. In my opinion, he'd been lucky to get another job. The highlight for me was discovering that his infamous book was no longer available on Amazon. That probably meant it had been dropped by his publisher. I considered digging deeper, but let it go. Sometimes the imagination is as good or better than reality.

So far, no one had linked any of these mishaps to me. It was time to move on to the next person on my list.

Dane's replacement at Keller and Eaves was a woman who'd had her own problems carving out a place in the company. I may have decided that Dane was a SOB and unworthy of my loyalty, but he had been popular with those at the top of the company. Unfortunately, the old-boy network didn't seem to welcome a woman into their ranks. It was rumored that my new boss wasn't included in after-work get-togethers and that her opinions were often ignored in meetings. She had my sympathy, but I wasn't about to stick my neck out on her behalf, not that it would have done any good. Besides, my guess was that she would sooner rather than later move on—by choice or forced by circumstances. So, I backed off taking on leadership roles, while still helping colleagues when they needed it. I let myself be labeled as a worker bee, doing a good job, but no longer striving to prove myself. It was much less time-consuming and stressful to stay in the background. And it gave me more time to work on my list.

When I was sent to Vancouver BC with two teammates to interview a new client, my role was to make sure the two "front" team members who would be meeting directly with the client were prepped and had everything they needed for the interview. I was also required to be available to provide support for anything that came up during their meeting. So, while they were with the client, I was free to do what I pleased, as long as I remained on a short leash. It was like going on a working holiday, one where I was on-call almost 24-7.

Even though I had to be ready to jump at a moment's notice, I couldn't see sitting in my hotel room on the off chance the "front" team members *might* need something. I decided I wouldn't go far, but I wanted to at least see what there was to see in the nearby neighborhood.

It was a lovely day, only a few clouds in an otherwise blue sky. The city was alive with people walking briskly to their destinations, food smells mixed with other less desirable odors, and a low level of noise associated with a thriving city scene. I wasn't particularly interested in shopping for anything, but it was good to be outside.

Just around the corner from a row of boutique shops with artistic window displays were several storefronts with more eclectic offerings. Obviously aimed at clientele with wide-ranging interests, including one shop with a window full of sex toys. I was about to turn back when I noticed a sign above a shop window that said "Crossdresser – Transgender Costumes." In the showcase was a very realistic face mask on a disembodied head. The "aha" I felt was almost physical.

Without hesitation, I went inside, browsed the available costumes, and made a list of items to purchase. Then I left and walked the main street until I located an ATM to withdraw some cash. I realized I was taking a chance that the withdrawal could be connected to the purchase I was about to make, but it would be a leap. And who would be interested?

I tried not to appear rushed or uncomfortable when gathering up my purchases, but I didn't want to be interrupted by a call from one of my teammates either, so I didn't linger. When I put the items I wanted on the counter next to the cash register, I told the clerk that I was buying them for a play my local theater was putting on. The indifferent young man behind the counter barely glanced up as he murmured something that sounded like "Uh huh." He accepted my cash, put everything in a bag, and went back to the novel he'd been reading when I came in. Sometimes bad customer service is a good thing.

I quickly went back to the hotel and deposited the cache in my suitcase. I was about to head out again when I got a call. The deal was close to being completed with our prospective clients, and my two teammates were going to lunch with them. Could I please make copies of the updated proposal they had sent me and leave them at the front desk for pick-up when they got back from lunch?

"Sure," I said, smiling to myself. In the overall scheme of things, being treated like a gofer was an insult that didn't even make the B list.

Back home in my condo, I unpacked my masks and hairpieces and set them out on the bed to view. The female masks were billed as "handmade realistic soft silicon head masks" suited for a "man who wants to be a woman, such as crossdresser, transgender, drag queen, lady-boy, cosplayer, or just for fun." The male faces were for similar applications but from the female perspective. I'd purchased four masks: an attractive female, an old lady, a middle-aged Asian male, and a young square-jawed male. I'd also purchased two wigs for females and two for males. Except for the short-haired male wig, I would be able to mix and match with the masks to create slightly different appearances. Add a hat or a hoodie and I would be prepared for a fair number of avenging activities, each as a different person.

If Detective Peters was right about them getting close to charging someone with Dane's murder, it definitely seemed prudent for me to keep a low profile until things were more settled. I decided to target individuals at or near the bottom of my list and do so with what I thought of as pranks or pokes, small or medium-sized annoyances to spoil their day, not to impact their lives. It was unlikely these incidents would be identified as part of a larger picture. Those involved would probably complain to a few friends and relatives and then move on. That was fine with me. After all, they hadn't been part of a conspiracy to make my life miserable, they'd just been unfeeling and inconsiderate in small ways that had fueled my insecurities and self-loathing. For that, they'd earned a few bumps in their otherwise complacent lives.

After choosing some likely candidates, I mentally reviewed my list of strategies and added a few that had been bouncing around in my mind. They seemed to fall into three categories: annoying, even more annoying, and possibly criminally annoying.

At the least annoying level, one idea I liked was to put a snake in someone's mailbox or inside their house, maybe both. They wouldn't know the snake was non-poisonous, so that could be upsetting, especially if it was a good-sized snake. I was also fond of the idea of spamming someone with hundreds of unwanted subscriptions. All I had to do was sign up an individual, and they would be bombarded with all sorts of magazines and newsletters. Just a small upset, like having crows knock over your garbage can and scatter its contents. Another easy, one-shot activity included placing an obnoxious sign in someone's front yard, as if they had chosen to place it there as a statement of belief. Something that made them look bad—something racist or misogynistic or a bit crazy.

The annoying actions seemed like things that might be attributed to local kids, bored teenagers with no particular axe to grind, just young people out to have some fun at someone else's expense. On the other hand, the second level of pokes involved some vandalism or what might be labeled as mischievous or borderline criminal behavior. For example, if someone was particularly fond of their car, tires could be slashed and car doors keyed. Or, tires could be removed, leaving the car stranded. I'd heard of a thief who'd removed the tires from a car parked in the owner's garage, and the owner didn't notice until he tried to back it out. That was a nice touch. Another appealing idea involved a wheel boot. If I could get my hands on one, I would get a twofer poke—their confusion as to whether it was an official if perplexing act and then, once they realized it wasn't official, having them try to figure out how to get the clamp off.

Or, I could spray paint a garage door with a threatening message that suggested they owed some drug dealer or gangster money. Or maybe print some vile message suggesting the person was a pedophile. Perhaps an enterprising neighbor or passerby would snap a picture and put it on social media before they got a chance to paint over it. One could hope.

What I rated as third level pokes had more serious consequences for the victim, but they didn't involve bodily harm. Someone was going to end up with drugs in their car or house and an anonymous tip made to the police. Then there was the unlucky victim who would have sex toys or edible panty arrangements delivered to them at their place of work, suggesting they were in a compromising relationship with someone. Or, it could work the other way around, the unlucky victim could allegedly be responsible for sending sex toys or edible panties to a co-worker. Male to female or vice versa. Or male to male or female to female. The victim would deny they did it, but it's difficult to prove a negative.

In addition, there were a variety of easy tech hacks—objectionable tweets sent from someone's computer about their boss or their company. Or a sex text apparently sent to their wife instead of a mistress by mistake. Or a wife sexting her husband instead of a lover. Oops. The possibilities were endless. It was like foiling someone's desk at work, only much meaner. And no one would end up laughing. Except me.

My first prank and poke target was Tim Colson, a bully who'd made life miserable not only for me but for a number of other vulnerable kids in grade school. I know putting him on the list was reaching a long way back, but memories of him tormenting me then were as vivid as if they'd happened yesterday. Back then, to avoid running into him, I always peeked around the corner before entering a hallway, ducking into a bathroom or the nearest classroom if I saw him coming. During recess I tried desperately to become invisible on the playground. I would sit next to the steps and put my head down. Or I would hang out behind the slide or next to the lone tree in the play area. Anything to keep him from noticing me. When we did come face-to-face, he would start chanting vicious nicknames, chasing after me until he got tired of the game. He would also make comments about how no one would want to screw me because I was ugly. At the time, I wasn't even sure what that meant, but I knew it was an insult.

If he hadn't come to the reunion, he might not have made it to the top of my prank list. But the minute I heard his distinctively unpleasant laugh at the reunion, a wave of memories washed over me, painful moments that were part of my childhood psyche. Then I saw him, standing in a small circle of people who looked like they wanted to be anywhere but there. No longer the awkward, pimply-faced kid, but a man with a bulging belly, sagging jowls and thinning gray hair. Almost unrecognizable, except for the laugh, a high-pitched sound half way between a hoot and a warlock cackle. It was a sound I associated with cruel teasing and not-so-funny jokes made at my expense.

That evening, as I'd approached the group he was talking with, no one was laughing except him. Had he said something intended to be funny? Did he still aim to put people down with cruel humor, or were his jokes stale leftovers from the past? Either way, it looked to me like he deserved a slap on the wrist.

At first, I thought Tim's punishment didn't require anything too dramatic. In some ways I felt sorry for him. He was pathetic. A failed stand-up comedian with a lousy script. But the more I thought about it, the angrier I got. He needed to get over himself. And perhaps I could play a part in helping that along. Still, to be fair, I needed to know more about his current life before deciding his sentence.

At the reunion, they'd given out contact information for most attendees, although I had deliberately failed to fill out that part of the form. But I had Tim's address, so one day I drove by his home. It was in a residential neighborhood filled with cul-de-sacs that all looked alike. A veritable maze with street names commemorating the trees that had been removed for the development: Spruce, Three Pines, Red Oak . . . The form had also listed his occupation: construction worker. And his marital status: married with four kids. I was glad I'd decided to minimize his punishment. After all, his wife and kids weren't on my list. I'd already made lives miserable for family members of other targets. I didn't want to make that a standard practice.

Tailing him to his work site didn't tell me much other than that he was part of a handful of men in work clothes and hard hats who were putting up the framework for what the sign said was going to be an apartment building with 50 units. Not particularly interesting work to watch. Nor could I get close enough to hear anything that was said. I didn't bother hanging around.

Then one afternoon I drove by his home hoping for inspiration and saw his wife and kids get into a dilapidated, dirt-streaked station wagon. When they ended up at a mall, I continued to follow them. The first thing I noted was that the kids paid little attention to anything their mother asked them to do. Whether it was to stay nearby, quit shouting, or stop hitting each other. The oldest kid, a teenage boy wearing a black T-shirt with a skull on the front, kept punching the two younger boys, for no reason as far as I could tell. Then he pulled a candy bar out of his pocket, ate it in two bites, and threw the wrapper on the floor. When I overheard him viciously taunting his sister and saw him pulling her hair until she cried, I decided a hefty comeuppance would be appropriate for both father *and* son. Two peas in a pod as they say.

Reporters frequently called out an area on the outskirts of the city known to be frequented by drug dealers and prostitutes. Several police cars cruised by as I was wandering past the strip of shabby shops lit up by passing cars and a few streetlights that hadn't been shot out. I was disguised as a middle-aged Asian male, unsure what I would do if approached by a cop before I completed my mission. It turned out it didn't take me long to find what I was looking for. The young man selling the coke and methamphetamines barely looked at me. He wouldn't have noticed if I was an alien. All he cared about was making a buck off some addicted schmuck so he could feed his own addiction.

Planting the drugs in Tim's truck during the day while he was at work was easy. I did it in plain sight disguised as an old lady. The elderly tend to be invisible, especially old women. Getting into character had been fun—the slightly bent stance, the uneven walk, the jerky movements. I paused next to his truck as if I needed a few moments to catch my breath, waiting until I thought no one was looking. Then I slipped the Slim Jim between the window and the rubber seal, wiggling it until the lock button popped up. It was lucky Tim drove an old truck; a newer model would have required more expertise to break into. Once inside, I quickly pushed the bag of drugs under the driver's seat and relocked the door.

After that, all it took was a disposable burner phone and a single phone call to the police. They seemed eager to make an easy arrest.

They stopped him as he was approaching his truck and apparently asked to search it. He had no reason to resist. At least that's what he thought.

I'd been sitting at a nearby bus stop waiting for it to happen. After it did, no one paid any attention to the old woman who slowly climbed aboard the bus, fumbling in her purse for the fare.

Two days later his unpleasant son was picked up for having a switch blade in his backpack at school. According to the anonymous caller, he'd threatened several kids with it. The bag of roofies was a little extra I threw in as a bonus. Planting the switch blade and roofies had been a piece of cake. I used the old run-into-someone-on-the-sidewalk trick. As the old lady fell, she'd dropped a bag of groceries that spilled everywhere and grabbed at his pack to break her fall. She then hit him with her cane and loudly insisted he pick up her spilled food. If there hadn't been other people around, he probably would have hit her back and moved on. But even bullies have some limits.

I wondered if later he would put two and two together. Even if he did, and if the police found his story credible enough to search for the old lady, since she didn't exist, they wouldn't be able to find her.

10

JUST DESSERTS

I've never been afraid of snakes or bugs, but when I was young, I remember other girls screaming when they saw even a tiny garter snake or a spider of any size. The garter snakes never hung around long enough to pose any kind of threat, and the poor spiders only wanted to be left alone to eat other bugs. I felt sorry for them. The spiders and snakes, that is. And the screaming and thrashing around seemed to me like part act and part uninformed histrionics. "Oh, I'm a helpless girl who needs a brave male to save me from the nasty *whatever.*" Still, I realize there are some innate fears shared by large groups of people. I was counting on that.

My next victim was near the bottom of my list and chosen partly as a matter of convenience. She was a former grade school classmate who clerked at a Fred Meyers where I shop, and she lived not too far away in a small house in a row of houses probably built in the 60s. When we were in grade school, she could always be found hanging upside down on the bars at recess, showing off her agility and her colorful underpants. She hadn't been the brightest bulb, about a 50 watt, so I might have excused her exhibitionist behavior if it hadn't been for the way she picked on me. For that abuse, she upped her wattage to 220, bombarding me with insulting comments whenever there was someone in earshot, memorializing the "fugly" label. She didn't single me out for any particular reason that I knew of, most likely it was because I didn't fight back. People like her enjoy attacking someone who won't defend themselves. It's a guaranteed win.

I used a drag queen disguise to buy the snakes in a large chain pet store. The clerk had scaly skin on his arms, as if he was a distant relative of the reptiles he was selling. Unlike the clerk in the costume shop, he at least pretended to be interested when I volunteered how I was going to use them in my act. But he didn't ask for a free ticket to the show.

While he was ringing up my purchase, I smiled and waved for the camera on the wall behind the counter. It felt in character. Then, as he bagged and boxed the pets I'd chosen—one western hognose, one ball python and one medium-sized garter snake—the clerk tried to get me to buy a carrier and a tank for each snake. But I said I was already set up. In truth, I didn't need any place to house them, even temporarily, because I didn't plan on keeping them more than a few hours. As soon as it was dark enough to make my deliveries, they were history.

The week before I'd watched her house at night to see if she had an established routine. She did. It included opening her bedroom window at night about ten inches. And there was no screen. Not a very safe practice, but one I was pleased to see. Furthermore, there didn't seem to be any activity in the neighborhood during the early morning hours, and no night owls with their lights on after about 11:00 pm. Of course, there was always the possibility that someone would get up in the middle of the night, see me, and report a prowler to the police. I was counting on the trees and hedges along the street to camouflage my movements.

That night, as I sneaked toward her house, I apologized to the harmless but scary-looking snakes, although I didn't think their tiny heads held enough brain cells to appreciate what was about to happen to them.

The black garter snake with the yellow strip along his back went into the mailbox on top of some existing mail. Hopefully she would check her box before the mail carrier dropped off more. People who deliver mail have enough to put up with without having to worry about checking each mailbox for snakes. Garter snakes aren't venomous or particularly aggressive, but I envisioned my target reaching into the box without giving the interior a thorough look first and the snake leaping toward the light to escape, maybe even slithering across her arm in the process.

The hognose went into the garden shed. To someone unfamiliar with the breed, they look very "snaky." A lot like a rattlesnake. But they have an upturned scale at the end of their snout that they use for digging; hence the name "hognose." In spite of their size and appearance, they are actually shy and gentle creatures. At least that's what I read. To me, it looked sufficiently menacing to give my target quite a fright, perhaps startle her enough to make her wet her colorful underpants—assuming she still liked panties she could show off. I sincerely hoped the snake got away before she attacked it with a garden tool. I'd like to think it glided off into the neighborhood, adapted its eating habits to what was available in the area, avoided being killed by a crow or raccoon, and lived out its years in relative comfort and freedom.

Last, I slipped the python in through her open window. It was almost three feet long with beige splotches that resembled tiny alien heads on a dark body. They apparently like warmth, so maybe he would cuddle up with her on the bed. I could picture her rolling over and gazing into his tiny snake-eyes as she awoke. That sent chills down my back just thinking about it.

Unfortunately, I would never know if the snakes managed to scare her sufficiently to justify my choice of attack. But as I went over all of the possible scenarios in my mind, I felt confident the snakes had been worth what I'd paid for them. If one day I found out she loved reptiles and had adopted three snakes she'd found as pets, I would be extremely disappointed. Although happy for the snakes.

Next, I went "off list" to choose a victim. It happened because of an exchange I overheard at work. Chad, one of my least favorite co-workers, made a comment about another employee who was a bright, hard-working, and gentle soul who happened to be transgender. Chad, on the other hand, was a self-centered slacker who had repeatedly challenged my suggestions on a previous project, not because he had any ideas of his own, but because he enjoyed putting people down almost as much as he liked boasting about his antique car collection. From what I knew of him, he qualified as misogynistic, homophobic, and transphobic. He represented so much of what I disliked about people in my past, how could I resist taking a break from my personal target list to focus on him? I had spent so much time thinking up ways to retaliate against people that I had punishments to spare. And he was a deserving recipient.

The obvious approach was to hit him where it hurt the most—his car collection. I considered the usual things— punctured tires, smashed windows, keyed doors, and even theft. But that didn't send the message I wanted. He needed to be somehow publicly shamed for his misguided views. Because of my own experience, public shaming was one of my favorite punishments. It needed to be based on something the "victim" was currently doing, something that deserved to be called out.

Slowly, my plan evolved.

First, I needed a subject that would get him talking. Second, I needed eyes and ears to get his comments on record. Finally, I needed to make the sound bites I collected public, plus making sure that HR received a copy.

It didn't take me long to figure out ways to jumpstart the process. All I needed was something he would see when he was around others that would trick him into making a politically incorrect comment. It didn't matter if the provocative language of the message was consistent with his phobic views on social issues or the exact opposite; either way I was confident that his response would make him look bad. Perhaps I could put a flyer promoting gender equality on the wall next to the coffee pot, with a few statistics about disparities in pay or advancement within corporations. Or, I could mock up a solicitation to support trans-gender kids and leave stacks of them on breakroom tables. Or, I could copy some propaganda from a white supremacy group and put it on the bulletin board, highlighting a few inflammatory statements. Then there were the issues of critical race theory, bathrooms for transgenders, why we needed a woman to run for President, on and on. So many possibilities.

Nor did it take much effort to figure out how to record him. Fairly sophisticated spy equipment is readily available to the average citizen these days. Tiny wireless cameras. Voice activated audio recorders. Whether for personal security or to spy on someone—sellers don't care as long as they are making money.

I bought a computer to use for the design and production of message content and immediately reported it stolen. Just in case someone searched the cloud, or wherever computer information is stored these days, to see if they could track where the propaganda had come from. My intention was to toss it in the water somewhere after removing and destroying its hard drive. I also purchased some spray paint that was perfect for small jobs around the house . . . or for leaving messages on mirrors and walls.

It seemed to me that there were two obvious locations at work where I could catch Chad badmouthing either individuals or entire groups of people: the break room and the men's restroom nearest Chad's desk. I had never been in the men's restroom and had no idea if men actually engaged in talk there or if that was a movie myth. But it was probably worth a shot. Especially if I gave them something interesting to talk about. It seemed to me that the break room was the most likely place to catch Chad in an indiscretion though. Again, it was a matter of putting out the right bait.

After considering and rejecting all sorts of topics and approaches, I decided to try one thing in the men's restroom and another in the breakroom.

Since a lot of people read things posted on the bulletin board in the breakroom, I was going to put up an article in support of the Proud Boys, highlighting their views on the superiority of the white race and use of violence to defend their rights. It probably wouldn't remain up for long, but it would certainly create a stir. If Chad was around for a discussion of the neo-fascist group, he just might say something he would later regret.

Meanwhile, there was one issue I already knew he felt strongly about, something that if vocalized and recorded would require HR to take some action. As painful as it was to write a disparaging comment about the transgender person in our department, that seemed like the topic most likely to provoke a reaction. In addition to what I'd over-heard Chad say before, I'd seen him mock his colleague behind his back with physically demeaning gestures that fit some stereotype Chad carried in his warped, pea-brain view of the world. I had little doubt that he would jump at the opportunity to further belittle his colleague.

Finding an article to put up on the bulletin board about the Proud Boys took less than fifteen minutes. They have quite a following in far-right circles. I printed it at home from my recently purchased laptop that would be headed for oblivion as soon as my plan was implemented. The next day, I waited until after hours when the office felt deserted before heading for the breakroom. Since I still often stayed late, I knew no one would think that was strange.

There was no one in the breakroom. The coffee pot had been turned off, but no one had bothered to dump out what was left. I poured myself a cup of coffee to justify being there, then quickly installed the listening device and tacked the article to the bulletin board. I was so relieved not to be caught in the act that I forgot the coffee had probably been there for a long time and took a sip. It was pretty awful, but I returned to my desk with it anyway. It was my prop.

I waited another hour. The cleaning crew had come and gone, and the security guy had made his sweep of the area and moved on. There was no guarantee that I wouldn't stumble across someone working late or an employee who came back to pick up something they'd left behind. If that happened, then I would be seen in a place I wasn't supposed to be with no reasonable story to explain my presence there. But it was now or never. I grabbed my oversized handbag with the equipment I needed in it and headed for the men's room near Chad's office.

There are only a few cameras in internal hallways, but there are cameras at the entrance to each suite of offices. Fortunately, the one on Chad's floor was pointed slightly askew, so all I needed to do was hug the left wall until I was out of range. There didn't appear to be anyone in the vicinity, but there was always the possibility that some man I hadn't seen was still there and would suddenly decide to take a leak. I needed to act quickly and get in and out fast as possible. Otherwise, it would be *me* and not Chad who ended up being reported to HR. And vandalizing a men's room was not something that would look good on my resume.

When I arrived at the restroom, I knocked, poked my head in, and asked, "Anybody in here?" I was prepared to say that a colleague had asked me to check to see if he'd left his wallet next to one of the sinks. I wasn't sure it made sense for someone to do that, but I doubted anyone would question me. After all, there's nothing to steal in a restroom. I was probably okay until I actually started writing out the message.

When no one answered, I went inside, set up my spy equipment, and spray painted a politically incorrect and despicable message about our transgender employee across a bank of mirrors. I didn't linger to appreciate my artwork but made a beeline for the door before the paint had a chance to drool or dry.

As far as I could tell, no one saw me as I exited the restroom and hurriedly slipped past the camera at the end of the hall. Nor was anyone around when I returned to my desk. I was fairly certain that my mission had been accomplished in secrecy. And very relieved.

I didn't stay long after I'd completed my tasks. Now all I had to do was wait.

The next day seemed longer than usual. Time always passes slowly when you're waiting for something to happen—water to boil, the mail to arrive, the microwave to heat your dinner, or, in this instance, everyone to leave the building so I could check the listening devices I'd illegally installed. I'd already noticed earlier that someone had removed the Proud Boys' article from the bulletin board in the break room. It hadn't been up long, so I doubted many people saw it, and I didn't know whether Chad had been in the break room or not before it was taken down. I had no way of knowing what had happened in the men's room on the floor above either. But I held onto a tiny shred of hope that one of my traps had snapped shut on the intended victim.

When I got an opportunity to retrieve my listening device from the break room, I was pleased to hear Chad's voice came through loud and clear on the recording. When someone asked, "Who the hell put this up?" he enthusiastically defended the Proud Boys and their efforts to save the downtrodden white male being discriminated against by government, minorities, the press, large companies—apparently by every group that wasn't composed exclusively by straight, white males or that promoted diversity. Listening to the exchange, his views might make him unpopular with peers, but I wasn't sure it was enough to get a warning from HR.

Later that evening when I sneaked into the restroom on the floor above my office to retrieve my other listening device, the mirrors looked like an ad for a cleaning product, not a smudge or even a tiny trace of the message I'd left the previous evening. I hoped that Chad had seen it and made a few comments before the cleaning staff had worked their magic. There was undoubtedly buzz about the nasty message resonating throughout the organization, but my plan would only be successful if a conversation including Chad had taken place in the men's room.

I put on my headphones to listen to the recording. At first there was nothing but silence. I fast-forwarded until there was the sound of someone entering. He managed to use the toilet and leave without saying a word. Then, there were several voices talking at the same time, like a group had come in together. Although I couldn't understand what they were saying, random words that popped out made it clear that they were reacting to the message I'd sprayed on the mirrors. Then things got calmer and I could make out what was being said. I heard a couple more men come into the conversation, but no Chad. I was almost giving up when he joined the conversation.

"Hey, I hear someone painted something on the mirror." There was a pause while he apparently read the message. Then, "Holy shit, that bastard nailed it, didn't he?"

I admit to being dismayed that there seemed to be agreement that the "bastard" had indeed "nailed it." I'd hoped for more from colleagues and was relieved that I didn't recognize any other voices. I was elated when Chad continued to dominate the conversation. He was a lemming charging over a cliff. A drunk looking for a bar fight. A rat who couldn't resist the smell of peanut butter in a trap. The recording might be illegal, but it would make him the company poster boy for discrimination.

I made a USB copy for our HR department and put it in inter-office mail marked: "Attention – Urgent." Then I surreptitiously left another flash drive on the IT receptionist's desk. Right next to her scotch tape dispenser and a copper paper clip container. I was counting on her taking a look to see what was on it so she could pass it along to the right person. Perhaps while cursing the person who'd left it on her desk without a note or instructions.

Then I scattered a dozen more flash drives around in public locations, like Santa Claus on a drunken spree. Two at a nearby Starbucks. One on the counter at a Geek Squad service area. Four at a local social gaming spot, a Barcade. And four at a community center that had an area devoted to computers for low-income kids. For good measure, I left one on a desk at the local library. These were random drops within walking distance of the office. And just in case there were cameras around, I wore a wig and baseball cap, nondescript clothes and kept my head down while trying not to look like someone doing something they didn't want anyone to see. Which isn't as easy as you might think.

Hopefully, no one would trace the USB flash drives back to me and one or more people would check out what was on the thumb they found and become angry enough to share its contents with friends and colleagues or post its contents on social media.

That night I got rid of the computer I'd used to print the article and switched the setting on my printer back to "save jobs."

Although I'd given it my best shot, success wasn't guaranteed. But the next day I was pleased to hear through the rumor mill about an irate IT employee who'd stormed up to Chad and accused him of being a "fucking lowlife" and called him several creative slurs that people seemed reluctant to repeat. It was only a few hours later that social media started posting and commenting on Chad's rants. I had included Chad's name and position within the company on the drive, so our company was soon bombarded with complaints and demands that Chad be fired immediately. By late afternoon reporters were hounding members of the board and the executive team with questions about the authenticity of the information and what was being done to remedy the situation.

Everything happened rapidly after that, proving that corporations can act quickly when bad press is involved and no one at the top is in trouble. By the next morning, Chad was gone, and the CEO made a public statement apologizing for not recognizing sooner that Chad was a "troubled man who should not have been on the payroll."

One reporter noted that there had been at least one internal complaint at Keller and Eaves prior to the incident. That was something I hadn't known but reinforced my belief that he deserved to be fired. Multiple social media sites posted Chad's comments, but my favorite was a YouTuber's video of Chad leaving the building, head down, metaphoric tail between his legs, overlaid with my audio. It got 10,000 hits within the first two hours.

All in all, it was a gratifying outcome. And no one seemed to notice the role I'd played in his fall from grace.

Things were going so well, I'm afraid I got overconfident.

11

FOILED!

Initially I'd decided family members were out of bounds. Not because they didn't deserve to be on my list, but because I thought it was too dangerous for me to target any of them. As long as I wasn't murdering or assaulting people, I doubted anyone would be looking for connections between me and my acts of revenge. But I could easily become a suspect in a transgression against a family member. Depending, of course, on whether it was something that came to the attention of the authorities. All things considered, it seemed smart to avoid drawing attention to myself by seeking retaliation against a relative.

Then my mother made one of her guilt-trip calls and babbled on about various family members. It was her way of checking in with me without actually carrying on a conversation. I pictured her telling someone that she had talked with me "just last week." The dutiful mother fulfilling her obligation to her disappointing offspring.

One of the relatives she updated me on was my Uncle Harry. She waxed eloquent about his cauliflower and artichokes and praised his green thumb in such glowing terms I could almost visualize him kneading the earth with oversized leaf-green thumbs. However, in my childhood memories, he wasn't revered for his gardening expertise, but cursed for his black heart. At family gatherings he would talk about me as if I was an object to be critiqued instead of an insecure little girl with an unfortunate face.

"I can't imagine whose side of the family she takes after. Got any uglies on your side?" he once asked my father while I was standing just a few feet away. Another time he told my mother, "Maybe she was switched at birth. If I were you, I'd check up on the other mothers who gave birth at the same time. See if any of them looked like they broke the mold." And on more than one occasion he said to my sister, "You should be thankful you don't look anything like your sibling." Statements like these went beyond "insensitive." In my opinion, they catapulted into the "mean" category. Especially since they were said when I was within earshot.

Not only did he reinforce my parents' underlying guilt about bringing an unattractive child into the world, he made me question whether I should ever have been born. And he made my sister hate me even more. Green thumb and black heart. Yes, Uncle Harry deserved a plate of retribution served with his praiseworthy produce.

Even after I decided to put Uncle Harry on my list, I argued with myself about the wisdom of doing so. In the end, I decided that a discomfiting minor poke would violate my rule against targeting family members only a teensy bit and wouldn't immediately call attention to me. After all, I hadn't been around Uncle Harry much in ages. And my mother's bragging about his vegetable garden hardly screamed "catalyst for revenge." Not that she would necessarily remember her own rambling comments made during her duty call.

After considering a variety of options that would allow me to remain at arm's length from what was happening to my uncle, I began signing him up for a zillion subscriptions to all sorts of magazines. Well, maybe not a zillion. And not all at once. I wanted to annoy him, not make him suspicious. I used the "toss the frog in cold water and slowly heat it to a boil" approach. Besides, there aren't as many magazine racks in stores as there used to be, and there are more cameras everywhere. Even wearing disguises, I had to be careful. If I thought I wouldn't be seen, I removed "blow-ins"—loose subscription cards—or ripped out ones that were attached in some way. Sometimes I actually bought the magazines to obtain the subscription cards. But especially with the oddball and erotic subscriptions, I preferred surreptitiously removing the sign-up forms, like patients in waiting rooms ripping out recipes from Sunset Magazine or Better Homes and Gardens. Once I had the cards, it was easy to disguise my handwriting and put in my uncle's name and address. And I always checked the "bill me later" box so he would have to cancel in order to avoid being charged.

It seemed unlikely that he would consider the possibility that an actual live person was responsible for his sudden popularity. He would probably assume he was the target of a scam in which someone had sold his address to magazine publishers. Nor did I have to feel guilty about the minor theft I was committing; there was no real collateral damage. If someone bought the magazine and wanted to subscribe, they would find a way to do so. And some of the magazines I signed him up for didn't deserve to be published in the first place.

The thought of his mailbox bursting with unwanted and often undesirable or salacious magazines and catalogs was not only pleasing, it felt appropriate. Some of the more sexual or off-beat subscriptions would surely make his mail carrier raise their eyebrows. Maybe he or she was a gossip, and if they told even a single neighbor about my uncle's copious and unsavory interests, it would get around quickly. Someone might even say something to his face. He could claim he was being spammed, of course, but the allegations would linger in the air like a bad smell. Uncle Harry would find out what it was like to be made the butt of a joke because of something over which he had no control.

If I had called it quits at that point, things wouldn't have gone sideways. But the more I thought about Uncle Harry, the more I wanted him to suffer. How could I let him off with a single, benign act of payback? He had hurt me so many times. I wanted to hurt him back. I wanted him to feel wronged.

Since he apparently loved his garden, the most obvious way to get back at him was to take it away, to destroy it. Stomp on his cauliflower. Pull down his green beans. Trample his tomatoes. Extract his green onions. Crush his cucumbers. In short, demolish whatever he was growing. I could even spike his fruit trees. That would be hard for me to stomach, but for Uncle Harry, I could do it. Afterwards, I would leave the gate open in case there were any animals in the area who needed a midnight snack and didn't mind if their food was in less than perfect condition.

I chose a moonless night and dressed like a cat burglar. There was no one on the unlit street when I parked in a row of cars around the corner from a convenience store and walked the four blocks to his house. I hadn't been there many times as an adult, but I knew my way around based on studying street views online at the library. And, as luck would have it, there was a tree-lined alley that ran behind the row of houses where he lived. Since his garden was in the back, that offered convenient and secretive access.

When I heard a dog barking, I wasn't worried. It didn't sound close. Although I would have preferred silence. If someone was prowling around. I wanted to hear them coming. But I didn't really expect to encounter anyone out and about at this time of night in this sleepy neighborhood. I just wished the mutt would shut up so I could be sure.

With a tinge of guilt and regret, I was spiking his prolific and innocent peach tree when I thought I heard a footstep nearby. I paused, then slowly turned. There was a dark figure against a faint moonlit sky only a few feet away and moving in my direction. That damn dog. His barking had obviously attracted notice.

"What are you doing?" the person demanded in a loud angry voice as he got even closer. He had a shovel in his hand, and I didn't think it was for digging a ditch. I started backing away, but he wasn't about to let me run off.

"You no-good hooligan," he screamed as he charged.

I was thinking about his use of the antiquated term "hooligan" as I automatically responded by reaching for the gun I carry for self-defense when I'm out at night. Without really thinking about the consequences of what I was doing, I withdrew my weapon and shot him as he started to swing the shovel at my head. He collapsed literally at my feet. It was too dark to see his face, but I assumed he was both surprised and in pain, unless he was dead. I froze. He wasn't making any sound. No moaning, no cursing, nothing. His body was totally still.

I'm not proud of what I did next; I didn't hang around to see if he was still alive or call 911. I ran.

As I sped down the alley, I saw a neighbor's light come on. Unless Uncle Harry had a miraculous recovery and was able to sprint back to his house or had a cell phone with him and managed to call 911 on his own, I didn't think I was in danger of exposure from him. And in spite of the dog that continued to bark, it might take a while for a neighbor to conclude something was wrong and either call the police or take a look around themselves. Although if they'd recognized the gunshot for what it was, they could be calling the police at that very moment.

It was too late for strategy; my only choice was to get away as quickly as possible without looking like I was running away.

Taking a circuitous route to my car, I kept my hoody up and pretended to be jogging, a late-night exercise junkie or insomniac. The four blocks felt like a marathon. But eventually I made it to my car without anyone yelling for me to stop. I was lucky. Well, *lucky* about my flight from the scene of an *unlucky* crime . . . of self-defense. If he hadn't come at me with a shovel, I wouldn't have shot him. I wanted him to suffer mental anguish, not kill him.

The good news was that I didn't think anyone besides Uncle Harry had seen me, and I was fairly certain he hadn't seen my face. So, if he was still alive, I doubted he would be able to identify me. Nevertheless, I made a detour to my storage unit to drop off the gun before going home. It was a space I paid for in cash under a phony name, a necessary precaution given some of my clandestine activities. The area was locked up after 8:00 pm, but I had cut some wires in the fence near a tree so I could come and go when no one was around. I was too panicked to decide what to do with my weapon other than put it in my unit. Should I act surprised that it wasn't in its box if the police came by and asked if I had a gun? It was probably too much of a coincidence to report it missing now. But I definitely needed to dispose of it as soon as possible. If no one asked, then down the road I could go on a camping trip and claim my gun was stolen from my tent. But for now, I would have to hope that the fact that I owned a gun wouldn't come up.

Besides the bullet, had I left any other evidence behind? I'd been using gloves, so there were no fingerprints on the metal rod I'd been pounding into the tree when he surprised me. And I had somehow managed to hold onto my hammer. All of the other tools I'd planned on using for my midnight raid were still in my backpack. I knew I'd left footprints and would have to get rid of my tennis shoes. But I'd been planning on doing that anyway. Other than that, I thought I was in the clear.

The next day the local morning news covered the incident.

According to the reporter, one of Uncle Harry's neighbors heard another neighbor's dog barking and went out to have a look around, taking his own dog with him. When *his* dog started barking and raced off, he followed and found Harry lying on the ground. The reporter credited Uncle Harry's nosy neighbor with saving his life. But the way I saw it, it was the neighbor's dog my uncle should be thanking. Of course, if some other dog hadn't been barking in the first place, I might have heard Uncle Harry coming and got away without shooting him. Two dogs, one endangered my uncle's life and another saved it.

It wasn't clear whether Harry was able to talk to the neighbor or not. But according to the ambulance driver, he was unconscious when they arrived. The police were quoted as saying it looked like he'd surprise a burglar and had been shot with a handgun at close range. There was no mention of the shovel, the spike in the tree, or if anyone had been seen fleeing the scene.

Have you ever wanted to do the "normal thing" but wasn't sure what was normal under the circumstances? That was my problem the morning after I'd shot my uncle. If I hadn't been the shooter and had simply heard the news report, would I call my parents? What about my sister? Or would I just go to work as usual? And how would anyone know whether I'd even heard or read about what had happened?

After much deliberation and soul-searching, I called my parents. Dad sounded tentative when he answered, even though I was pretty sure they had caller ID and therefore knew it was me on the other end of the line. "Hello?" he said as if asking a question.

"Dad, it's me, Callista."

"Yes, I know." Then why hadn't he said, "Hello, Callista?" Or, in spite of caller ID was he hoping it was someone else?

"Are you and Mom okay?" I asked, playing the dutiful daughter.

"You've heard about Harry?"

"Yes, I saw it on the news. Do you know how he is doing?"

"We're getting ready to go to the hospital," he said.

"Do you want me to come? I can be there in about two hours." Please, please say "no," I silently pleaded with the gods.

"No, your sister, Clara, is going to meet us there." Did he think I didn't know my sister's name?

"Okay, but I could come too."

"No, that won't be necessary."

A flicker of anger whipped my adrenaline. It was like not being asked to a party you didn't want to attend in the first place. But I was still jealous of Clara for being the child my parents turned to for support. Struggling to keep my voice even, I asked, "Is there anything else I can do?"

"No, ah, but thank you for offering." That sounded so formal, like he was talking to a casual acquaintance rather than to his daughter. Did he hear the distance his words and tone put between us?

"I'll go ahead and go to work then. But don't hesitate to call if you decide you need something. And please let me know how Uncle Harry is doing."

"I will." He hung up abruptly without saying goodbye.

I sat there, seething over feeling shut out, but relieved at the same time. I was glad I'd called though. And glad, for once, that I'd been rejected. It would give me time to decide if there was anything I should be doing to cover my tracks. Besides getting rid of my tennis shoes. I'd washed them the night before and managed to separate the sole of the left shoe from the bottom to make it look like that's why they'd been tossed. Just in case someone found them in the dumpster I'd dropped them in. The dumpster was in an alcove alongside a strip mall grocery I'd stopped at once on my way to the office. I'd noticed the dumpster because a youngish woman in shabby clothes was going through it, one item at a time, her shopping cart already half filled with her finds. Now I was glad I hadn't taken the time to give her a few dollars. She might have remembered me from that. But I wished I could have dropped off my expensive tennis shoes without damaging them first, in case they were something she could use.

When I arrived at the office, I heard murmuring as heads turned towards me. By virtue of being related to a crime victim, I was currently a bit of a celebrity. Soon I found myself the center of attention from colleagues mouthing condolences but probably just hoping to learn some gruesome details.

"Really," I said, holding up my hands, "I only talked briefly to my dad. He and my mother and sister were headed to the hospital. They're supposed to call me later with an update on his condition." Not that I intended to share anything they told me with colleagues.

"Don't you think you should be there with them?" a woman's voice I couldn't quite place asked. I looked around, trying to figure out who had said that, identifying two possibilities.

"I can go over after work if I'm needed." I wanted to add "bitch," but didn't. What right did anyone have to cast covert aspersions on my relationship with family members? Push a little more, I thought, and I'll figure out who you are and put *you* on my list.

"I heard he's in a coma," someone said, changing the subject.

"My dad didn't know. As I said, I'm hoping to learn more later."

"Were you close to your uncle?" another voice asked.

Ignoring the question phrased in the past tense, I extricated myself from the group, saying, "I need to get to work."

An hour later an enterprising reporter managed to track me down via phone and was pleased when I didn't hang up, but displeased that I didn't know anything. "Call my sister Clara," I advised. "She's at the hospital." You want to be in charge, sis, you take the heat.

Late afternoon I got a call from Detective Peters. "Sorry to hear about your uncle," he said.

That didn't sound like the opening line from an official about to ask if you shot someone, but I was still leery.

"I was about to check in with my parents to see how he's doing."

"I talked to one of the officers. They operated, and he's stable but still unconscious."

"That sounds promising," I said. And possibly dangerous for me. Why was Detective Peters even talking to someone from another jurisdiction about what had happened? After a very brief pause, I asked, "Do you know if they have anyone in custody?"

"Sorry, I don't have any insider details. You probably heard that for some inexplicable reason, someone was spiking a fruit tree in his back yard. He must have caught them in the act."

"Yes, I heard that. Who spikes someone's fruit tree? Was it blocking their view? Or dropping leaves that got blown into their yard?"

"I'm not sure, but I'd say it was someone who doesn't like him."

"An enemy of Uncle Harry's? I'm sorry, but I can't picture him as someone who has enemies. And that still doesn't explain why they were spiking his tree."

"People do strange things. That's what keeps me in business."

"Well, I certainly wouldn't want you to lose your job." I tried to sound jaunty, but it came out flat.

"You know what they say—*crime is common; logic is rare.*"

"No, I didn't know 'they' said that." Again, my jauntiness fell flat, at least to my ears.

"We detectives are lucky most criminals aren't that smart." He paused. "They'll catch the guy who attacked your uncle."

"I hope so," I lied. "Well, thank you for calling."

"I'll let you know if I hear anything. Meanwhile, stay away from gardens at night."

"Gardens *and* graveyards," I said. And hopefully, from the police.

12

SHOOT FOR THE MOON

After the fiasco at Uncle Harry's, I considered lying low for a while. It was the smart thing to do. But then, there wasn't anything terribly smart about setting out to get revenge for past wrongs in the first place. Nor do most stories of revenge that I've read about have happy endings. Eventually, someone usually gets caught, if not by the police, then by one of the victims. And things usually go sideways from there. It occurred to me that I should be thinking more about consequences and spending less time focused on emotional justifications.

With fear of getting caught looming large, I did some soul-searching about justice, the ability of people to change, and my own motivation for seeking revenge.

One of the more memorable sermons from my church-going days was by a pastor quoting from Deuteronomy about the nature of God's vengeance. At the time I was startled by the savageness of it. Although it's obviously an entirely different situation when it's an act of God rather than a human response to injustice. Still, the description in Deuteronomy 24:42 makes my puny efforts pale by comparison: *"When I sharpen my flashing sword and begin to carry out justice, I will take revenge on my enemies and repay those who reject me. I will make my arrows drunk with blood, and my sword will devour flesh—the blood of the slaughtered and the captives, and the heads of the enemy leaders."*

When first compiling my list, I remembered this Biblical passage and could picture "arrows drunk with blood" taking out the bullies from my past, their corpses lying on the ground in a neat row with me standing over them holding an impressive wooden bow. God didn't wait for his enemies to self-destruct, so why should I? In a just world, what "goes around" *should* "come around." An *eye for an eye.* I revere the concept, but based on my experience and reading about what happens to people, not only in my local community but all over the world, what's "right" or "good" doesn't necessarily prevail. In fact, I would say it seldom does.

None of the people on my list were my enemies in the traditional sense of the word, but they had wronged me or sinned against others who hadn't deserved it. Wars had been started over less serious grievances. So, I didn't feel it necessary to guilt myself for considering ways to punish them.

Granted, I wasn't an avenging angel out to right the wrongs of the world. All I wanted was a slice of justice for my own limited life and suffering. And since I had sworn off killing those who had sinned against me, not "devouring flesh" with a sword, but simply giving people from my past a taste of what it's like to be the target of someone's venom, that meant I wasn't really a bad person either—was I?

To be honest, before now I hadn't spent much time thinking about whether I was a good person with a few warped tendencies or a bad person overall. I've assumed I was good enough, by most standards. I had never deliberately gone out of my way to hurt anyone . . . until I started on my revenge journey, that is. Until then, my life's focus had been on proving I was worthy of respect. It was failing to achieve that goal at Keller and Eaves that turned my life around and started me down a dark path of retaliation.

Now that I was taking a step back and looking at the big picture, one thing I felt I needed to consider as a part of this equation was the possibility that the people on my list had become better people, individuals who would no longer make my little list if I was judging them in their current state. It was possible their childhood meanness had transformed into positive adult traits. Perhaps I was the one caught in a moment of time, like a bug in a piece of amber. Was revenge served cold a rational or simply an emotional choice? Was I becoming as ugly inside as I was on the outside?

Should I call it quits and simply accept my past and my future as "fugly"? Or should I accept that appearance is everything and consider plastic surgery? I had the means to do so. I didn't need to be beautiful, just a little less unattractive. Other people didn't hesitate to change their looks—a nip and tuck here and there, Botoxed lips, neck lifts, breast augmentation. You name it, someone's done it to their face or body to improve their image. Why shouldn't I benefit from what was medically possible? Maybe there was still a chance for a normal life, a family, a happy future. Perhaps all I had to do was end my fixation with past wrongs and focus on the here and now.

On the other hand, Miss Jean Brodie believed loyalty to ideas and people was solidified at an "impressionable age," which happened to be about twelve in the classic novel about her. The Catholic Church considers eight the age of accountability. And there is research to suggest our personalities are set as early as age seven. Based on what I've read and experienced, it *was* possible that the people on my list had experienced miraculous come-to-Jesus moments and were now enlightened, kind, and virtuous. But I had my doubts. I already knew of several who hadn't; why would the others be any different?

And even if I accepted the notion that people were capable of change and earning redemption in the eyes of the church, did I personally believe that absolved them of past wrongs? Or was there something left on the balance sheet that needed reconciliation? Could someone have an epiphany and become self-aware, ask for forgiveness, and make amends? Like an alcoholic reaching Step 8 in

AA's Principles: ". . . an *accurate and unsparing survey of the human wreckage he has left in his wake.*"

Even though no one had asked me for forgiveness, as I considered the yin and yang of what I'd been doing, I found myself softening toward my mission a little. And considering cosmetic surgery more seriously. Then I remembered Hugh. He had made so many people miserable when we were younger. And after seeing him at the reunion, I had little doubt that he was the same old Hugh. Still, if his worst crimes were the ones I had personally experienced, maybe I could bury those memories and move on. Unless the rumor was true and he really was guilty of raping someone at a party in front of a group of other boys. It may have been an act of youthful bravado, a misguided sense of what constituted masculinity among teenage boys trying to outdo each other by boasting about their sexual exploits. But understanding "why" didn't wipe away the pain and lasting impact something like that may have had on his victims. I needed to know if it was rumor or reality before I could burn my little list.

"Karen? This is Callista." I'd placed the call in spite of my reservations about calling attention to connections between me and the people I targeted.

"Callista. It's good to hear from you." She sounded like she meant it.

"I was wondering if you'd like to have lunch? We didn't really get a chance to talk much at the reunion."

"That sounds good. Let's do it." With her acceptance I felt a rush of adrenaline and a twinge of fear. Once I'd talked with her, I would be somewhat exposed. But she could be a wealth of information, and any source I used presented some degree of risk.

We met at an out-of-the-way Chinese restaurant mid-afternoon. The booths had high-backed wood walls that went all the way to the ceiling. They may not have been soundproof, but they provided a feeling of privacy and seemed to at least muffle nearby conversations.

I'd checked it out in advance and had reserved a booth at the back. It was across from a giant aquarium where lethargic fish roamed strands of seaweed and disappeared briefly now and then behind an assortment of rocks and phony looking castles.

Karen was right on time, as I expected she'd be. I was already seated with an open menu in front of me.

"I've never been here before," she said as she sat down and slid to the center of the seat to be directly across from me.

"Me neither. A friend recommended it." Not true, but it seemed like an innocent deception.

The waiter came to bring us a pot of tea and to ask if we had any questions. I had lots of questions, but not about the menu.

We both studied the menu and made small talk until he returned to take our orders. I got a #2 and she got a #14. It was that kind of place.

After a brief exchange about the weather, I decided to get to the point. "I'll be honest," I began. "I have a reason for wanting to talk."

"I assumed it wasn't for my scintillating conversation." She gave me a shy smile.

I paused. "It's about someone who was at the reunion. Someone whose behavior toward me when we were in school was despicable. I'm curious to know if he's changed."

Karen lost some of the color from her face as she glanced down at the table. "There were a number of people at the reunion who gave me grief in junior high and high school."

"Was one of them Hugh Graham?"

She looked up, then reached for her tea. Her hands were trembling. When she saw me noticing, she withdrew her hands and put them in her lap. "What do you know about me and Hugh?" she asked, her voice softened by a slight tremor.

Until that moment, I hadn't been thinking of Karen as a victim in the rape rumor. "I'm sorry," I said quickly. "I wanted to ask about the . . . incident . . . but it didn't cross my mind that *you* might have been involved."

"Involved? What a strange word to describe what they did to me." A single tear appeared at the corner of her left eye, threatening to roll down her cheek. She blinked it away.

"Then the rumors are true."

She nodded. "For me and probably for others."

"I assume you run into Hugh, living in the same town."

"Hugh and his gang of four. Yes."

"Oh my god—did all five . . .?" I didn't know how to ask.

"I haven't talked about this with anyone," she said, looking down again.

"I'm so sorry. I . . . I didn't have anything like that happen to me, nothing that egregious. Hugh was mentally cruel to me, and I haven't been able to forget or forgive. But I understand if you want to drop the subject." I felt like I needed to let her off the hook, but I sincerely hoped she would tell me more.

"Maybe it's time," she said. "After all these years . . . maybe it's time." She sat up straighter and took a deep breath. "Yes, all five. But Hugh was the first, the leader. And he egged them on. I . . . I tried to get away, but one held my feet while another gripped my shoulders."

"I'm so sorry," I repeated. "I really had no idea."

"It was a long time ago." It may have been a long time ago, but it was clear that her bad memories were as vivid as mine. Probably more so since the assault on her had been physical.

"You didn't report it?" I asked, but I knew the answer.

"No, I was ashamed. I let him lure me into that back room. I should have known better."

"And afterwards?"

"He threatened to say I begged him to fuck me. Like he was some god and I was *nothing*."

We both drank some tea, letting the weight of her confession settle. After a long silence, I said, "I have to ask, why did you go back to that town?"

"Believe me, I never thought I would. Except to visit my mother. Unfortunately, she needs more help than an occasional visit, and I couldn't ask her to move. She's very attached to both her house and the community. So, I moved in with her and do what I can."

"Maybe I was lucky that he and his friends thought I was too ugly to screw."

"I knew he tormented you. I'm sorry I never stood up for you."

"I understand why you didn't. They were good at intimidation and crushing confidence. But I wish we had banded together to fight back." I hesitated. "I'm going to tell you something I've never told anyone." I hadn't planned on sharing this with her, but I suddenly wanted to unburden myself. "I heard them talking about having 'taken someone's cherry.' I didn't know it was about you, and I never tried to find out more. It was the rest of their conversation that was etched in stone on my mind. They were planning who to attack next, and someone suggested me. But I was rejected as 'gross.' Then they made a few comments about my cunt and wondered if it was as ugly as my face." I could feel my cheeks flush as I spoke.

"How awful for you," Karen said with what sounded like heartfelt empathy.

"Compared to what happened to you, it's nothing. But at the time, it was 'everything' to me."

The waiter brought our food and we sat there without speaking, immersed in thought and the aroma of Asian spices. I pulled the wood chopsticks apart and took a bite.

Karen picked up her fork. "I've never managed to get the hang of those."

"I've been known to let some noodles drop off."

After a few more bites, Karen put down her fork and looked directly at me. "Why did you want to know who they had raped after all this time?"

"I've been thinking about how he should pay for what he was like back then, and I wanted to know the size of the payment."

She raised both eyebrows. "What kind of 'payment'?"

"I don't want to involve you by saying more." Somehow, I felt safe in admitting that much to Karen. Like me, she had been victimized. I couldn't imagine her running to the police to warn them someone was out to get Hugh.

"I think we've established that I'm already *involved*."

"What I mean is, I may do something that could have repercussions, and I don't want you to get into trouble. I'd appreciate it if you would try to forget about our discussion today. Pretend that it never happened."

"I've wanted to get back at Hugh for years. Whatever you're planning, I'm in." She looked and sounded stronger and more determined than I could ever have imagined.

"I don't have a plan . . . yet, but I'm working on it."

"I'm serious. I would really like to . . . see him . . . beg for mercy. But I doubt you are thinking of something like that."

I actually laughed. "The same scenario has crossed my mind, but I don't want to go to jail. I'm considering doing something behind the scenes. I'm not sure what that looks like, but I'm going to shoot for the moon on this one. I want him to suffer, to feel enough mental pain to compensate for what he put us through. I know it won't be an equal trade-off. But I want to walk away feeling like he's paid a price for years of bad behavior. Whatever it takes. But please don't feel any obligation to participate. You have your mother to think of. I don't have anyone, so if I get caught, it only affects me."

"Don't worry about that. I'm with you. Let's shoot for the moon."

13

PARTNERS

As much pleasure as I had derived from coming up with ways to get even with people in the past, that pleasure was doubled by having a partner. I looked forward to my brainstorming session lunches with Karen. We always met in the same restaurant and sat in the same booth. I grew intimately familiar with the menu and Karen's eating preferences. And I also became intimately familiar with the depth of Karen's anger toward Hugh and some of his buddies. I had accidentally unleashed a tiger, eager to attack her prey.

In spite of the fact that we were becoming fast friends as well as allies, one thing I didn't do was reveal any of my past activities. I told myself it was because I didn't want her to have anything to hide if approached by the authorities. That way she couldn't be accused of being an accomplice. But deep down, an untrusting speck in my soul didn't want to give her any leverage over me either. It was best for her and for me if she was kept in the dark.

Karen assured me that she would be up to almost any act of vengeance, even if it involved some level of violence. For instance, we agreed that one of the more fitting punishments for Hugh would be to cut off his privates. We fantasized about drugging him, taking him to some hotel, and waiting until he woke up to threaten him with a knife. But neither of us could actually imagine going through with something so horrific. In addition to being bloody and distasteful, if something like that leaked to the press, they would be all over it, most likely portraying Hugh as the victim. The police would be forced to investigate. We could see the sensational headlines with our names in the opening paragraph. Hugh would deny the rape charges, and we wouldn't be able to prove he was a liar.

Unfortunately, we needed something that would publicly humiliate but not physically mutilate him. Public humiliation was still my favorite form of vengeance.

"Something like what happened to Taylor," Karen said one evening when we met for dinner instead of lunch. "That's what we need."

"Yeah, that was pretty funny, wasn't it?" I said, sensing that Karen was in her own way laying a trap for me. She was too respectful to accuse me directly.

Karen studied my face for a minute, then said, "I personally thought it was the perfect punishment for a mean-spirited woman who was also cheating on her husband."

"I agree. We need to come up with something comparable for Hugh." Her backhanded praise told me she knew it was me but was in silent agreement not to broach the subject if I didn't freely confess. I wondered how she would feel if she knew about Dane and Adriana. Even though she said she wasn't opposed to violence, I didn't think she would approve. And I wasn't about to find out. Unless the law came after me.

"Maybe we should be working backwards on this," she said. "What kind of outcome are we talking about here? Do we want him to have fifteen minutes of humiliating fame? Threaten him with exposure of past acts to make him squirm? Lose his job or his marriage, like those photos did to Taylor? She didn't even get custody of her kids, although I understand she has visitation rights."

"I do feel sorry for her husband and her children," I said, meaning it. "They didn't deserve to suffer." But that didn't mean I lost any sleep over what I had done.

"Hugh has four kids . . ."

"That we know of," I interrupted. It was meant to be funny, but it also triggered a thought that was struggling to take shape in my head. Karen beat me to it.

"I say we make him the poster child for violating the Seventh Commandment. Nothing salacious; just good old-fashioned adultery. It isn't quite like nailing him for being a rapist, but it would have consequences. If the rumors are true, it may be fairly easy to prove."

"You're suggesting we try to catch him at it? Assuming he *is* an adulterer."

"We can hire an investigator to see if he is actually as much of a Don Juan as he pretends to be. Otherwise, I say we frame him," Karen said with feeling.

"Hiring a detective could be tricky," I said, my mind immediately going to the practical side of things. "We don't want to use either of our names. That could come back to bite us." I paused before suggesting: "How about we hire someone in his wife's name?"

"I like that. But can we pull it off?"

"I don't see why not. If we approach it right."

"And if the detective doesn't find anything?"

"My money is on them finding *something*. Maybe we'll decide to change our approach based on what turns up. But if not, then I'm with you. I say we make something up."

"I like the way you think." Karen smiled. She had a pleasant smile, even when talking about framing someone.

"It will be more credible if we have pictures though."

"Can't they be faked?"

"Probably, but I think good fakes are hard to come by. Let's hope whoever we hire finds something that Hugh would rather keep secret."

Karen looked thoughtful. "We have to face the fact that this will be bad for his kids."

"Unless we uncover something that we can blackmail him with, keep it to ourselves, and just tweak him from time to time. Otherwise, the public options will impact his entire family. I don't see a way around it."

"I suppose it's possible his kids may have mixed feelings about him. Especially if he's as much of a loser as he was back when we knew him. Maybe they won't be all that sad to lose their dad."

"Most kids are attached to their parents, even if they are dirtbags." I had plenty of experience in that department. "I think we have to face up to that."

"Well, whatever we do, if it hurts Hugh, it will undoubtedly have a ripple effect in some way on his family. I can live with that if you can."

"I say we hire an investigator and see what he or she comes up with. Then we'll have a better idea about what direction to take and how much padding we'll need to do."

The next day I set things in motion. First, I researched local investigators, concentrating on those who specialized in infidelity and domestic investigations. After narrowing it to three, two men and one woman, I chose the woman on the assumption she might be more sympathetic to "my" situation as the wife. Although I was aware that was gender stereotyping and wasn't necessarily true, I had to make a choice without a face-to-face interview. It was my best guess under the circumstances.

Her name was Verla Thomas. She worked out of what looked online to be a tiny office in a community just north of downtown. The Thomas Detective Agency website listed services but not pictures of Verla. I assumed she didn't want whoever she was investigating to recognize her. I tried finding a picture somewhere else and failed. I'm not sure why I wanted to see what she looked like; it didn't affect my decision to try to hire her. But, like most other people, I liked having a face to go with the person. Ironic.

Next, I adjusted the settings on a burner phone I purchased to disguise my voice. When I got Verla on the line, our initial exchange confirmed for me that I had made a good choice.

"I need you to be discreet," I began.

"That comes with the job," she replied. She had a low, well-modulated voice that sounded confident and trustworthy to me. Although why I thought she sounded "trustworthy" I can't exactly pinpoint. It was a gut response to her calm demeanor and quick responses.

"And I have some special requirements."

"Tell me what they are, and if I can't comply, I'll let you know up front."

"I'm concerned about my husband getting his hands on something that would make me look bad if we end up in a messy divorce. So, I'd prefer you not keep any detailed notes. Almost anything in writing can be twisted or taken out of context. For that matter, I'd prefer you not keep track of any communication. That's why I'm using a burner phone, and I assume you aren't recording this conversation."

"No, I wouldn't record any client conversations without permission. And unless what you want me to do involves complicated instructions, I don't need to keep a file on the case. Any information or pictures I gather will be turned over to you; I won't keep duplicates."

"Good. As you might have guessed, there are children involved. I want to make sure he can't put his hands on anything that later becomes an argument for retaining custody or getting joint custody."

"Understood. Anything else?"

"I'll be paying you in cash. But I don't want to come to your office. There are cameras everywhere these days."

"No problem. I have a PO Box that is perfectly safe."

Once we agreed on the ground rules, I explained that it was a bad marriage, that I suspected him of having affairs, and that I wanted any evidence she could find that would ensure that I kept the children if we divorced. She asked questions that told me she understood the situation and knew exactly what was needed. As soon as I dropped off a deposit, she would begin surveillance. As early as this evening if that's what I wanted. I said it was. Then she gave me a private contact number to call in a few days to see what progress she was making on my case. Or, she would text me on my burner phone if something came up that couldn't wait. If she found anything, anything at all, she would make arrangements to get the information and proof to me without my husband's knowledge.

Karen and I were willing to invest a fair amount of money in the attempt to find some legitimate dirt on Hugh. We knew that would simplify our task. And if we were able to use facts rather than made-up stories, it would provide some insulation against prosecution if we were caught. But one way or the other, our goal was to make Hugh pay. Still, if our detective couldn't find anything, we were fully prepared to go with Plan B. That, of course, would require even more expenses and greater ingenuity and risk. I was hoping it wouldn't come to that. Partly because I wanted to believe that he was still a bad person.

It was just three days later that I got a text from Verla; she wanted to talk to me. After our conversation, I could hardly wait to tell Karen the news. I gave her a call and arranged to have dinner at our usual restaurant. I could tell she was dying to ask me about the last-minute arrangement, but we had agreed to avoid talking about things over the phone. When I first suggested that "rule," Karen had resisted, pointing out that there was no reason for anyone to be listening to our conversations. But I had insisted, and she had finally gone along with it. What she didn't know, of course, was that I was constantly worried that I might come under investigation for a past crime. I couldn't rule out that possibility completely, and I didn't want to take any unnecessary chances.

As soon as we were seated, Karen leaned toward me across the table and said, "Well?"

"I heard from our detective today," I said, casually, like it was an everyday occurrence.

"And . . .," she prompted impatiently.

I couldn't help but smile. "Should we order first?"

"Come on, Callista."

"Okay. I just want to savor this moment." I leaned forward until our heads were only about twelve inches apart. "It's not what we expected, but it's something to work with." I forced the smile off my face and sat up straight. "Not that it's exactly *good* news. Well, good news for us, but not for his family."

"That sounds a bit scary." Karen, too, leaned back.

"It is, actually." I kept my voice low even though there was no one nearby. "He apparently hits his wife and children when he's drunk."

Karen slumped back against the wall of the bench. "Noooo. That is so sad. So wrong."

"Look at it this way, it makes our task easier, and we will be doing the family a favor."

Karen stared at me, not blinking. "But didn't that make the detective suspicious about who she was dealing with? I mean, the wife would already know that was happening."

"When Verla called me with her report, I was pretty sure she guessed I wasn't the wife. She's a smart woman. So, I confessed that I was actually a friend who sensed something was terribly wrong with their relationship and that I'd assumed he was having an affair. I explained that my friend refused to talk about her situation, and I couldn't stand sitting around and watching her suffer without doing something. That I knew she wouldn't have the stomach to have him followed, but I thought if I could hand her the evidence she needed, she might work up the courage to leave him.

"I also explained that I'd never liked him, and it didn't surprise me that he was abusive. And now that I knew the situation, I intended to do everything I could to make sure my friend and her kids were safe. I thanked her for the information and asked her to keep watching him for a few more days."

"Quick thinking."

"The bottom line is that I'm not sure Verla cares who I am . . . she was clearly upset by what she discovered. Said she almost didn't catch him because he was obviously headed home after an evening of drinking with his buddies. But she had a gut feeling and decided to stay with him a little longer. She saw his wife peek out the window as he went up the walk. She almost left at that point but stayed to check her email. Then she heard screaming.

"She got out of her car and ran up to look in a window. Hugh had his wife backed up against the wall. She said things happened so fast she barely had time to snap shots of him hitting her. But the angle and lighting were both good for taking pictures.

"Then one of the children came to see what was happening. She took several snaps of him standing in the entrance to the living room in his pajamas, rubbing the sleep out of his eyes. She heard his mother yell for him to go back to bed, but he started running toward her instead. When he got close, Hugh struck out and knocked him to the floor. Verla managed to get in two quick shots that captured the entire unpleasant incident.

"She was about to call the police when Hugh collapsed in a chair, and the wife and child ran from the room. It looked to her like he'd passed out, so she was torn. It's her experience that if the wife stays with an abusive husband, they usually deny there's a problem when police show up. And at least for a while, the wife and child were probably safe. So she left.

"That's why it made my 'confession' so easy. She wants to see him pay for his behavior almost as much as we do. It's definitely more than a job for her."

Karen's face was puckered in concentration. "So, what's our plan? Turn him in to the police?"

"I think we have to do that, but only as part of the original plan. If this is a pattern of behavior, his wife may have already decided to stay mum. She might not be willing to testify against him. She might be afraid to testify."

"You think we need to make this public, right?"

"Yeah, I say we make a list of places to send the pictures, anywhere we think they could have some repercussions for Hugh."

"A reporter or two for sure. They might shy away from targeting a specific person, but there's always the chance that could get them started on a larger story."

"Department of Health and Human Services?"

"I think there's some agency within that department that focuses on children. I'll check it out."

"Other family members?"

"Yes. And of course we should post it on social media."

"I know someone who can do that."

Karen paused and looked at me with a strange glint in her eye, but she didn't press. "Do we warn his wife before we set things in motion?"

"Maybe we should. Give her time to pack up and get out."

"What if she doesn't want to leave?"

"Knowing her relationship is going public might be all it takes to help her make the right decision for her and her children."

"I'll get the names and locations of some safe places for her to go."

"There's one problem with this that we need to consider. We don't want Hugh to think his wife is responsible for all of the publicity. That could make things even worse for her. How do we deal with that?"

We ate in silence for a while, our meals lukewarm but still tasty. After several minutes of chewing and swallowing, Karen, her voice suddenly animated, said, "We could give ourselves a group name and release the information that way. A group dedicated to helping abused women."

"I like it. But how did they, er, 'we' know to be watching him? The group had to be contacted by someone to get involved."

"We can claim it was a neighbor who alerted us to the problem, without getting specific."

"That might do it," I said. "Take it a step further and make a plea for people to look out for signs of abuse in families in their neighborhood."

"A group with a mission."

"Okay, that sounds good. But if someone researches this group, they won't find anything. No history. No office. No nothing. Just a name."

"Maybe we refer to it as a 'newly formed organization.' They key is to convince Hugh that the complaint didn't come from his wife."

"What if he confronts his neighbors? Demands to know who made the complaint."

"If he's an abuser, why would he want to do that? Wouldn't he be worried that they had overheard or seen past incidents?"

We slowly worked our way through what was left of our meal. I don't know about Karen, but I was so caught up in thinking about what we were considering doing, I ate automatically and was surprised to suddenly realize that my plate was empty.

After ordering another pot of tea, we went over next steps. "I'll tell Verla our plan," I said. "It may be best though if she doesn't know the organization isn't real."

"All we have to do is come up with a name that sounds convincing."

"I doubt she'll ask many questions. I'll also see if she has other ideas about what we might want to do with the evidence she gathers. There could be things we aren't thinking of."

When we left the restaurant, I was happy. Hugh was going to pay bigtime for his transgressions against women and children. And, indirectly, against Karen and me.

We were within days of pulling our evidence together and taking the final step in our plan to make Hugh's life miserable when Hugh almost ruined everything.

It was late Friday evening, our detective's last night of surveillance. She had followed Hugh back to his home from a bar where he'd been drinking with his usual buddies. Although his driving was apparently erratic, he made it home without incident or without being stopped by the police. He left his car in the driveway and started singing loudly as he headed for the front door of his house. He was halfway there when his wife came out to hurry him inside. He resisted, and things quickly escalated, arms flailing and voices getting louder.

Out of the corner of her eye, Verla apparently saw a neighbor peeking out the window at the drama unfolding in Hugh's front yard, a phone in her hand. She was busy documenting everything when Hugh knocked his wife to the ground and stumbled toward the front door of their house on his own. Verla said she put down her camera and started to go over to see if his wife was okay, but stopped when the woman pulled herself up and followed her husband inside.

Verla said she had no doubt the neighbor had called the police, but she hung around to make sure just in case.

Hugh and his wife were inside and things were quiet by the time two police officers arrived. Verla saw his wife answer the door and shake her head as if puzzled by why the police were there. After a short exchange, the two officers left, apparently convinced things were fine. It was just a nosy neighbor overreacting.

That evening, after Verla told me about what had happened, she added that she hoped we "nailed the son of a bitch."

A week later, we did just that.

14

———

WADA

We called our faux group WADA—Women Against Domestic Abuse. To give it some credibility in case Hugh or his lawyer investigated, we created a logo and established a PO box. Then, for good measure, we had my hacker friend set up a Facebook Page and a Twitter account. We decided against sending the pictures Verla had taken to a local reporter as our goal had shifted slightly. What we wanted most of all was to get Hugh's wife and children to a safe place. Verla went by to see her when he wasn't there, showed her the pictures and gave her some resources she could turn to for help. The outcome wasn't what we'd hoped for—she'd burst into tears and yelled at Verla to leave and never come back.

After much discussion, we decided to forge ahead as planned. We posted the pictures on the WADA site, naming Hugh but blurring the faces of his wife and children. We also sent copies to the police and social services.

We hoped enough people would see the pictures about Hugh to shame him and to prevent him from continuing to abuse his family for fear of criminal prosecution. What we didn't anticipate was that the WADA post would go viral on the media. A local news team picked up the story, and our faux group and Hugh's face had their fifteen minutes of fame. Several social service employees told reporters that this was the kind of organization the community had needed for some time. Even the police acknowledged it as "helpful."

Once the WADA name was out there, we started getting messages from abused wives seeking advice and help. That was something we definitely hadn't anticipated. Now we had to decide what to do about the organization that didn't actually exist. If we simply walked away, would WADA be forgotten? Or would someone investigate and eventually link the phony creation of the group to us? And what about those abused women who needed help?

Although we hadn't done anything technically illegal, if they traced the site to Karen and me, we would have a lot of explaining to do. What if we were forced to admit our connection to the detective we'd hired? We could argue that we'd heard rumors through the local grapevine about Hugh's treatment of his wife and family. But it's a big leap from feeling sorry for someone you've never met to hiring a detective to see if the rumors were true. The bottom line was that neither of us wanted the attention that being associated with the organization would bring. Although for different reasons.

For me, the real downside of exposure was having someone poking around in my affairs and perhaps stumbling across enough coincidences to encourage poking around even more. What happened if they started seeing connections, with me the spoke in the wheel of any number of unexplained incidents? That could eventually lead to some serious charges, maybe even a re-evaluation of Adriana's role in Dane's death.

For Karen, it was mostly about not wanting to be seen as a troublemaker. The school board might not like that. And some parents might not like it either. Of course, there was also her connection to Hugh that she didn't want made public.

Over dinner at our usual place, we discussed how to handle what was happening.

"WADA is obviously something a lot of women need," Karen

said. "I'm starting to change my mind about it. I mean, maybe we should keep it going."

"Keep it going? It doesn't exist, so how can we keep it going?"

"We could raise some money, hire a few staff, you know."

"No, I don't know." I was irritated because of the risk it posed for me. But at the same time, in a way I liked the idea.

"We could partner with other groups; we wouldn't have to do everything on our own."

"What is the 'thing' we would be doing that other groups aren't doing already? There are hotlines and helplines, counseling, legal assistance . . ."

"They all focus on the victim; we went after the predator."

"I thought there was no 'we' in this. That the real 'we' was going to remain anonymous."

"I'm not talking about us. I'm talking about the organization."

"But the organization *is* us. And we could have a lot of explaining to do if anyone starts looking seriously at why we went after this particular predator."

"Think about how many women need a push to walk away from bad situations. We could be instrumental in helping them take that first step."

"That's the point. They tend to stay with their abuser. Just look at Hugh's wife. And how would *we* identify abusers if no one wants to speak up?"

"Maybe friends, relatives or kids would come forward if they could do so anonymously. Then we could expose the abuser. Just like we did with Hugh."

Our food was getting cold. I took a few bites, considering the pros and cons of what she was suggesting. The planner in me started to spin ideas and identify obstacles and challenges. Our initial notoriety would fade; we would have to advertise. It would be a sideline for both Karen and me, so we would have to hire someone to do the work. Clients would probably be few and far between, possibly unable to pay for services. We would need to raise money to support our activities. And some abusers would fight back.

"Where do you suggest we get the money to fund the organization?" I asked. That seemed like the biggest barrier. "Hiring our detective wasn't cheap. And that kind of work requires time and expertise."

"I have some savings. And I could afford to contribute a little something on an on-going basis."

I stopped eating and stared at her. The look on her face was so earnest, so determined. "You really want to do this, don't you?"

"At first, I just wanted to get back at Hugh. But now, yes. I really want to do this."

I sipped my tepid tea. "We'd have to make it a legitimate organization. After the fact."

"I've looked into that. We'd need a board, officers, a tax number, and some permits and licenses. We'd need to file with the county and state. And figure out what hiring a few employees entails. Maybe apply for a few grants."

I laughed, choking on the tea I'd just started to swallow.

"What's so funny?" Karen sounded put off by my laughter.

"I can picture the title of the grant: 'We need money to pursue predators.'"

"We can massage the mission statement so it looks like we're filling a gap without sounding like we simply want to harass and expose the bad guys."

"Okay, I'm in." I made up my mind just like that. Whether to please Karen or to find an outlet for my simmering anger about past treatment, I wasn't sure.

"What?"

"I said 'I'm in.' But I don't want to be 'in' in an official capacity. I'll help you figure out how to make it work, contribute a little money to get it started, maybe even volunteer from time to time. But that's all."

"Why don't you want to participate officially?"

I hesitated, but I'd already decided on my limits of sharing my past with Karen, and this didn't make it any easier. "I'm asking you to accept my desire to keep my involvement at arm's length. Can you do that?"

She quickly capitulated. "Of course. You can get as involved as you feel comfortable doing."

With that unofficial handshake, we started exploring our options.

Two days later Karen called to tell me that Hugh's wife and children had disappeared. "I called a few friends and relatives," she explained. "I wanted to make certain they were okay. But no one knows where they've gone."

"Hopefully they went somewhere to start a new life. Maybe some organization helped them get away. If I were her, I wouldn't want to wait around for Hugh to decide he wanted another go at me or the kids."

"I was hoping to talk to her, see how she felt about what happened. I suppose that's silly."

"We may never know if they have a happy ending or have been scarred for life. But we did what we thought was right. We have to remember that." We both knew that wasn't the whole truth, but I was trying to make her feel better. Our initial actions had been for all the wrong reasons, but it was by far not the worst thing I had done.

I was heading home from the office when I almost literally bumped into Detective Peters.

"Imagine running into you here," Peters said. "Right in front of your place of work at quitting time." He gave me a big smile, and I automatically smiled back. He had that effect on me.

"Imagine," I said. "Although I usually work later."

"Then I would have had to run into you next to your cubicle."

"You sound determined." I said it lightly, but I experienced a tingle of unease.

"I'm hoping you have time for a drink?" It was part statement, part question.

"As an officer . . . or a gentleman?" I asked, feeling a bit foolish in doing so. There was no way he was considering it a social encounter.

"I'm not wearing a tie. But I don't have my badge out either."

I hesitated for a moment before saying, "I'd love to have a drink and perhaps unravel what no-tie no badge means in police vernacular."

We went to a nearby restaurant and asked to be seated in the bar. When he ordered both hors d' oeuvres and liquor, I relaxed a little. But just a little.

"So, Detective Peters, what's on your mind?"

"Call me Jay." Another attempt to put me off guard?

"Okay, *Jay*. What are we doing here?" It was a direct question that I hoped would throw him off guard. But he was like a professional tennis player and lobbed my question back.

"We are enjoying each other's company." He raised his eyebrows a fraction of an inch. "Aren't we?"

"I always find our conversations . . . interesting," I said with exaggerated caution.

He suddenly got serious. "I've valued your observations in the past. I hope you've never felt like I was interrogating you."

"There's a book by John Marquand called *Point of No Return*. It poses the question of how much what you do for a living influences and eventually takes over who you are. What I have no way of knowing is how much of our conversation is in some way *official*." I hoped my honesty would get honesty in return.

"Fair enough. I suppose if you said something that I suddenly realize relates to a case I'm working on or have worked on, I wouldn't be able to ignore it. But I can honestly say that I'm not here with an ulterior motive today."

"You were just in the neighborhood?"

"It's a bit out of my way. And . . . I confess, you were on my mind because of the headlines about WADA." He laughed. "What a name. A play on Yada Yada do you think? The Seinfeld or the religious version?"

"Acronyms are often a bit strange. But I like the sound of it." I tapped my fingers on the table to accentuate the rhythm as I chanted, varying which syllable was accented. "WÀDA, WADÀ, WÀDA, WADÀ." When Karen became a visible part of the group, he might wonder about whether I, too, was involved. Maybe I should forewarn him so I could sidestep possible suspicions.

He was still smiling when he asked the critical question, "Are you familiar with the group?"

"A little. I'm glad they called out that, ah, I was about to say 'bastard.'"

"Do you know Hugh Graham, or were you tempted to call him a bastard because of what he's allegedly done?"

"Both. We grew up together."

"I thought I remembered you being from the same town."

"The operative word is 'from.'"

"You left and never looked back, huh?"

Was that a loaded question? "For reasons I can't explain even to myself, I went to a reunion not too long ago. It wasn't particularly fun for me. But I did become reacquainted with someone I'm staying in touch with. In fact, we now have dinner on a regular basis."

"Male or female?" He quickly added, "If you don't mind me asking."

"Female." Why had he asked that question? "Her name is Karen. We had dinner last week, and she mentioned volunteering with WADA. We were both impressed by their investigation of Hugh."

"Are *you* considering volunteering too?" That sounded like a landmine question to me, but I stepped on it anyway.

"She's trying to talk me into it. To keep her company. It depends on the kind of volunteer work they need. I am sympathetic with WADA's mission as I understand it. If no one points a finger at the abuser, too often the victim doesn't fight back. On the other hand, I don't like the idea of neighbor spying on neighbor. There needs to be some middle ground."

"Were the two of you surprised at Graham's behavior toward his family?"

"We both had him pegged as a narcissistic loser, but neither of us suspected him of being an abusive husband and father."

"I assume neither of you dated him in high school."

"I didn't date in high school," I said flatly.

"Oh? If you don't mind my asking, why not?"

It almost sounded like he didn't have a clue, but that was so unlikely, I started reconsidering whether I could read him at all. "No one asked me out."

"Your male peers were probably intimidated by your intelligence. Smart girls don't always fare well in high school."

Not for the first time, it crossed my mind that he had prosopagnosia, face blindness, but according to research, even people with that disability rated attractiveness the same as people with normal facial recognition. "Thank you. But over the years, I've come to be at peace with my, ah, unattractiveness."

"I find that very few people are happy with their looks. I certainly wouldn't mind looking like Brad Pitt."

I shook my head. "If you could choose any face, why him? Might as well go for George Clooney. He's even better looking now than he was at 30."

"Okay, I'll settle for George. So, who would you choose?"

I pretended to give it some thought, although I'd fantasized about that very question enough times over the years that I could have given him a prioritized list of ten off the top of my head. "I prefer striking over perfection, so maybe Natalie Portman or Lady Gaga."

"Lady Gaga? Really?"

"Or Toni Collette. I think having a distinctive look is good. Memorable."

"I'm still hung up on Lady Gaga. Really?" He laughed out loud.

"Well, for better or for worse, we are stuck with the faces we have for now. Maybe in our next lives."

The conversation dissolved into small talk about what we liked and didn't like—music, movies, TV, food. I kept waiting for him to make his move, to ask the question his police persona wanted to ask, but nothing else related to any of my current or past crimes came up.

He offered to drive me home, but I said I preferred to walk. It might not have been gracious, but I wanted our encounter to end while everything was still positive. While I could fool myself into thinking it had been a friendly meeting, nothing more. Unless he'd been testing the waters to decide if I was somehow linked to what had happened to Hugh. But even if that had been his goal, and he figured out that Karen and I were responsible, we hadn't done anything illegal. My fear was if he made that leap it would lead straight to other things in my past, eventually taking him all the way back to Dane's death.

15

WHAT'S NEXT?

"I have a lot to report," Karen said as we were relaxing with a final cup of tea after a satisfying dinner of orange chicken and spicy green beans.

"Charging ahead?"

"Full speed. Hugh isn't the only abusive husband out there who needs to be stopped as soon as possible."

"I'm sure there are enough if spread end to end they would stretch from coast to coast."

Karen pushed a yellow notepad across the table. There were three names at the top identified as "president, secretary and treasurer." "It was surprisingly easy to find three people to agree to be on the board of directors. I've named myself as the registered agent, and I'm in the process of filling out the articles of incorporation to become a 501(c)(3). There are a lot of rules governing the on-going operation of a non-profit, but nothing too formidable."

"What did you tell the three prospective board members about WADA?"

"I told them that I'd investigated the organization because I had decided to volunteer with them and that I'd discovered they were an informal group functioning unofficially. Furthermore, I explained that they were concerned the news coverage had made maintaining their approach untenable. They were happy for us to adopt the name to leverage our new nonprofit."

"Sounds somewhat plausible."

"If I can get the official WADA up and running quickly, I think I can pull this off."

"Karen, you amaze me."

"I couldn't have done this without you."

"It's been fun working with you. And I should mention that I told Detective Peters that you were thinking about volunteering with WADA. And that I might too."

"You talked to Peters about WADA?"

"I ran into him and he asked some questions about Hugh and WADA."

"Anything we need to worry about?"

"I don't think so."

"Well, I'm going to hold you to your promise to volunteer from time to time. You and I can work on some 'special projects' together."

"I'm going to leave the undercover work to the professionals. But I'll be happy to do some behind-the-scenes grunt work."

"Think of all the good we can do."

"Think of all the trouble we could get ourselves into."

"Do you have something better to do with your life?"

"I'm living it. Isn't that enough?"

"Look, I admit that until you came along, I was living a pretty mundane existence. Doing all the things I felt I *should* be doing. There is no end to the *shoulds* that can weigh you down. But now, now I keep thinking about what's possible. How we can help people who are in desperate need."

"I'm not the do-gooder type."

"That's not what I'm suggesting."

"It sounds to me like you have an organization that can manage anything legal that comes along. We stepped over the line once; I'm not sure I want to make it a habit."

Karen took a deep breath and let it out slowly. "You're right. I know that from time to time the organization will be walking a thin line between what's legal and the gray areas of ethical behavior and potential liability. The problem is that predators don't operate in the light of day. They hide behind closed doors, bravado, and intimidation."

"I'll be happy to strategize off the record, maybe run a few errands or put up some posters, but that's it. Am I clear? Are we good?"

"Clear and good. I appreciate all that you've done already."

That night, lying in bed, my mind couldn't let go of what Karen had said: "Think of all the good we could do." I had enjoyed planning and sharing Hugh's takedown with Karen. And I would have loved doing something more with her for WADA. But I could picture it so easily getting out of hand. She and I both had an addiction to the idea of payback. If we went too far and crossed a line, it could mean bad trouble for her and endgame for me. I needed to take a break. If nothing popped up to call attention to what we'd done, then perhaps I could return to my own little list in the not-too-distant future.

Two weeks later Karen informed me that all the paperwork for WADA was complete and they were waiting on the state for confirmation. She said that she and the other board members were scheduled to meet the following week to set goals and identify what they needed to achieve them. They were all very excited and looking forward to helping victims of abuse.

As for me, I was starting to feel like things were back to normal.

I'd been assigned to an interesting project at work and was working long hours again. Karen was spending more and more of her spare time on WADA. We were, however, still meeting for the occasional lunch or dinner.

Then I got a call from her just as I was about to leave the office.

"I need your help," Karen said. She sounded frantic.

"Anything," I said, knowing it realistically depended on the ask.

"We have a woman named Nora who wants to go to a safe house with her two children but whose husband is preventing them from leaving their home."

"How is he doing that? Are they locked up?"

"We don't know their exact situation for sure. We arranged to meet her, but she didn't show up. And she isn't answering her phone. We sent someone by, pretending to be a friend, but her husband answered the door and said she wasn't available. Our representative saw her peeking around the corner from inside the house. She apparently waved and made a thumbs down motion before disappearing."

"Why don't you have the police check it out?"

"That's the problem. Her husband is a police officer. Initially she told us we couldn't involve the police for that reason."

"What do you want me to do?"

"I intend to rescue them. And I can't do it alone."

"By 'rescue,' do you mean break in and whisk them away without her husband catching us?"

"Something like that."

"We aren't Navy Seals," I said. But my mind was already starting to work the problem.

"I know, but we can't abandon them. From what she told us, the situation is bad for her as well as for the children. He's an angry, physical person who is slowly becoming more and more violent. She said he never used to be that way, but his job is causing some sort of breakdown. And there may be drugs involved."

"There's no way to anonymously suggest to his supervisor at the department that he needs help?"

"She didn't seem to think so."

"Maybe you could approach Detective Peters, see what he would suggest."

"I've thought of that, but going through channels takes time. I'm not sure how much time she and her kids have. I don't want that on my conscience."

"So, you're thinking we do some surveillance, try to figure out when he isn't home so we can break in and help them escape."

"Yes, exactly."

"That sounds pretty straightforward, actually. Unless he has cameras connected to his phone, or there's a house alarm system, or he has her locked up . . ." I paused to let the potential obstacles to her plan sink in.

"We can take some tools with us in case we have trouble getting in. The key is to get in and out as quickly as possible."

I thought about it, but not for long. She was right—it was an intervention that could succeed if we did it right. "Okay," I said. "But we need to plan for every contingency. Let's start by looking at a Google map. Once we have her and the children, we will need to get away fast."

We did surveillance for two nights. Her husband was apparently on the third watch at work from 8:00pm to 5:00 am. He left at 7:30 and returned at 5:30. We weren't sure how long that schedule would last, but it seemed like good timing for a break-in. We decided to make our move the next night a couple of hours after he left for work.

There was no place to park in the back of the house, so we planned on taking them out through the front. We were going to leave Karen's car on the street at the edge of the property. I'd leave mine around the corner, just in case we needed backup. Ideally, we would put the family in Karen's car, and I would follow in mine.

We had observed that the lights went off at exactly 10:00, so we were fairly certain they were on a timer. Only two rooms had lights on after the husband left—one on the lefthand corner in back, and the other next to it facing the back yard. There was no television glow from any room that we could see. No other lights at all. It made us suspicious about how much freedom the wife had once she was alone with her children.

We chose 10:30 as our entry time. It was dark then. Most neighborhood dogs had been walked. Children put to bed. Blinds pulled. Neighbors were probably still up, but if we waited until later, our coming and going might stand out more. We would go around back, knock on the window we thought was the master bedroom, and see if we could communicate with Nora. If there were no unlocked windows and she was unable to assist in our entry, we would have to break in. We were counting on being able to pick the lock on the back door, but we were prepared to break a window if necessary—although we obviously preferred to keep things as quiet as possible. In addition to being worried about cameras and alarms, we also hoped to avoid motion sensing lights, barking dogs, and nosy neighbors.

Nora's husband left at 7:30 pm on the dot, wearing his uniform. We also wore uniforms, of sorts, dark clothes and baseball caps. Our dark backpacks contained everything we thought we'd need to gain entry.

Karen parked out front and waited for me to join her before we made our way along the wood fence to the back yard. There was a light on in the house on the other side, but their shades were drawn. There were no lights on at the house near where we'd parked. No dogs put up a fuss at our presence. And no spotlights suddenly switched on.

I went over to the back door to see if I could pick the lock while Karen tapped on what she assumed was Nora's bedroom window. Out of the corner of my eye, I saw her trying to open the window. When that failed, she joined me on back porch.

"I thought I heard something," she whispered, "but I couldn't make it out."

"Well, for a police officer, he has a pisspoor lock on this door. And I don't see an obvious camera."

"How long . . ."

"I'm working as fast as I can. Just remember, we need to look for an alarm shut-off when we go in. Assuming there's an alarm system. Nora may be able to give us the code. But we have to be quick."

The door opened with a loud click. There was no chain lock. And no keypad for an alarm that I could see. Karen headed for what we assumed to be the children's room and I headed for Nora's. The door was locked, but the key was in the lock. He obviously didn't anticipate she would figure out a way to remove it from the inside. Moments later I learned why.

Nora was drugged. That was one contingency we hadn't counted on.

"Nora," I said, shaking her. "Nora, we have to get you out of here." I patted her face and pulled back the covers. She mumbled and seemed to be aware of my presence, but she apparently couldn't talk. I wondered what he had given her. I had no doubt it was to make sure she didn't find a way to take off while he was gone. As I tried to get her into a seated position, I realized she also had one hand cuffed to what looked like a bathroom hand grip attached to the wall next to the bed. He wasn't taking any chances.

Karen poked her head in. "I've got the kids," she said. "Do you need help?"

"No, go ahead and take them out to the car. Nora has been drugged. I'll get there as soon as I can."

"I want mommy," a little girl voice said.

"She'll be with us in a few minutes," Karen assured her. "Let's go wait in the car."

"Where's daddy?" the boy asked. He sounded afraid to me, but I didn't have time to think about that. I had to get the cuffs off and somehow manage to get her to the car.

The handcuff was harder to pick than the back door had been, but I finally got it off and was trying to get her to support herself a little so we could leave, when I heard sirens in the distance. There must have been either a hidden camera or a silent alarm after all. "Let's go, Nora," I urged. I felt her tremble as she said something that sounded like "yes" and tried to take a step. But her leg gave out and I had to hold on to keep her from falling.

"What the hell," I said, "I can do this." I crouched down, got my shoulder under her, grabbed her around the bottom, and managed to stand under her weight. Fortunately, she wasn't that heavy, but it wasn't easy. I headed for the back door, praying that Karen had already taken off with the kids.

Staggering but determined, I made it to the back fence and managed to drop Nora on the other side before climbing over. Then I started dragging her toward what looked like a children's playhouse. We barely made it inside before the siren ended with a burst of sound. Lights started going on all over the neighborhood. I pictured eyes peering out from behind curtains, everyone wondering what was happening.

If they have dogs, it's over, I said to myself, cradling the sleepy woman in my arms and whispering to her to keep still. She either understood or had succumbed to whatever drug he had given her because she slumped against me, her breathing steady but barely perceptible.

I could hear men shouting but I couldn't make out the words. I also saw flashlights moving past the playhouse, but no one came to check it out. Where was Karen? Had she managed to get away? Were there any camera shots that could identify us? So many questions. For the moment, all I could do was stay scrunched up in a child's playhouse with a woman who was basically unable to move.

When things got quiet, I knew I needed to make my move. At any minute they could start doing a more thorough search of the area. So far, we'd been incredibly lucky, but luck always runs out. I tried to rouse Nora and felt her shake her head. "Can you hear me?" I asked.

"Yez."

"Good. I need you to try to help me get you to my car. Do you understand?"

"Yez. Kids?"

"They went with Karen. I'll take you to them, okay?"

I pushed open the door to the playhouse and managed to crawl out, dragging Nora after me. A dim light from the house ended just a few feet away. More good luck. I stood up and pulled Nora to her feet, steadying her as she swayed. "Do you think you can walk if I help you?"

"Try." She was shivering. There hadn't been enough time to find any clothes or shoes for her. She was barefoot and only wearing a thin nightgown. I put down my pack and took off my jacket and forced her arms into it. She said something that I thought was "thanks."

I put one arm around her waist and started propelling her toward her neighbor's house, staying just outside of the dim circle of light. She couldn't exactly walk, but she managed to stagger along with me supporting her weight as much as I could.

There was a large rhododendron in the front yard. It grew all the way to the ground. I pushed Nora under the canopy and told her I would be back in a few minutes. Then I raced to my car. It was right where I'd left it. I'd already made sure there were no internal lights that would come on when I got in and started the engine. Within minutes I was back at the rhododendron where I'd stashed Nora.

Both of us were fueled by adrenaline at this point. I half carried her to my car and shoved her on the floor in back. "Sorry," I apologized. "Stay down."

My heart was racing as I drove away. Realistically, I knew that not every neighborhood had hidden cameras everywhere, but then we'd also missed something at the house too. When I was far enough away to start breathing normally, I got out my phone. There were several messages from Karen. I punched her number and she answered before I even heard it ring.

"Are you okay?" It was clear she was trying to sound calm. Like before, we had agreed against phone calls, but under the circumstances, breaking the rule seemed necessary.

"We went out for something to eat after the movie, but I should be at the party soon," I said.

"Great. I look forward to seeing you."

We hung up.

"Kin I gettup?" Nora said.

"Why don't you stay down. We'll be at the safe house in about ten minutes. Your kids are already there."

I heard her crying.

"I can only imagine how hard this is for you," I said. "But it's almost over."

I kept my eyes on the rearview mirror looking for police cars. There weren't many cars of any kind on the road, but each time one was about to overtake us, I worried that it was an unmarked police car and that lights would suddenly start flashing. Except for the flashing of turn signals, however, they were all false alarms.

Karen was waiting on the steps to the safe house and raced out to the car when I pulled into the driveway. I got out. "She's in the back. We'll need to help her inside."

"Is she hurt?"

"Drugged, I think."

"Oh."

Between the two of us we hauled Nora out of the car and bundled her as fast as we could into the house. Once inside, I felt immense relief, my knees suddenly weak.

Two women were there to greet us. They took one look at Nora and pulled up a chair for her. "We need to get her some slippers," one of the women said.

"Are the kids okay?" I asked.

"We've put them to bed," the other woman said. "It's probably better if they don't see their mother like this."

"Is there anything else we can do?" Karen asked.

"No, you've done more than enough. We can take it from here."

As they left with Nora, Karen turned to me. "I waited as long as I dared. When you didn't come out, I was so frightened."

"I was hoping you would leave when you heard the sirens. In fact, I was counting on it."

"I didn't want to." Karen stepped toward me and gave me a big hug. "I knew you'd figure something out. Thank you."

"Let's go," I said. "We aren't in the clear yet."

16

DIG TWO GRAVES

Each day that went by after we rescued Nora and her children, I felt more confident that we'd gotten away with it. There was no news coverage that I could find. No mention of a woman and two children being "kidnapped." No mention that they were even "missing." My thought was that Nora's husband was afraid of what she might say if the search was made public and they caught up with her. He was probably looking for her on his own or with help from some of his fellow police officers. I could imagine the kind of story he made up to cover himself. "My wife is emotionally unstable . . ." "My wife has a drug problem . . ." "My wife was brainwashed by liberal bitch friends . . ." And of course he would say, "All I want is for her to be safe and to have my children back."

Before Karen's plea for help, I'd been trying to keep a low profile. Given my role in helping Nora escape, it felt even more essential that I avoid doing anything that could attract attention from the police. With that in mind, I started putting in extra hours at work, not with any hope of recognition or promotion, just to occupy myself. Karen and I kept in touch, but we had fewer meals together, both of us consumed by our work.

When Jay called and asked me out to dinner, I was only somewhat concerned. "Will this qualify as a date?" I'd asked. He'd replied: "I'm not intimidated by smart women." And apparently not by unattractive women either. So I agreed. But not without some soul searching. Even if it was only a friendly dinner, would I be able to act normal around him given the secrets I carried and knowing full well that he was a police officer at heart?

We met at a restaurant after work. That morning I'd dressed with an eye to what would be appropriate for work while being date-worthy too. A couple of the males in my area gave me a onceover during the day, a sign that what I was wearing was flattering to my well-proportioned figure. Unfortunately, no amount of makeup could make my face attractive. Once again, I considered cosmetic surgery. I was tempted by rhinoplasty in particular. I considered my up-tilted nose with its front facing nostrils to be my worst feature. Having a shapely nose in the middle of my face would be a good start.

It wasn't a fancy restaurant, but there were table cloths and nice photographs of quaint villages that looked Italian hung on the pale beige walls. The lighting was dim, but it was still bright enough to see what you were eating. Jay was waiting for me at a table for two under a picture of an ancient olive tree, its gnarled roots like brown octopus limbs stretching out from its base. He jumped up to help me into my chair and gave me a warm smile.

An antipasto platter and a bottle of wine was delivered to our table moments after I sat down. As I draped the strap of my purse over the back of my chair, my phone started vibrating. I could hear the buzz through the thin leather of the purse, like a small bee trying to escape. Although I'd put my phone on vibrate, I hadn't really expected any calls. I don't get very many. I wanted to ignore it, but I was having a hard time.

Jay raised both eyebrows and nodded toward my purse. "Go ahead if you think you should answer it. I'm okay." He smiled to reinforce his permission and understanding.

"I'll just check." The instant I saw who had called I was uneasy.

Karen knew I had a date with Jay. She wouldn't interrupt without a good reason. "I need to pick this up," I said, trying not to sound as alarmed as I felt. I tapped the tiny telephone receiver—a strange relic for a modern cell. Then, "Oh no," I muttered when I heard her frantic voice. "Are you okay?" Then, "Are you sure?" I listened to more of her excited explanation before saying: "I'll be there as soon as I can."

"What is it?" Jay asked as I put the phone away.

"It's Karen. Someone attacked her. She's been taken to the emergency room and is waiting to be checked out. She needs a ride home." I gazed reluctantly at the food and the man across the table. "I'm sorry," I said as I pushed back my chair.

Jay got to his feet. "I'll go with you."

"You don't need to."

"I want to, please." He signaled to the waiter. I didn't hear the exchange, but minutes later I was in his car on the way to the hospital, a box with the antipasto in it on the back seat. The pungent aroma of garlic and another spice I couldn't quite place hovered in the background.

When we arrived at the hospital, Jay let me off at the emergency room entrance while he went to find a place to park. The small room was filled with people sprawled on benches and chairs, a few on the floor. At least half of them were on their phones, anxious voices overlapping with anxious voices, a cacophony of unintelligible conversations. The person at the main desk barely glanced at me when I asked about Karen.

"If she isn't in the waiting room, then she's in with a doc," she said. "You can take a seat."

"She called for me to pick her up," I said. "Will she come back through here? And can you give me any idea how long it might be?"

"I have no idea how long. You can see how busy we are. You'll have to take a seat and wait."

I stepped back and looked around. There were a couple of vacant chairs in the far corner. I waited until Jay arrived, explained that I was unable to get any information on Karen and asked him to see what he could find out. At least when he leaned down and showed the woman his badge, she gave him eye contact. But either she couldn't or wouldn't provide much more information than she'd given me. She told him that Karen hadn't been officially admitted as a patient, and when she was released, she'd come back through the lobby. Probably within an hour or two.

Jay went down to cafeteria to grab some coffee for us while we waited. Karen didn't miraculously appear while he was gone. But someone was rushed through on a stretcher. I caught a glimpse of red on a dark shirt as they vanished through two double, swinging doors.

"This is an incredibly busy place," I said when Jay returned.

"For some, it's the only place they can come if they're sick."

"I thought it had to be a real emergency."

"That is a matter of interpretation. They aren't supposed to turn anyone away. But they can make them wait. It's sad. They do the best they can under the circumstances."

The coffee was strong, a dark mass inside an institutional Styrofoam cup. "I'm surprised a hospital would still use Styrofoam," I said as I took a sip.

"Maybe they're government surplus. I know we still have them at the precinct."

I took another sip. "Not how I expected to be spending the evening," I said. "Sorry."

Jay took a long swallow before saying, "Let me make a call." He got up and went over to an empty space near a window. It seemed like he was away more than the six minutes it showed on the large clock on the wall behind the main desk. Hospital time is slower than regular time.

"Did you find out what happened?" I asked as he sat back down. I was fairly certain that was the reason he'd stepped away to make a call.

"Yes. It seems that the father of a boy she's been counseling on the side didn't like what was happening and went to the school to confront her. It was after hours. Not a lot of people around. She was alone in her office.

"A couple of kids and another teacher heard the shouting and tried to intervene. But . . ." He paused. "According to the report, the man was fairly belligerent. I know from experience situations like that can escalate fast and witnesses often disagree about who did what first. When she fell, she apparently banged her head against the edge of a desk. That can be nasty."

"Did you learn anything about her attacker?"

"*Alleged* attacker. But he does have a rap sheet. Bar brawls. Minor drug charges. That sort of thing."

"Do you know his name?"

Jay hesitated. "It will probably be in the news. But don't even think about going there."

"What do you mean?" My mind had already started down the path I was certain he was referring to, but I wasn't about to admit it.

"I can see it in your eyes. You're angry. You want to retaliate on behalf of your friend. That's a normal reaction. But he's in custody; the criminal justice system will handle this."

"You don't know what I'm thinking." I tried to control the defensiveness in my voice but failed.

"I know what I'd be thinking," he said. "But you need to be there for your friend, not interfere with police work."

"Sure, I'm angry, and I'd like to punch him out. But I'm not a fighter." I took a sip of now cold, bitter coffee. "And I wouldn't know how to hire a hit man. But it would be tempting. The guy sounds like scum." Was I saying too much? It's so hard to know what other people would say and do under the circumstances. All I knew was that I was angry as hell.

"Like I said, you need to be there for your friend. People who are victims of an attack often become either irrationally fearful or obsessed with wanting revenge. Neither is healthy."

"But both are understandable, right?"

"Absolutely. But there's a saying: '*While seeking revenge, dig two graves . . .*'"

"*. . . one for yourself,*" I finished for him. "I understand how self-destructive harboring hate can be." I didn't think it was necessary or wise to elaborate. "In addition to Karen, the person I feel sorry for is the *alleged* attacker's son, the boy that she was apparently trying to help. Imagine how he must feel about what happened."

"Yeah, it can go one of two ways for him. Either he will feel guilty for provoking his father by seeking help, or he will want to get back at him for what he's done to Karen. Since he's young, he might not be able to take his dad on physically. That's likely a good thing. But I doubt this will have a happy ending."

"You see this kind of thing all the time, don't you?"

"More than I'd like, yes."

"How do you cope?"

"Whenever possible, I try to help the victims of crimes."

"I thought your job was to catch the bad guys."

"Don't misunderstand me, I'm no bleeding heart. I don't waste much time feeling sorry for criminals. But I try not to become too jaded. It's like a cancer that has the potential to take over your body at any moment, but in situations like these, you do have control over its spread."

I knew he was right. I had let my emotional cancer metastasize. And although I wasn't sorry for my past acts, my circumstances had changed. Now I was not only more vulnerable, I had more at stake. More to lose. And Jay was right; I could control my future behavior. The question was whether I wanted to take his advice and walk away or whether it was too personal to do that. Karen was the closest friend I'd ever had. How could I let an attack against her go unavenged?

Jay wanted to stay with me until we knew what was happening with Karen, but I urged him to go home. He had to go to work in the morning, and there was no guarantee how long it would take for them to decide to admit or release her. If they said she could go home, I would get a taxi or call an Uber. I might even stay with her overnight to make sure she really was okay. And if she was admitted, I wanted to be there with her.

He finally agreed to leave. "Call me if you need anything," he said. "And we have a raincheck on this evening, right?"

I nodded. "Leaving that antipasto platter wasn't easy."

"Oh, I could go get it for you."

"Please don't. Garlic and the aroma of ailing bodies and antiseptic don't go together. But thank you."

He smiled, then added: "And if you get any crazy ideas, give me a chance to talk you down, okay?"

I was touched by his concern, although a bit uneasy about it too. Why was he worried about what I might do? I experienced a speck of guilt as I nodded "yes" while at the same time my mind was multitasking, trying to think up ways to get back at Karen's attacker. How to inflict pain on him, but without getting caught. Yes, I could control my future behavior, but I might not choose pacifism.

The hour and a half wait felt much longer. I kept trying not to check the time, but it was hard to concentrate on anything. I'd check my email, look at a news app, scan Twitter, anything to pass the time. I even tried some online Solitaire, but I've always found that boring.

When Karen appeared at the entrance to the waiting room and scanned the room looking for me, I leapt up and hurried over to her. "I'm fine," she said before I could ask. "Let's get out of here."

I called an Uber, and we went outside to wait. "How do you feel?" I asked. She had a not very subtle bandage around her head, covering most of her forehead.

"They gave me some pain pills but told me not to take them unless I feel like I have to. And they said I should stay awake for a couple of hours."

"No problem," I said. "I'll go home with you. We can drink tea and talk."

Karen looked straight ahead and said in a low, flat voice: "I want him to suffer for what he has been doing to his son . . . and for attacking me."

"He's under arrest," I assured her.

"That's not what I mean."

"I know what you mean, but that's not a good idea."

"Why not?"

"Because you would be the primary suspect if we retaliate."

"But think about his son, Brian. What's going to happen to him now? He's eleven, a vulnerable age. Even if his mother doesn't kick the asshole out, he will probably be furious with Brian. He will never consider that it was his own fault he got arrested. People like that never do. And even if she does tell him to leave, or if she gets a restraining order, you and I both know how worthless that can be."

"You weren't seriously injured, were you?" I asked. The bandage on her forehead looked impressive, but her color was good and she seemed strong.

"Mild concussion is the verdict. I'm supposed to go home and rest."

"Did he threaten you with a weapon?"

"Just his fists. I thought he was going to beat me up."

"But he didn't actually hit you?"

Karen sighed. "It all happened so fast. I don't know if he pushed me or if I fell trying to get away from him. The next thing I knew I was on the floor and there were all these people fussing over me. I could hear Clint screaming as he was being hauled away."

"He sounds like a violent man."

"He is. And he needs to be stopped."

"I know what you're saying. Jay and I discussed it. You need to give the criminal justice system a chance."

Karen gave me a pathetically disbelieving look as if to say, "How could you be so naive?"

"Don't worry, he won't get away with this without consequences. He'll most likely get some jail time and will be out of the picture at least for a while."

"But what if he gets out on bail?"

"He has a record, so my guess is that he will be held without bail. I'll look into it tomorrow first thing, okay?"

The Uber I'd called for showed up and we put our conversation on hold. But as soon as we got to her place, she repeated her concerns about Brian's father, Clint, over and over, a broken record of anger and a demand for justice. "If only WADA had more resources to handle this sort of thing," she bemoaned while I boiled water for tea.

"If he goes to jail, you'll have time to figure something out." I poured two cups of tea and asked if she wanted sugar or milk.

"No, thank you." I could tell she was starting to wear down. "I'm so tired," she said.

"Drink your tea and you can lie down. I'm going to stay here tonight."

"You don't have to do that," she protested. But I could tell she was relieved.

She talked a little about Brian while we sat there at her kitchen table, the aroma of Earl Gray spiraling up from our mugs. He sounded like a nice kid who deserved better than he was getting. He was lucky to have an advocate in Karen.

While she got ready for bed, I made up a place for myself on her couch. Then I went in to say goodnight. "It will be okay," I assured her as I tucked her in as if she was my child instead of my friend.

"Promise?" was the last thing she said before nodding off.

I found some soda crackers in her cupboard and ate a few with another cup of tea before trying to find a comfortable position on her uncomfortable couch. I knew I needed to get some rest. Tomorrow would be a busy day. I had a couple of graves to dig.

17

THE PERFECT NOSE

Brian's father did not get bail. I would like to say that I had a hand in it, but it was actually a public defender's ineptness that sealed his fate. The overworked and pressed-for-time public defender is a stereotype that is more real than not. And when I talked to the one representing Brian's father, I could sense right off that he wasn't going to put a lot of effort into getting his client bail.

"He's going to plead 'not guilty,' although I tried to get him to take a plea deal." The thin man with the sloping shoulders sounded frustrated but resigned, like someone used to being disappointed by his clients. "My client claims he didn't hurt the defendant *that much*. He also claims it was an accident. And he wants his day in court." I must have looked concerned because he quickly added, "Don't let that upset you, there are witnesses and cameras that say 'guilty as hell.'" He blinked pale blue eyes that were slightly bloodshot and fluttered the long fingers on his right hand as if to swat away what he'd just said. His eyes landed on the scattered piles of folders on his tiny desk, battered fake wood with a couple of drawers on one side, lined up in a row of similar tiny desks in a sprawling office space populated by people hunched over their own piles of papers. "I'm sorry, I shouldn't have said that. Of course I'll give him the best defense possible."

I couldn't help noticing that he needed a haircut, and there were white flecks of dander sprinkled across his poorly fitted brown jacket. Didn't he know professionals weren't supposed to wear brown suits? I've never understood why, but I knew it wasn't fashionable.

"I know you will do your very best," I assured him. "But I'm a friend of his *latest* victim." I hit the word "latest," not that I felt like I needed to. "I'm here because she asked me to assess the situation. She's, well, a bit afraid of him at this point. And she wants to know whether she has to worry about him being set free to come after her again."

He looked around, but no one seemed to be listening to our conversation. If you worked in an environment like this you probably got used to tuning out what was happening around you. "You shouldn't be here," he whispered. "And I shouldn't be talking to you."

"Yet here I am, and here *we* are," I said softly, leaning slightly forward. "But don't worry, I don't think either of us has said anything that would jeopardize the hearing. And you're right—I shouldn't be here. Sorry." I thanked him and quickly made my way past the row of desks and overworked employees of the state.

I'd been concerned that Brian's father would get some wild-eyed bleeding-heart public defender who would somehow see him as a victim of society and come up with an effective strategy to get him released on bail. In spite of his past history. And in spite of the fact that he'd apparently been drunk when he attacked Karen. How do you argue it was an *accident* when he sought her out at work and was heard screaming threats at her? Still, his lawyer could have tried for a plea deal by promising his client would get treatment and counseling. But it sounded like Brian's father wasn't interested in a plea deal; he had dug in his heels, determined to fight the charge of gross misdemeanor. And, after talking to his public defender, I was fairly confident Clint would get an adequate but not a passionate and creative defense.

Even after I reported back to Karen on my impression of Clint's public defender, she continued to worry about Clint and what he might do if he got off. But she worried needlessly. At his hearing, the judge didn't buy that Karen had interfered with his parental rights by counseling his son to disobey him. On the other hand, the prosecution made a strong case against release. She depicted him as a raging bull who had shoved Karen down and would have continued beating her if not for the intervention of others. That, along with declarations from Karen and witnesses, made a strong case that, if released, he would be a threat to Karen as well as to his son.

A month later at his trial, he was convicted to nine months in prison, along with a $1,500 fine. Karen was relieved if unsatisfied. And I assume his family felt similarly relieved, even though it was only a temporary stay from fear. After the incident, Brian had stopped by to apologize to Karen for what his dad had done, and she had assured him it wasn't his fault. The good news was that, after his father's conviction, Brian's grades improved and he turned out for the football team. It appeared as though having his father in prison had done more for him than any amount of counseling.

Unlike Brian, Karen's return to normalcy was a slow process. The wound on her forehead ended up requiring some surgery, and she developed an infection afterwards and had to be on antibiotics for a month. She ended up with a visible scar. That upset her, but I told her it made her look exotic, like someone with a mysterious past. *She* thought it looked like she'd had a birthmark removed.

It was fortunate that she had her work with WADA to take her mind off of Clint and any thoughts of revenge. I, on the other hand, couldn't let it go. I kept worrying about what Clint might do after he was released from prison. If he hadn't been repentant after the assault, what made anyone think he would admit personal responsibility for his actions after spending time in prison? My guess was that his anger toward Karen would intensify rather than dissipate over time. I could picture his first drunken spree after his release ending in another attack. Against his son or against Karen. I felt it was up to me to make sure that didn't happen.

One evening I asked Karen if Brian had any good memories about this father. I was angling to find out about hobbies, some way to predict his movements after his release. I was thrilled when she mentioned that Clint was an avid hunter who took off every year in his camper on hunting trips. Brian had gone hunting with him from the time he was old enough to get a license. He'd told Karen about feeling close to his father then but quit going because Clint usually got drunk after a day of hunting. Even back then, Clint's drinking made him querulous and eager for a fight.

From my point of view, the timing of Clint's anticipated release from prison couldn't have been better. He was due to get out shortly before hunting season. Since his conviction didn't prohibit him from owning a gun, my guess was that he would be anxious to return to his seasonal hunting routine.

Some years ago, I'd taken a self-defense class that had several sessions on guns, including some target shooting practice. I'm embarrassed to admit that I not only enjoyed target shooting but was good at it. A natural aptitude the trainer said. Even though it had been a while, I was pretty sure that with the right gun and scope I could take out a knee-cap from a fair distance. An unfortunate hunting accident like that would make life harder for Clint and make it difficult or impossible for him to physically assault someone, at least for a while.

Since I was refraining from all extra-curricular activities until Clint was released from prison, I had some time on my hands and plenty of accrued vacation time. I decided to go ahead with the rhinoplasty.

The surgeon I chose had an excellent reputation but almost lost me as a patient when he twice asked, "Are you sure that's *all* you want done?" I gave him the benefit of the doubt because I assumed he was used to dealing with people's vanities and probably thought I would want to see huge improvements after surgery.

"It wouldn't take much to take care of that chin while I'm at it," he said after the second time I assured him all I wanted was a nose job. "Some minor augmentation would dramatically change your face."

"Let's put that on my bucket list, okay?" I was tempted, but I couldn't visualize what kind of chin I needed to go with the new nose. And in spite of hating my face, it was the face I was used to. I wasn't sure how I would feel about looking in the mirror at an entirely different person. Doing a little at a time, like wading into the lake rather than diving in, felt like the best approach for me.

At work I told everyone I was going on vacation without being too specific. Colleagues told me to have a good time but didn't ask many questions. Other people's vacation plans are never as interesting as your own.

I told Jay I was taking some time off, again without getting too specific. He said he envied me the down time; we both spent far too much time at work. I asked why he didn't take some time off, and he lightheartedly asked if that was an invitation to join me on my vacation. I wondered if I'd said "yes" if he would have considered it. Since the night of our "almost first date," Jay and I had occasionally gone out for drinks or dinner. But our relationship was basically stalled at the starting gate. I didn't mind. It was nice to have someone other than Karen to go out with from time to time, and it seemed safer to keep him at a distance.

Karen was the only one who knew about my rhinoplasty. Like the surgeon, she had encouraged me to have several things done at once, but she also seemed to understand why I wanted to proceed slowly. "Having someone mess with your face is unsettling," she agreed. "That's why I'm going to keep what's left of this scar."

"It's hardly noticeable when you wear make-up," I assured her, although that was a bit dishonest. There was something about the jagged raised line that called attention to itself. She'd told me that people undoubtedly noticed but politely refrained from saying anything. Except for the occasional youngster who would forthrightly ask, "How'd you get that scar?"

In spite of being incredibly busy at work and with WADA, Karen checked in every day after my surgery, either by phone or in-person, to see how I was doing and to give me an update on how she was doing. I'd been told it would take three to four weeks for my nose to look "normal." Well, the "new" normal, that is. I'd scheduled a three-week vacation with the surgery the Saturday before my vacation actually began. Given two weekends with three weeks in-between, I felt like it was enough time for the recovery to be close to complete.

The first week I avoided mirrors. After that I'd look in the mirror several times a day, checking to see if the swelling had gone down enough for me to tell what I was going to eventually look like. I'd turn my head this way and that and ask myself whether the new nose was an improvement. Although the real question was, did I look less unattractive?

The strange thing was that I didn't *feel* any different. Although I'm not entirely sure why I thought I might. Nor did I look that different, except for the almost perfect nose that had taken up residence on my face. I half expected it to wash off and my old pig nose to reappear. And now I wished I'd gone ahead with the chin augmentation so my perfect nose wouldn't be lonely, a standout feature lost among the facial irregularities and splotches. Although there were also fewer splotches thanks to a dermatologist recommended by the surgeon. She had performed miracles with some experimental treatments and creams.

Every time she came by to check on me, Karen assured me that my nose was lovely. Then she would quickly add that what I looked like shouldn't matter, but that she wanted me to feel good about myself. I knew that was a contradiction. If it didn't matter what I looked like, then how could an "improvement" make me feel better about myself? Still, I appreciated her encouragement. I don't think I could have gone through the process without her support.

The evening before my return to the office, I stopped by Karen's to pick her up for dinner, and she wasn't quite ready. While I waited, I noticed the calendar she had attached to the side of her refrigerator.

I'm not sure why I looked, but I did. She had the same date marked on hers that I did on mine: Clint's release date. Assuming he didn't get out early for good behavior. I'd already decided exactly what I wanted to do when he got out, but I was definitely not going to tell Karen. Because the outcome I intended involved committing not one, but several criminal acts.

The dinner was my first outing since the surgery. We went to our usual restaurant. It was a test of sort. I wanted to see if anyone there took a second look or if they were so used to the overall effect that they wouldn't notice. There was still a little swelling left, but not enough that people who didn't know what my nose was supposed to look like could tell. To be honest, I was becoming fond of it. It was like hanging up a new picture on a wall surrounded by familiar paintings that had been hanging there so long you scarcely noticed their details any more.

After we were seated, I asked Karen, "Do you think our waiter looked at me longer than usual?"

"I was trying to decide, but I couldn't really tell."

When the waiter came back to take our order, he looked directly at me, pencil poised over his order pad, while I took my time deciding what I wanted. As if the menu wasn't as familiar to me as every millimeter of my old face. I didn't get any indication that he observed anything unusual about my appearance. His eyes didn't linger on my nose, and his expression remained neutral. When he didn't react, I wasn't sure if I was disappointed or relieved.

The next morning, I braced myself for my return to the office. If anyone thought about it at all, they might put together my three-week absence and my new nose. I wondered if anyone would dare ask. Or would they simply whisper about it behind my back?

The first person from my team that I ran into simply said, "Hey, you're back. How was your vacation?"

"Good. Glad to be back though."

Everyone was busy with what they were doing, so no one said more than a brief "hello" and "welcome back" and "hope you had a nice vacation." I was beginning to wonder if anyone would comment on my new nose. Then, one of the admins stopped by with a question about my schedule, paused and took a second look. "Did you do something with your hair?" she asked. I almost laughed and considered saying, "No, I did something with my nose." Instead, I gave her a bland shake of the head.

By the end of the day, it was as if I'd never been away. At various times I'd chuckled to myself about "being nosy," "sticking my nose into other people's business," "keeping my nose to the grindstone," and reminding myself that "a smile is happiness right under your nose." I admit to being a bit surprised that no one did a double take. It had been a three-week ordeal for me. And it had cost a lot. I'd considered arguing to the insurance company that it was "essential" surgery, but I knew the claim would be denied. Mental well-being did not justify a medical procedure to the insurance industry.

I stayed late that first day back to catch up on a few things. It was the cleaning woman who finally said something to me about my nose. We'd never done more than exchange the occasional "how are you this evening" in the past, but tonight she asked about my vacation.

"It was good," I said.

Then, she took a second look at my face and said, "It looks nice."

"Ah, what looks nice?"

"Your nose. It's narrower and points down. Very nice." With that she returned to her cleaning. Her accurate observation a simple statement of fact.

It made me wonder if other people noticed and felt uncomfortable saying anything or if they didn't think a "nice nose" was worth commenting on. On the other hand, when I thought about it, I might not be able to pick some of my colleagues out of a lineup. And I definitely couldn't describe their individual noses. So why should I expect them to be more observant than me?

I was about to leave for the day when Jay called. "Welcome back," he said. "I've missed you."

"It hasn't been that long," I said.

"Well, it's different when I know I can't see you . . ."

"Different than when I'm here and we don't see each other?" That wasn't a very nice thing to say and I regretted it immediately.

"I know, it's strange, but that's the way it is. Anyway, I thought maybe we could catch a coffee. I'm working late, but I could take an hour's break if you could. You can tell me about your vacation. Make me jealous."

Fifteen minutes later I as waiting for him in a Starbucks, feeling nervous, not at all sure how I'd feel if he didn't say anything about my nose. And, at the same time, almost afraid he *would* bring it up.

I bought coffee for both of us and waved him over when he arrived. The minute he sat down he stopped and leaned forward to study my face. "Your nose," he said. "It's different."

"Yes, I confess. I had a little adjustment done. What do you think?" I tried to be jaunty about it. Like I was asking if he liked my new hairdo.

"I like it." He continued to stare. "I think I understand why you did it, it's a good nose, but I hope you didn't feel like you needed to change your appearance."

"I've always hated my . . . face." I'd started to say "nose," but if I was going to be honest—

"It's an unusual face," he said. "But it has character." He was talking as if my face wasn't "me," but some separate object. Unlike most people who acted as though my face represented everything about me.

"Do you like the way *you* look?" I asked.

"I don't think about it much."

"Well, I've had to think about it all my life. Because most people are turned off by my appearance."

"What makes you say that?"

I almost laughed at what appeared to be his genuine naivete.

"Kids make it really clear what they think about the way you look. They gave me nicknames."

"Nicknames?"

I suddenly didn't want to talk about it with Jay. If I told him too much, maybe he would start seeing me as fugly. Once labeled, the word might as well be stamped on my forehead. "Can we change the subject? Toast my new nose and leave it at that?"

He raised his cup. "To your new nose. May it pass the sniff test." He took a sip and said, "That didn't make sense, did it?"

"Not really, but I appreciate the gesture." And I did.

18

BEST SERVED COLD

Months before Clint's release date, Karen started bringing up ways to get even. I had to do some fancy talking to make her see how anything we did would just make it harder for Brian. Apparently, after serving his time, Clint was going to be welcomed back with open arms by his wife. It didn't make sense to me, but if that was the plan, I thought the best thing Karen could do when Clint returned was to keep an eye on Brian to make sure he was okay. Other than that, I did everything I could to convince her that it wasn't smart to get in the middle again. I argued the case so well that I almost convinced myself that *I* should let it go. Almost, but not quite.

I hated lying to Karen, but I was determined to protect her. And, indirectly, I was concerned for Brian and his mother. Of course, by consistently lying to Karen, I was also providing cover for myself. I needed her to tell the authorities how adamant I'd been about staying clear of Clint and his family. She wasn't a good liar, so she needed to believe I meant what I said.

My hunting accident plan was slowly evolving. And, although as plans go it seemed fairly solid, I had some misgivings. It involved a number of fairly complicated steps. And every step needed to work in order for the plan succeed.

Shooting him in the leg was the easy part. I was pretty certain I could find a good location to shoot from, especially if I waited until the end of the day when he was returning to his car. That way I wouldn't have to track him in the woods. The lighting might be a bit tricky at dusk, but I was confident I would be able to hit my intended target. Since it didn't seem like a good idea to try to get in any target practice, I was using visualization to prepare myself. It's a method some athletes use to improve performance and enhance their competitive edge. It supposedly helps to instill a heightened state of mental awareness. And it seemed to be working for me. Each time I visualized shooting Clint in the knee, I felt closer to achieving my goal.

It was getting to the site without being seen that worried me the most. Having my car captured on camera or running into other hunters.

The final plan was elaborate and required the acquisition of a number of items: a tracking device to put on Clint's RV, a used bicycle, a license plate to put on the *borrowed* motorcycle while I was using it, a motorcycle helmet, and a hunting rifle. I also needed to learn how to hotwire a motorcycle and figure out where I could "borrow" one for the evening without getting caught. Each of these tasks required careful preparation as one slip-up could cause the entire plan to unravel.

In addition to gathering all of the resources I needed, there were a host of other things I had to do to pull it off. First, I had to leave my car in the driveway that evening. I often did that, so it wouldn't be that unusual. My neighbors would see it and be able to swear it had been there all evening. Second, I had to be especially mindful about fingerprints and DNA. I would of course wear gloves when riding the bicycle and motorcycle and when handling the rifle, but I also needed to wear a hat under the helmet to avoid leaving any hairs attached to it.

Finally, there was evidence disposal after the fact. I would toss the helmet alongside the road as if it had fallen off a motorcycle. Hopefully someone would consider it "finders' keepers." And in case I left some strands of shirt or shoeprints in the woods where they could be found, I needed to get rid of everything I wore for the attack, including my shoes. With luck, I might be able to return the motorcycle before the owner noticed it was missing. If not, I would leave it near where I'd picked it up to make it look like it had been taken by a joyriding kid. As for the bicycle, I would drop it off out in the open where I hoped some light-fingered youngster would find it.

The many-faceted plan required precision, some skill, and lots of luck. It also involved committing a whole series of crimes. The prospect of pulling off such a complicated scheme was both frightening and exhilarating.

I was wearing my young square-jawed male mask and a wig with long hair pulled back into a pony-tail when I bought the tracker. The pony-tail protruded from the back of a baseball cap with a long, curved brim that partially hid my face when I kept my head down. There was quite a line in the large box store I'd chose for the purchase. My theory was that busy checkers wouldn't be paying attention to individual customers, and also, other individual customers wouldn't be around to answer questions by the time the police got interested—if they ever did. I paid in cash to further blur the trail.

One down.

A few weeks later I went on a weekend hiking trip and stopped at a roadside swap meet where I was lucky enough to find a functional used bike. I was wearing a wig and fake tattoos on my face and neck; my hope was that anyone I talked to would remember the tattoos but little else. In addition to the bike, I bought a number of food items that lots of people were buying. If it ever came up, although I doubted it would, I was prepared to admit being at the swap meet and making some food purchases, but not a bicycle. Unless I inadvertently left prints on the bike, I doubted anyone would identify me as the person who bought it.

Two down.

The Goodwill was filled with bargain hunters when I came across a battered motorcycle helmet that was more than adequate for my needs. Again, they would have to link the helmet to me through DNA for it to become evidence. And if they found the helmet without my DNA, and even if they suspected the helmet had been worn by the shooter, they would find it extremely difficult, if not impossible, to track down where it was purchased and by whom. But, if by some wild coincidence, they questioned the clerk at the Goodwill, he might remember my face, but I doubted that he could swear to me having purchased that particular helmet on a day when he'd been waiting on customers non-stop.

Three down.

The gun was the trickiest purchase. I needed a common hunting rifle, preferably a bolt action .30-06 with a telescopic sight, something that was good at 400 yards since I wasn't sure how close I could get. I thought about getting a rifle at a gun show where they didn't require background checks, but I was leery of cameras, and paying in cash for something like that might call attention to the purchase. If I traveled to another state to get a gun, they might still be able to track the sale to me. Besides, that would make it look even more suspicious, especially if I no longer had the gun in my possession when they did their investigation. Of course with no gun or other strong evidence, it would all be circumstantial, but a good prosecutor might be able to connect the dots and get an arrest and possibly a conviction. That's why I considered the gun acquisition to be a chancy make-or-break act.

In the end, I decided to steal a gun. Ideally, I would have targeted some random hunter, but how do you identify a hunter that you don't know? The best I could come up with was a friend of a relative who I knew hunted. It was only one degree of separation, but on the other hand, I'd had no recent contact with either this particular uncle or his hunter friend. And I was fairly certain no one had a clue that I had listened to the two men talk about hunting at a large family gathering years ago. They'd initially attracted my attention because of their loud voices, but I remember becoming both fascinated and repulsed by their conversation. They were discussing gory details related to hunting, how you needed to "dress the carcass" immediately so it wouldn't spoil, what kind of knife you should use, where to cut and what to discard. It had all seemed unnecessarily cruel and distasteful to my inner-child sensibilities.

My family ties could be described as loose at best, and I had never shown any interest in hunting that I could remember. But if by some longshot the police made a connection between the rifle, my uncle's friend, and my family, that still didn't necessarily point the finger at me. And even if someone noted my connection to Karen and Clint, it seemed to me that the worst-case scenario would be labeling it a "suspicious coincidence." They would need more, much more, for an arrest. At least that's what I was counting on.

When I went online to check, I discovered that my uncle's friend still lived two blocks away from him. I remembered the house from the outside, but I don't think I was ever inside. That was a bit of a problem. But not an insurmountable one. My guess was that most people without young children keep guns in spare rooms or closets. And if the gun I was after was kept under lock and key, I would manage. All I needed to do was find a time when both he and his wife were away for an evening.

Surveillance was undoubtedly a lot easier before everybody became camera happy. Now you never knew who might be watching you watch them. The first night I parked in a strip mall lot and walked the eight blocks to his house. I was wearing my Chinese man disguise. As I got close, I pretended to be jogging and went around the block a couple of times. It was awkward. There was no place other than a laurel hedge around the house across the street to stay even partially out of sight. I hung out at the end of the hedge under an aging tree and tried to look like I belonged. I did some stretches and drank from a plastic bottle, like I was resting up before jogging some more. A dog came by and sniffed me up and down but didn't bark when I remained still and let him sniff. Eventually it lost interest and moved on.

At five o'clock, the couple got in their car and drove off. They had been dressed casually. They could have been going anywhere, but I knew that a popular pastime for a lot of retirees was going out to early bird dinners, and the timing was right. I continued to watch their house, occasionally jogging around the block, hoping no one was counting how many times I did. As daylight faded, I felt more comfortable. The only streetlight was far enough away that I now blended into my surroundings, another shadowy shape. They returned at 6:30, went inside, and turned the lights on in what I guessed to be the living room. I could make out the faint glow of a TV through the thin curtains.

The next night was a Thursday. I parked in a different place and went through the same routine again. It was tedious and tense at the same time. The constant worry was that someone would notice me, think I was casing the neighborhood, and call the police. But my only encounter was with an older couple walking their dog. They said, "Nice evening," and I replied "yes."

This time they stayed home. At 7:30 I called it a night.

Friday evening they left at 5:00 again and returned at 6:40. My guess was they had gone out to dinner again. I wasn't sure an hour was sufficient time to break in and steal a rifle, so I was hoping they might stay away longer on a Saturday evening. If they left around dinner time, I was going to give it a try. I was getting tired of surveillance.

Saturday, I got lucky. They left the house at 4:30, this time on foot. I followed them at a distance. They went to my uncle's. Apparently, they were still friends. And since it was around dinner time, I was optimistic that they would stay there for several hours. I hurried back to their house and quickly made my way around back as if I had the right to be there. Their back yard was surrounded with a 6-foot wooden fence. It was still light, but I didn't see any neighbors' windows that had a direct view of the yard. And I didn't hear any voices to indicate there were any backyard parties taking place. It was a "go."

They must have had the original locks on their back door because it didn't take me long to get inside. When I didn't see a keypad to disarm an alarm, I breathed a sigh of relief. I'd been counting on them not having one. A lot of older people in middle-class neighborhoods didn't bother with alarms. But if there had been one, I would have had to make tracks and come up with plan B.

YouTube is a great resource for criminals. I had watched several YouTubes on a burner phone on how to break into a gun storage cabinet, and although I wasn't sure any of the techniques they suggested would work, I was ready to give it a try. But I didn't have to. My uncle's friend kept his four rifles in a rack at the back of his closet. I sincerely hoped he didn't have grandchildren. Although the .30-06 Springfield was not loaded. But it did come with a scope. And I found a box of shells under some blankets on a shelf above the rack. I couldn't have asked for more. It was almost too easy. I put everything in the duffle I'd brought for the purpose and quickly let myself out.

Less than a half hour later I pulled into a spot in front of my storage unit to drop off the stolen rifle along with several purchases I'd made earlier. Some boots that were a size larger than I usually wore that I'd picked up at a used clothing store. An old leather jacket that was cracked with age but fit like it had been made for me that I'd found at a consignment shop. And a motorcycle license plate from a junkyard where I went to purchase a hubcap that I didn't really need. My theory was that by purchasing all of these items well in advance of actually committing my target crime, the trail leading from them to me would be very cold.

The only thing left to arrange was a just-in-time motorcycle theft.

19

SHOWTIME

My short-term goal was to stay out of trouble. I was obeying traffic laws when driving, not posting anything on social media, not making waves at work, and only crossing the street at crosswalks. I'd set my personal list on the back burner and was concentrating on living a normal life. A normal life with a slightly different face. Each day that passed I grew fonder of my shapely nose. I promised myself that if I managed to pull off Clint's hunting accident without getting caught, I would buy myself a new chin. One small body part at a time.

Karen got all hot and bothered when Clint was released from prison, but my mantra to her became the cliché I didn't believe in: *what goes around comes around.* So don't worry, I told her. It's a matter of time. Some day he will get what he deserves. At least that much was true, and sooner rather than later.

After letting her vent and repeating the platitude numerous times, she seemed to accept the truth of my lie. People like to tell themselves that things will even out in the end. At the same time, we all know that good people have bad things happen to them, and bad people do bad things and go unpunished. Life has never had a reputation for being fair. That's why I was going to put my finger on the scale of justice one more time. This time for Karen. And to some extent, for Brian.

The hardest part for me was waiting the two months for hunting season. Although I knew it was probably good to have some time between his release from prison and any act of retribution, it was still hard. Each night I mentally crossed off another day on my calendar. At least he hadn't ended up with a felony charge instead of a misdemeanor. A felony conviction would have prevented him from owning a hunting rifle. And it seemed fitting that a hunter would be hunted. Even if the goal was to wound and not kill.

The more I thought about it, and the more times I visualized what it would feel like at the moment I pulled the trigger, the more I liked the plan. Although, if I'd had my druthers and thought I could get away with it, I would have been waiting for him at the prison gate with a gun aimed at his black heart.

I knew Karen was disappointed with what she probably considered my tepid response to the situation. At the same time, I knew that was also a good thing. I wanted her to find my repeated attempts to placate her as irritating as sand in an oyster. If she stayed upset with me, the more authentic she would sound if or when she was questioned after I shot Clint.

Meanwhile, I continued to occasionally see Jay. Although in our conversations we were learning more and more about each other—our pasts, our opinions, our likes and dislikes, our views of the world—there remained some distance, some blank spots carefully side-stepped. At least that's how it was for me. I couldn't speak for Jay. But because of how we'd met and him being a police officer, I remained on guard, wary of hidden agendas. Then there was the nature of our relationship, something we never openly addressed. Was he seeking companionship from time to time because he was lonely? Did he see me as a woman or just as a buddy? Was my appearance really a non-issue for him, or did it disqualify me from being anything but a friend? Ironically, I enjoyed being with him but wasn't attracted to him physically. So, if he felt the same, it shouldn't matter. But I couldn't help but wonder.

My reasons for continuing to meet with him remained somewhat undefined in my own mind. Since Karen was my only real friend, having someone else to get together with, however limited our relationship, was something I enjoyed. In addition, he was also a sort of weather vane. I wasn't entirely certain I would recognize a change in his attitude toward me if he started to suspect me of criminal activities, but I hoped that I would. Meanwhile, being friends with "the enemy" was a bit exciting. Like poking a hornet's nest or running with the bulls at Pamplona.

Then, one evening over dinner, he informed me that Adriana had been found guilty of 1st degree murder and was going to prison. I had been following her trial after she was charged. I'd even attended a couple hours of testimony. But I hadn't realized that the jury had returned a verdict.

"Do you think she'll get life in prison?" I'd read that women were less likely to get a death sentence. I didn't know if I could live with myself if that happened.

"The judge is ruling next week. But my guess is that it will be more like 20-25 years. Even though they determined it was premeditated, her lawyer sowed some doubt by arguing that they never determined what type of poison actually killed him. So, the case against her was partly circumstantial."

"But they still found her guilty."

"She didn't testify, and she somehow looked guilty. I know that shouldn't count, but juries don't always stick to the facts alone."

"But how could they determine cause of death if they couldn't find what killed him?" I happened to know that if the mushroom toxin wasn't identified within 2-4 days of ingestion, it could be almost impossible to detect. And since they initially thought he had a bad case of food poisoning and that he would recover, they probably hadn't looked too carefully at the possibility it was something in his coffee rather than in something he ate.

"The prosecution testified that some mushroom species produce two rounds of illness like that."

"But I thought she only served him coffee?"

"All I can say is that the jury was okay not knowing the exact cause of death. And they liked her for it. It's hard to know sometimes what makes jurors vote in a particular way."

Yes, it was hard to know. I was sad for her. But if she got out in twenty years, she would still be a relatively young woman. She would still have some time to live a normal life.

Two nights before the opening of hunting season, I had dinner with Jay. It felt like I was tempting fate, that my building adrenaline rush would reveal that I was planning something, something I needed to keep secret. In less than 48 hours after our dinner together I would be tracking Clint's movements, hoping to end his reign as a bully and abusive father—unless he had lost his interest in matching wits with a deer. After all of my subterfuge, preparation, and planning, that would be a huge disappointment.

I needn't have worried. Right on schedule, the next afternoon Clint's GPS indicated he was on the road in his camper headed in the direction of an area popular with local hunters. It was a place I had already scouted under the pretense of enjoying the many hiking trails in the heavily wooded forest there. I hoped that was indeed where he ended up instead of going farther away. The farther away he went, the more complicated my motorcycle heist became. As it was, if he ended up where I thought he might, I should easily be able to pick up a motorcycle tomorrow and make it to where Clint was hunting well before dusk.

There were variables of course. Like if he got his limit early in the day and was already back at his camper when I arrived. Or if he didn't return on the main trail but took some circuitous route back. Or if he just decided he would rather drink than hunt and was working on getting smashed rather than bagging a deer. There were lots of ways he could foil my plan. But, as long as I didn't get caught stealing a motorcycle, a failure wouldn't be the end of it for me. It would simply require a new approach.

The next day was clear and cold. A great day for hunters. Of all sorts.

There was a tavern popular with motorcyclists 7.7 miles from my home. I'd driven past it a number of times before thinking of it as a good place to "borrow" a motorcycle. To get there by car only took a few minutes, but I was planning on bicycling there so I could leave my car in the driveway. Since I wasn't used to bicycling, I'd been building up leg strength on my stationary bike at home rather than riding in the neighborhood or near my storage locker where someone might see me. The bike was currently chained up in front of a grocery store. I'd driven it there late the night before and dropped it off when no one was around.

Not only didn't I want to be seen riding a bicycle anywhere near my house, I didn't want to be seen leaving my house either. When it was time to go, I slipped out the back in my dark clothes and hoody with the helmet, a change of clothes and the rifle in a pack large enough for a backpacking trip. Although it was daylight, I was pretty sure no one had witnessed my departure. And once I'd put some distance between me and my home, I felt anonymous.

I put on a hat under the helmet for the ride from the grocery to the tavern. It took more effort to maintain my balance and to pump my way up small slopes than it had riding my stationary bike, even though I'd increased its resistance levels to build leg strength. Fortunately, it wasn't that far, and I made good time. I left the bicycle chained to a fence that separated the road that ran behind the tavern from the building next door. Still wearing my helmet, I calmly walked over to a small, older motorcycle with what I thought might be its original red paint under streaks of dust and dirt. It was parked alongside several impressive Harleys that looked like they could have been props in Easy Rider.

Older motorcycles were supposedly easier to hotwire than newer ones. I had to take that on faith, since I hadn't had access to the real thing for practice. Instead, I had watched so many YouTubes at the library on how to hotwire a motorcycle, I could go through the process in my sleep. I had even memorized what to expect with particular motorcycles by brand and year. Although I couldn't determine either the brand or the year of the motorcycle before me without taking a closer look, with luck, it wouldn't be any worse than putting together an IKEA cabinet.

All of the YouTubes claimed that unlocking the handlebars of any older motorcycle without a key was a simple task that only required a screw driver or a Bic pen. I'd considered the Bic pen approach to be a macho exaggeration, but I couldn't resist trying it. When it worked as promised, I was both very surprised and very pleased. I quickly pushed the motorcycle around to the side of the building where I wouldn't be as visible while trying to get it started, removed my helmet in order to see better, and took a deep breath to calm myself. My calm only lasted a few seconds. Although I had done a lot of visualizing in lieu of hands-on practice, what I was looking at bore no resemblance to anything I'd studied on the videos. Granted, the YouTube experts had all acknowledged there were engine variations, but it was as if I was looking at a different kind of machine altogether.

"Need help?" a male voice said. I was angry with myself for letting him sneak up on me, my heart thumping as I kept my head down and fought to keep my voice steady.

"Nah," I said. "She's finicky, but I've almost got it."

"Well, give a shout if you need help—I'll be at the bar."

I thanked him without looking up, relieved he was moving on so quickly.

Even though the light wasn't all that bright at the side of the building, and I was wearing a mask and a knit cap, I wasn't thrilled about being spotted. What if the guy said something to the bartender or some customer about seeing someone working on a bike outside? What if another biker came out to help or to check on their own bike?

Under the circumstances, if I couldn't get it started in the next few minutes, it might be prudent to call it quits. Although nothing about what I was doing was prudent, anything but. Unless someone challenged me, I might as well keep at it until I got the bike running.

As I studied the mechanism, things started to make sense. I had the speaker wire ready, and I finally identified the ignition wires. Next, I removed the cap and located the bridge between two of the three ports on the connector, stuck my wire to the bridge, and held my breath.

The engine sputtered then caught.

I put the plastic cover back, pulled on my helmet, jumped on the bike, and sped away.

It was exhilarating. And a bit tricky. Although I'd been thinking of it as a large and bulky bicycle with a powerful motor, I quickly realized that size alone made the balancing act exponentially more difficult. As soon as I found a place to pull over next to some bushes that I could hide behind, I did. After changing the license plate, I practiced shifting gears and breaking. I wouldn't be making any fancy turns or doing anything creative, but if I was careful, I might be able to get to my destination without wiping out.

If someone had told me I would be riding a motorcycle on a main highway without ever having ridden one before, I would have said they were crazy. But there I was. Doing something both technically and physically challenging, on my way to commit a serious crime.

So many things could go wrong. I could end up smeared across the road or stopped by the highway patrol. Or I could already have ended up on a camera somewhere, and, despite my disguise, maybe there was some way I hadn't thought of that I could be identified. But at this point, I was committed. The only thing to do was to keep an eye out for traffic and potholes, stay within the speed limit, and trust my karma.

One of my biggest worries was that I'd be unable to get the motorcycle going again when it was time to make my escape. I would know *how* to do it, but would it work a second time? Or what if someone else knew how to hotwire a motorcycle and made off with it while I was lying in wait for Clint to walk down the trail? I'd tried to think of all the possible glitches with my plan and how to cope if something went wrong, but I knew the unexpected could be a showstopper. Yet, there I was.

When I arrived at the campground where Clint had his camper, I checked to make certain he hadn't returned early and was already drinking with his buddies around a campfire. Relieved that there was no sight of him at his campsite, I found a sparsely populated spot on the opposite side of the campground from where Clint was parked and left my motorcycle and helmet behind a clump of brush next to the tree line. I didn't see anyone as I headed into the woods, paralleling the trail I hoped Clint would take back from his day trip. It was the perfect plan, as long as all the players used my script.

The hill above the main trail that I'd identified on my hiking trip to the area was just the right distance to shoot from, close enough to ensure a hit, but far enough away to allow for escape. Unfortunately, it wasn't as easy to access the spot through the woods as I'd anticipated. There was more ground cover than down below, including lots of blackberries. But I wasn't about to let a few thorns keep me from reaching my post.

The sun was disappearing from sight by the time I got settled in. Now another fear seeped into my mind, something I should have thought of but hadn't. What if Clint was wearing so much gear as to be unrecognizable at a distance? What if I guessed wrong and shot the wrong person? It had taken a series of lucky breaks to get this far; I might not get a second chance. My only other worry was what happened if I took my shot and missed.

When I heard voices coming down the trail, I readied myself by slowing my breathing and focusing my mind. Two men came into sight. They were laughing and talking loudly. I could tell both by sight and by their voices that neither one was Clint. All of my muscles suddenly relaxed and I almost dropped the rifle.

Lying on the ground trying to keep my rifle at ready with sticks and roots poking me was truly uncomfortable. As the earth cooled, I could feel my body's core temperature getting lower. I told myself that the discomfort would keep me alert. He could come down that trail any minute. Any minute now. All I needed to do was stay alert.

But if he didn't come before it was too dark to safely take the shot, I would have to call it off.

The trail was filling up with shadows when Clint and a buddy finally appeared. I recognized his voice before I got a glimpse of his face under his red hunting cap. I zeroed in on his legs through the scope and followed his progress as they came down the trail. The two men were a little closer together than I liked, but I had a clear shot that I took as they drew even with where I was lying in wait.

The rifle lunged in my grasp even though I'd thought I was prepared for the kickback. As I looked down at the two men, I realized my first shot must have missed its mark. They were standing there, looking around, as if confused by what they thought they had heard. The fact that they were no longer moving made my second shot easier. Right on target. Goodbye kneecap.

I didn't hang around to see what happened next.

20

OOPS

I knew I was making too much noise as I crashed through the brush, but my adrenaline was pumping like a runaway train, and every microbe in my body screamed *get away*. At the edge of the woods my brain finally took control, and I paused to put the rifle in my pack and reconnoiter before leaping out of the woods onto the road. My hands were shaking and my raspy breathing echoed among the trees. A predator on the move.

When I didn't see anyone in the vicinity, I stepped out onto the road and headed briskly in the direction of Clint's camper. I needed to remove the tracker before I could leave. If I left it in place and someone discovered it, it might look like a planned shooting instead of an accident. There was a couple one campsite down from Clint's, but they seemed pretty focused on getting a fire going. Trying to look purposeful rather than sneaky, I retrieved the tracker. Clint had graciously parked so that it was attached on the side facing a row of trees instead of the road or another campsite.

As soon as I had the tracker back, I made a beeline for my motorcycle, trying to act normal while still moving fast. Taking deep breaths to get myself under better control by increasing oxygen to my brain. I was a lot more anxious than I'd anticipated. There were too many opportunities to be seen by some hunter or camper.

My hands were shaking as I took out my hotwiring tools. "Calm down," I told myself. Even if someone saw me now, they wouldn't necessarily connect me with what had happened to Clint. I was counting on it taking them some time to get a response from a 911 call. And, after making the call, they would most likely be focused on Clint's injury rather than on finding the person who had shot him.

I heard some people shouting in the distance at the same time my motorcycle came to life. Thank heavens for small things—at least I wouldn't have to walk home.

No one tried to stop me as I drove out of the campground, careful not to speed. Once on the road, I congratulated myself on how smoothly everything had gone overall. It would have been nice not to have taken that second shot. That kind of muddied the "accidental" shooting argument. Although it was still possible it could be seen as an accident, some wild-eyed hunter taking a shot at a deer near the path at dusk . . . twice. Missing both times. It *was* possible.

Suddenly I realized that I had congratulated myself too soon. There was one thing I hadn't counted on . . . running out of gas.

I couldn't believe I hadn't checked to see how much gas was in the tank of the motorcycle I'd taken. It was so basic. So obvious. Not exactly something a master criminal mind would overlook. It made me wonder what else I had missed. I was running literally on empty, miles away from my destination. And safety.

Several cars whizzed past as I rolled the motorcycle off the road and over some bumpy terrain to get it under the shadows of a clump of evergreens. It suddenly felt like I was trying to steer it through molasses, resisting my determination to get it out of sight. Marginally satisfied that no one would notice it beneath the trees as night descended, I took off my helmet, got out a screw driver and quickly removed the license plate. I considered putting its original back on like I'd intended, but decided it might slow down the process of figuring out where it had come from if I didn't. Although it could have been reported stolen by now. Still, gaining a little time might make the difference between getting caught and getting away.

At a break in the traffic, I crossed the road and started walking. I still had the helmet and the license plate. It seemed wise to get further away from where I'd left the motorcycle before discarding them. Make the evidence harder to piece together. Other than that, I didn't have a Plan B. I couldn't call for an Uber or hop a bus or thumb a ride. The only option seemed to be to walk, even though I was at least 20 miles way from where I'd left my bicycle. If I could keep up the pace, I might be able to get there in about eight or nine hours. A long walk, but not impossible for someone as motivated as I was. And it would still give me time to sneak home before daylight.

When the ambulance and firetruck screamed past, I was fairly certain I knew where they were headed. It had taken them long enough. I wondered where they were from and if the EMT on board were used to working on people with gunshot wounds.

After walking about an hour, I dropped the helmet in a ditch. It could have been a spare that fell off the back of a motorcycle. Or, it was old, someone could have tossed it. People did things like that. Two hours more and I flung the original license plate out into a field of tall grass. I wasn't sure it was the best spot to leave it, but I didn't want to have it on me any longer. It was bad enough that I had a rifle in my pack.

Cars whizzing past thinned out as it got late, but no one slowed down to see what my situation was. Would the police connect a person walking along the highway with a possible fugitive fleeing from the scene of a crime? If it was truly a hunting accident, the guilty hunter wouldn't have to make a getaway on foot. And why would anyone think it was anything but an accident at this point? During hunting season there were always accidents. It might be a day or so before some detective had second thoughts about what had happened. If anyone did. And by then I would have covered my tracks as best I could.

When I came to the first gas station, it was already closed.

Perhaps that was just as well. If I'd been tempted to steal a car, that might have complicated things even more. It was best if I kept walking. Even though I was already feeling fatigued, and I had miles more to go.

There was one thing I managed to do as planned—disposing of the rifle. There was a bridge over a swift-running stretch of river that I had tested by dropping pieces of wood in to see whether they sank or were carried off. Hopefully the rifle would quickly disappear downstream like the wood had.

I waited until there were no cars before tossing the rifle and the fake license plate in the water, pausing long enough to watch as they were swept away by the current. It was possible that one or both would be washed ashore at some point, hopefully not within eyesight of the bridge. And hopefully, wherever they ended up, they wouldn't be found right away. Even if they were, it was possible they wouldn't be connected with the shooting, at least not immediately. I was counting on that.

There was one other thing that made my stomach roil with anxiety. What if some police officer thought it was suspicious for someone to be walking along the highway late at night and stopped to ask me where I was headed? Or what if they stopped to ask me if I needed help? The mask I was wearing would look real enough in the dark, but what if they shined a light in my face? What would I say then if they asked why I was wearing a mask? *I'm on my way to an early Halloween party? I was planning on robbing a bank, but the banks were closed? I'm hiding from my ex-spouse?* Should I whip the mask off or take a chance and leave it on if approached by someone official? Worrying about what I would do or say under those circumstances kept my mind off the blister I could feel forming on the little toe on my right foot. At least for a while.

When I finally remembered I had an extra pair of shoes that actually fit in my pack, I felt really stupid. Once things start going downhill, they seem to accelerate. I went behind some roadside bushes and changed into the more comfortable shoes. It didn't stop the blister from being annoying, but it eased the pain a little. I left one oversized boot in the bushes and kept the other for a couple of miles before flinging it into the woods.

My pack was lighter, and I was rid of the bulk of evidence that could tie me to the scene. No motorcycle. No rifle. No helmet. No shoes. But I was still a long way from home and declaring "mission accomplished."

The darkness made walking difficult. The side of the road sloped in places, and there were holes and humps and rocks. To make things worse, I was frequently blinded by oncoming headlights. My feet hurt. My blister was getting worse. And my mind swirled with doubts and misgivings. It was one of the longest and most difficult hikes I'd ever attempted. But I kept going. There was no other choice.

By the time I reached the tavern, the parking lot was empty and everything was completely dark. Except for the neon sign proclaiming the tavern's existence. Both feet felt like I'd run a marathon, and the Kleenex I had put in my shoe to ease the pain of the blister on my toe was shredded from rubbing back and forth. If I'd known I'd be spending the night walking, I would have brought different shoes.

There was one thing that hadn't gone wrong—the bicycle was still where I'd left it. I'd been trying not to think about what I'd have to do if someone had managed to break the chain and stolen it. I was so tired that for the last few miles I'd been calculating and recalculating how close to home I dared ride the bike before abandoning it. What I wanted was to ride it all the way home to avoid having to walk further. But I knew I shouldn't do that.

When I reluctantly ditched the bike near a grade school as planned, I sent a silent plea to all larcenous grade schoolers. Please take my bike and keep it for as long as you want. Smear the handlebars with chocolate and splash mud puddle water over the tires. Destroy it as evidence. Please.

The last few miles were killers. So much for the 2.5 miles per hour as the average for most adults. At least it wasn't the average for *this* adult. My gait had become slower and slower as my feet got heavier and heavier. Each step a conscious effort. But I was getting there. And unless something else went wrong, I would be home before sunup.

I didn't see any neighbors' lights on as I sneaked in the back way, and I didn't turn any on once inside. I would have to get rid of my clothes first thing tomorrow. And I needed to check the yard for shoe prints. It would be a shame to jump through every other hurdle and to be caught because of a shoe print comparison between ones found along the road and some in my own backyard. Highly unlikely, but possible.

Before disposing of my clothing in the myriad of nearby clothing collection boxes, I wanted to make sure I'd removed any telltale dirt or DNA, so I put everything I'd worn in the wash, including my shoes.

The shower in the dark was soothing. Then, as soon as my head hit the pillow, I fell asleep, despite my aching legs and sore feet.

I awoke to a knock on the door and immediately felt a panic stronger than I'd ever experienced before. My clothes were still in the washing machine. What would I do if it was a police officer at the door? I quickly put visions of a swat team getting ready to ram my door out of my mind. The knocking was insistent, but no one was yelling for me to open up.

"Sorry, I slept in this morning," I said, as Karen rushed past me into the room.

"Have you heard?" she asked.

"Heard what?" I said, yawning.

Karen stopped and seemed to see me for the first time. "Oh, I woke you up, didn't I?"

"Yes. Want some coffee? I do." I turned toward the kitchen.

"So, you don't know," Karen said, trailing after me.

"Know what?" I yawned again, this time for effect, as I turned on the water and started to fill my Keurig.

"Clint has been shot," she said, sounding elated.

I shut off the water and turned toward her. "Shot?"

"Yes. It was a hunting accident. I saw it on the news this morning."

"I don't suppose he's dead."

Karen frowned. "No, but the reporter said he was going into surgery. So, there's hope." She smiled.

I turned back to making coffee. "You don't mean that," I said.

"Yes, I do. I have absolutely zero sympathy for that man."

"Well, if the police question you, try not to sound so gleeful."

"Why would they question me?"

"Well, if it's a hunting accident, they probably won't. Not sure why I said that—not awake yet."

"I believe it does prove you right—sometimes what goes around comes around."

"Not often enough," I countered. "But it would be satisfying to think he got a little comeuppance, even if it was an accident."

"What else could it be? He was shot while on a trail coming back from a day of deer hunting."

"Do they have the shooter in custody?"

"The reporter was asking for anyone who was in the area to come forward and talk to the police. As if another hunter wouldn't know that they'd shot someone. So, I'd guess *no*."

"And they didn't say how badly he was injured?"

"No, just that it required surgery."

"Couldn't happen to a nicer guy," I said. "Come on, Keurig, fill the damn cup." I needed to clear my head so I didn't say anything I would regret later. And I needed to get going. The sooner I got rid of the clothes and shoes I'd worn, the better.

21

TAKE IT ON THE CHIN

My chin augmentation surgery was scheduled for the week after hunting season opened. My thought had been that it would take me out of commission during the investigation of Clint's hunting accident. And it also gave me an excuse to avoid seeing Jay until things settled down. When he called three days after the incident, I didn't answer but let him leave a message. The message was that he was hoping we could get together for coffee. The fact that he'd mentioned coffee instead of dinner wasn't that unusual, but it still set off a red flag for me following so close after Clint's "accident." I was glad I had an excuse to ask for a postponement.

The chin surgery was far more painful than the nose surgery. I could barely talk, but I'd been told the swelling would go down in a week or two, and that I would feel much better then. And I would have a lovely jawline instead of a receding chin.

Karen came by the evening of the 3rd day to see how I was doing. "You don't look that great," she said when I let her in.

"It doesn't feel that great," I admitted, my words slurred as I fought back tiny stabs of pain. "You'll have to do most of the talking. But I'm glad you're here."

"You told me not to bring anything, so I didn't," she added.

"Your company is all I need."

"That's sweet." We sat down in the living room. "Well, since you want me to talk, I'll tell you about the visit I got from your friend Jay."

I blinked. With my chin bandaged, it was easy to keep my expression neutral. But that wasn't how I felt inside. My stomach had reacted badly to her announcement, like I'd taken a gut punch.

"He came by at school, just as I was getting ready to leave, and asked if I had a few minutes. He was all serious sounding, and it didn't feel like I could say 'no.' He suggested we go to a nearby coffee shop for our talk, which made me even more uneasy. I mean, if he only had a few questions, why couldn't he just ask them?

"Once there, he got right to the point, asking if I'd heard about Clint, and I of course said 'yes.' Then he asked if I owned a gun or a rifle. I said that 'yes' I had a handgun but that I have never owned a rife. At that point he took out one of those pocket notepads and wrote something down. Then he asked some more, rather pointed questions, although he never came right out and asked if I had shot Clint.

"Could I account for my whereabouts on the first day of hunting season? I, of course, had to ask when that was, although I was pretty sure I knew since I'd heard about Clint's accident on the morning after he'd been shot.

"Next, he wanted to know if *you* had a gun, and I said 'yes,' a handgun. And that I was fairly certain you didn't have a rifle—why would you? Then he wanted to know if we'd talked about Clint's accident, and I told him we had. The day after it happened. I also told him that you and I agreed that it couldn't have happened to a nicer person. I could tell he didn't like me saying that, but it was the truth, so I didn't back down.

"Then I jumped in and asked him if he knew how Clint was doing, and he claimed he didn't. But why would he be asking me all of those questions if he wasn't investigating what happened?"

I shook my head and immediately regretted it. "Do you really think he suspects one of us?" I asked. My words came out as though through a muddy funnel, but Karen apparently understood.

"I couldn't tell for sure. I did mention that you had talked me into letting my desire for revenge go. That you tried to convince me that prison was punishment enough. I admitted that I wasn't actually convinced, but that I agreed with you that Brian's welfare was more important than revenge. And I told him about how several teachers had been helping me monitor Brian's behavior since his father's release."

"Did you ask if they have a suspect?" It sounded like I needed a speech therapist, but Karen acted as if we were having a normal conversation.

"Yes, but he pulled the 'I can't talk about an ongoing investigation' excuse."

I raised my eyebrows to acknowledge her comment.

"He did ask one strange thing . . . he wanted to know if either of us had a motorcycle. I assured him that I had never had the slightest inclination to be a motorcycle mama and that you had never mentioned ever owning one or even riding one. In fact, I laughed. Said I couldn't picture you on one. Because I can't. Sorry. I'm probably just responding to old-fashioned ideas about who rides motorcycles.

"Anyway, we ended the conversation talking about your surgery. He honestly doesn't get it. The shape of your chin doesn't matter to me either, but I can understand why you want to be more attractive. Especially after I saw what a difference changing your nose made."

Karen continued filling in the silence between us, talking about her work, local news, and a couple of movies she had seen. When she noticed I was getting tired, she apologized for staying so long. I tried to assure her that the distraction was much appreciated. But after she left, all I could think about was Jay asking her about motorcycles. Even if neither of us was a prime suspect, he was obviously considering whether we should be on the list. And more importantly, he was following up on motorcycle leads—why? Had they made a connection between the abandoned motorcycle and the location where Clint was shot? Had someone seen me drive off?

Each day I half expected Jay to call, but he didn't. Although he did text me a couple of times saying he hoped my recovery was going well. I let him know it was hard to talk but everything was fine. Hint, hint—don't come by to question me.

After two weeks I went back to work. My face was still swollen, but then I wasn't trying to hide the fact that I'd had cosmetic surgery. It wasn't as if no one would notice. And what they said behind my back couldn't be any worse than what they may have said before about my face. A couple of brave souls even acknowledged my condition and said that they thought my chin was going to be lovely after the swelling went away.

"People don't get to pick their relatives or their face," I said. "I'm stuck with my relatives, but decided I might as well have a nose and a chin that I like." They laughed, and for an instant I felt good. Then I got angry. Why should changing those two features make a difference in how people responded to me? On the other hand, that's why I was going through this hell, wasn't it?

I put off getting together with Jay until the end of week three after my surgery. The swelling was almost gone, and my face was starting to look normal. Well, better than normal actually. Having a chin that I could thrust forward or lift up for a haughty glare was very satisfying. And when I looked down my nose, no one was staring into my nostrils. This was how I should have looked initially. A few more nips and tucks here and there, remove a couple of moles, and I would have a face that might not be beautiful, but at least I would blend in instead of being noticeably unattractive.

My family didn't know about my cosmetic surgery yet. As far as they knew, I'd taken a couple of vacations that weren't exciting enough to send pictures. I couldn't help but wonder what they were going to think when they saw the new me. Except for paying for braces for my teeth when I was in high school, they had never suggested I make any changes. And they'd only agreed to the dental work because the dentist insisted it would help me avoid dental problems in the future. Maybe they felt like cosmetic surgery was too overwhelming. Or too expensive. Or maybe they felt my face was my physical cross to bear. Or *their* cross to bear. Although why they would think that either I or they deserved to suffer because of my appearance is beyond me.

When Jay asked me out to dinner, I assumed he was backing off on me as a suspect, but I knew I still had to be careful. We met at one of our favorite restaurants. He was waiting for me and looked rather startled when I sat down across from him. "Wow," he said. "It really makes a difference."

"For the better, I hope."

"It depends on what you mean by 'better.' You do look more, what's the word, 'standard.' 'Traditional.' I'm not sure how to say it. The important thing is that it makes you feel good about your face."

"It does," I said firmly. "My old face kept people from 'seeing' the real me. All they saw was my face. Now I'm hoping that will give my 'inner me' a chance."

"Doesn't it bother you that they didn't give you a chance before? I think it would bother me if I felt people I knew were responding to me differently because of a cosmetic change, that is."

"In all fairness, there are any number of filters people use all the time— How you dress or wear your hair. What they know about your background and economic status. Race. Sense of humor. All sorts of things. Facial features are just one aspect of the package. But a significant piece of the whole for most people."

Jay studied my new face. "I know it's still 'you' under there, but it takes some getting used to."

"Well, all I can say is 'get used to it,' because given what it cost, it's here to stay."

He laughed, reached across the table, and put his hand over mine. "I'm happy for you." I couldn't help but feel pleased that he was happy for "me" and not necessarily for "him."

Our meal came and we made small talk while we ate. Everything seemed like old times until our after-dinner coffee.

"Ever ridden a motorcycle?" he asked. Was there a hint of insinuation in the question?

"No, and I've never wanted to. I'm not a leather jacket kind of woman." I took a sip of coffee. "Karen said you asked her the same thing. Why?" I couldn't help but feel that what he said next was going to define our future relationship.

"It's about the Clint hunting accident investigation." He paused, as if considering his words. "I'm not in charge of it, but I admit to being a bit concerned that you or Karen might be involved." Well, that was certainly straightforward.

"Involved? Like in one of us shot Clint?"

"Maybe not one of you personally. But I know how upset she was when Clint threatened her . . ."

"And pushed her, injuring her head and giving her a concussion . . .," I added quickly.

"Yes. He's a despicable human being who deserved to go to jail for what he did."

"But didn't deserve to be shot?"

"The punishment should fit the crime."

"I thought it was a hunting accident, not 'punishment.'"

Jay hesitated. "It seems to me like a strange place for a hunting accident."

"Oh?"

"You ever been to that park?" Another direct question. No sneak attack at least.

"Yes, I have hiked there as a matter of fact."

"Then you are familiar with the main trail."

"I was only there once, but I think I remember it. As you start up the trail after leaving the parking lot, there's a hill on the left and a gully on the right. Am I picturing it correctly?"

"Yes. And the shot came from the top of the hill, not too far from the parking lot."

"Could someone have been following a deer along the ridge?"

"It's possible."

"But a woman was seen leaving on a motorcycle? Is that why you've been asking about motorcycles?"

"I can't comment on that."

Even if someone had seen me, how could they have identified me as female, especially given the mask and time of day? "Well, all I can say is that it wasn't me, and I'm positive it wasn't Karen either." I tried for what I hoped was a dramatic pause followed by a tone of indignation. "Can you really picture her—or me—as a sniper?"

Jay suddenly smiled. "Actually, I can picture you as a sniper. A cool, calculating one with a steady hand."

"Really? I think I'm flattered." And in a way, I was.

"But a deliberate shooting in that location took some planning."

"You think I'm not capable of planning?"

"I think you like a good mental challenge. But I don't see you as a villain."

I managed a shallow laugh. "I would hope not. But, for the record, I may not have shot the scumbag, but I'm not going to lose any sleep over it."

22

SUCCESS AT LAST

There were a few unsettling weeks after my dinner with Jay. I kept worrying that some other law enforcement person would come poking around and that there was something I had overlooked in the last-minute change of plans due to running out of gas. Had my rifle washed up on shore somewhere and they found an errant print? Had they figured out where the one set of footprints alongside the road ended and another began? Did they have dogs who were able to track me from the abandoned motorcycle back to my home? Over and over again I kicked myself for not checking the motorcycle for fuel. It would have been so easy to have brought along some extra to add just in case.

I worried most about the dogs. When I thought I knew how things would play out, I didn't consider the possibility that I would leave behind the kind of trail I did. Some solid guesswork, a sharp eye, and a sniffing dog could make all of my careful planning moot. Disaster—and all because of one tiny mistake. Well, perhaps not so tiny. Maybe I should say because of one stupid mistake. Tiny or stupid—either way it could lead them to me. And perhaps land me in prison.

The day after the shooting, I'd driven by the place I'd left the bicycle and saw that it was already gone. I didn't care what had happened to it as long as someone else's fingerprints were on it. The rifle and other incriminating items were more worrisome because I couldn't know for sure what had happened to them. There had been nothing in the news about someone finding a rifle in or along the banks of the river, although the police could have kept it out of the press. Nor had there been anything about a stolen motorcycle. Because of Jay's questions, I remained concerned that the police had connected the theft of the motorcycle to the shooting. I was also still worried about whether Jay seriously considered that I was somehow involved. I felt threatened by his police instincts and what I might have said to expose myself. At the same time, I was fully aware of the irony of the situation, and saddened by the thought that he suspected me of the crime.

After a month had gone by and no one showed up at my door to question me about where I'd been the night Clint was shot, or if I owned a hunting rifle, or if I had stolen a motorcycle from the nearby tavern—I started to relax. Not completely, but a little.

As for Clint, Karen was keeping tabs on him. For Brian's sake, she said. And probably because she was glad it had happened to him and wanted to make sure he was suffering. Over dinner one evening she announced: "His kneecap was so badly shattered that he may lose the use of his leg. That should slow him down."

"You mean Brian can run away if his dad decides to thrash him."

"You got it. He won't be able to physically bully *anyone* if he has to use a crutch to get around."

"Or, he could use the crutch as a weapon."

"He'd have to catch someone first."

"Unless they don't see him coming."

"Don't be such a pessimist. You always hear the clomp of a crutch." Then she blinked and did a retake, suddenly getting that I was teasing her.

"Do you know if they have any suspects yet?" I kept my voice casual, acting as though I wasn't following the case as closely as she probably was. But in truth, I was scanning multiple news sources daily, checking for any details that would tell me whether I was going to come up on the official radar.

"No, as far as I can tell, no one has come forward and confessed, and the police haven't found either the culprit or an eye witness. At this point, I doubt they will."

"If you did it, you'd tell me, right?" I kidded.

"I did mention I went to sniper school, didn't I?" Karen said with a grin.

"Maybe you should get a job with the FBI."

"Maybe *you* should."

"I think I would like that," I said, half serious.

"Really?"

"The TV version at least. It's probably boring most of the time, with lots of paperwork and no independent power."

"I see you more as the Equalizer."

"Love Queen Latifah. But I don't think the show is realistic."

"It isn't supposed to be—it's inspirational."

"In what way?"

"She makes sure the little guy gets justice."

"You know how I feel about that. What goes around seldom if ever comes around. And superheroes don't exist."

"Well, we made someone pay for past crimes once."

Actually, my scorecard was better than she knew, but I wasn't about to brag. "What we did to Hugh wasn't that big of a deal, although I admit the final outcome was much more satisfying than we originally intended. And we didn't need superpower skills or have to shoot anyone. I'd be lucky to survive my first attempt at that sort of thing. In real life, people shoot back at you, and they don't always miss."

· · ·

Two weeks after my conversation with Karen something wonderful happened: I was promoted to VP of Project Management at Keller and Eaves. I'd given up hope that I would ever be more than a project lead, so I was surprised and pleased, ecstatic to be more accurate. Everyone thought that Marcus Manning, one of my least favorite colleagues and Adriana's former lover, was a shoe-in for the position, so when it was announced that I had been chosen, colleagues started gossiping about why. To be honest, I'd had no idea that I was even in the running. Although I knew my past performance had been stellar, I didn't realize anyone higher up the chain had noticed.

On the other hand, I certainly didn't think Marcus deserved to be VP of Project Management. Setting aside how he always challenged anything I suggested when we were working together on the same team, I didn't see him as either creative or competent. Rather, I considered him a mediocre engineer with an inflated sense of worth. So many tall, good-looking men in my experience were like that. Maybe I resented him because his performance was always evaluated through an attractiveness filter. Of course mine was too, but with the opposite outcome, at least in the past. Could my new nose and chin have played a role in my current good fortune?

The promotion involved moving from my cubicle to an office with glass walls and a door with a plastic name plate with my name and new title on it. No view. But a real door, a huge status symbol in the company. The desk was manufactured wood, but not bad looking. There were drawers on both ends and a modesty panel facing out. Two chairs, one behind the desk and one in front of it. The one behind the desk looked and felt comfortable. The one in front didn't encourage visitors to stay for long. The only other pieces of furniture were a small bookcase with a few company manuals in it next to a narrow table for my printer. Home sweet office.

I was unpacking my box of personal belongings when I had my first official visitor: none other than Marcus Manning. His too perfect lips were turned down, his frown slightly menacing. "You didn't waste any time," he said, eyeing the objects strewn across my desk. He closed the door behind him but remained standing.

"Is that your way of saying 'congratulations'?" I asked.

He glanced over his shoulder before replying. Glass walls can be intimidating. "You don't deserve this promotion, you know."

I stood still and looked him in the eyes, unblinking. "Why are you here?" I asked coldly.

"To let you know that I will be watching you. Don't get too settled, because I doubt you will be here for long." It wasn't even a veiled threat, but an overt declaration of war.

"I know we've had our differences, but I can't imagine that it will do either of us any good to be at each other's throats." That was my way of saying that I was willing to play nice if he was. If he didn't, I didn't intend to lose the war.

Marcus smiled, a crooked, nasty grin. "I guess we'll see." Then he made a dramatic exit. If he'd been wearing a cape, it would have swirled around as he glided off.

I sat down and watched him disappear down the hall. He could be charming when he wanted to be and had a lot of friends in the company. If he was determined to make life tough for me, he would probably succeed. Nevertheless, I wasn't going to let him walk all over me. I'd put being a victim behind me. Now I was prepared to fight back.

The next Saturday, Karen and I went out to dinner to celebrate. I ordered a bottle of medium-priced champagne, and we toasted my new job.

"I always thought you'd eventually get a real office," Karen said.

"I feel like I've earned it ten times over, but I was beginning to think it would never happen."

"Do you think it's related to your new face?"

"That's crossed my mind. But I'd rather think it's based on performance." I took a sip of champagne. "Not everyone is pleased though. Remember me telling you about Marcus?"

"Adriana's boyfriend?"

"Yes. Not my biggest fan. Well, worse than that. He stopped by to threaten me."

"Threaten?"

"To warn me is perhaps more accurate. He says he's going to be watching, so if I make the tiniest misstep, he'll be there to point it out."

"Why would he do that?"

"Because he thought the job should have been his."

"Of course he did. Men." Karen shook her head. "By the way, I'm curious, do you still keep in touch with Adriana?"

"Funny that you mention it. It's been a while. But I went by to see her on Wednesday, and she acted real stand-offish. Not her usual grateful-for-visitors persona. We didn't talk about Marcus, but that's what I assume it was about."

"I thought he'd moved on. Didn't you say he dropped her?"

"For a while. But I think they're seeing each other again. Maybe he gets conjugal visits. The best of both worlds—sex without any complications."

"That's harsh. But why would they get back together?"

"Even though they've had an on-again, off-again relationship, they've known each other a long time. Maybe she convinced him she was innocent. Or maybe he just got over it. Still, I can't imagine that whatever kind of relationship they have will last that long with her in prison."

"She still claiming her innocence?"

"Yeah. And I heard that she has a new lawyer. But Jay doesn't think she'll make any headway. The evidence was too overwhelming."

"But you never felt like she did it, did you?"

"I don't know. There are days when I think she may have. I mean, she did serve him the coffee that supposedly killed him. On the other hand, maybe she only wanted to make him sick and gave him a deadly dose by mistake."

"Why would she do that?"

"You're right; that doesn't make sense. But Adriana as a hardened killer doesn't make sense either."

"Rejection can do strange things to people."

"Yes, it can." Karen had that one right.

CALICO CAT

Life was good. I loved my job. It was challenging, but totally within my capabilities. And I enjoyed being on the inside. Granted I was on the fringes, but hearing about short and long-term company goals and being present for exchanges about organizational strategic planning was fascinating. And I liked watching the interplay between the main players, noting the underlying messages and all of the jockeying to be top dog.

Although I was included at meetings, the hierarchy was physically staged, partly to control participation. There was a huge table in the conference room. The people in power sat at the table for meetings, while lesser players and support staff sat in chairs lined up along two walls. I didn't mind not having a chair at the table; I was thankful to be in the room. And perhaps someday I *would* have a seat in the inner circle.

Buoyed by my professional success, I decided to make some other changes in my life. I considered moving but liked the convenience of my condo. I decided my place could, however, use some upgrades. Like some new kitchen appliances and new furniture. Maybe after I spiffed up my kitchen, I'd have a few colleagues over for dinner. Start living a more normal life.

Another change I thought about making was getting a pet. I couldn't remember having any that was mine alone growing up. We'd had a few parakeets, a dog at one point. But they belonged to the whole family, and I never got attached.

There were strict rules about pets in the condo agreement, but dogs of a certain size as well as cats were allowed. A dog seemed like more responsibility to me than a cat. Nor would I have to walk a cat twice a day or find a place outside for it to go to the bathroom. And I couldn't face carrying around a clutch of plastic baggies to pick up poop. So, I decided I would get a cat. A calico if possible. I liked the way they looked. Especially ones with unusual markings. Maybe because I've always been different myself.

There was a shelter not too far away. I stopped in and was surprised to find I had to make an appointment to see any animals in person. I'd pictured going there, checking out what they had available and, if I saw a cat I liked, it was mine. That may have been how it used to be, but even though there are lots of unwanted animals around, the people in control of handing them out apparently have some very strict rules. And, as I was soon to learn, there was one rule I should have checked on in advance.

The sign on the door said "Animal Rescue Shelter." The volunteer who greeted me wore a badge that said "Marissa, Animal Rescuer." I almost said, "Hi, I'm Callista. I'm here to rescue a cat from the rescuer at the rescue shelter." But Marissa was so bouncy and earnest I decided I'd better not kid around.

After taking down my name on a form attached to a clipboard, she said, "Tell me what kind of pet you're looking for."

"A cat, a calico if possible."

She wrote something in a box; I was at a bad angle to read what it said. "Age?" she asked.

"Mine or the cat's?"

Marissa frowned. "Are you looking for a young cat or would you be satisfied with an older cat?"

"No preference."

She scribbled something that didn't quite fall within the box parameters on the form as her frown deepened. "Sex?"

I knew the answer wasn't "yes." "No preference," I said again.

Marissa raised her eyebrows. Was I supposed to know exactly what I wanted, like buying an article of clothing—size, color, material, style. Well, I didn't. I waited while she wrote something else on the form.

"I'm open to a cat that seems right when I see it," I began, but she cut me off.

"Do you have sufficient space for a cat?"

I wanted to ask how much space a cat needed, but I sensed that wasn't the right way to respond. "Yes, I have a two-bedroom condo on the ground floor with a small, but adequate fenced yard."

Marissa blinked and lowered her clipboard. "You don't intend to let the cat go outside, do you?"

"Well, yes. I thought I would put in a cat door so he or she could come and go as they please."

"I'm sorry." She set her clipboard on the counter. She didn't sound sorry.

"I don't understand."

"Cats should be kept indoors," she said firmly.

"But cats roam my neighborhood all the time," I objected.

"That makes them vulnerable, both to other animals and to disease."

"My yard is fenced," I said, even though it was clear I'd already lost the argument. And I knew that a fence wouldn't contain a cat, so I don't know why I said it.

Marissa made a sound that sounded like a cat with a hairball caught in its throat. "You aren't serious, are you?"

"I know cats don't like to be penned up," I began.

"It isn't penning them up to keep them inside. It's called 'keeping them safe.'"

"What if I promise to keep my cat inside?"

Marissa made that hairball noise again. "I'm sorry, but I don't think you're a good match for one of our cats."

Not a good match? I wanted to protest: we weren't talking about a life partner, just a cat. But it was clear the conversation was over.

"I would give a cat a good home," I said. "Keep that in mind when you have to put down one of your cats because you run out of space." I savored the word "space."

I could tell Marissa wanted to deny they ever put down an animal, but although she might be rude and unreasonable, she was apparently not a liar. At least not about a well-known public fact.

Once outside, I was in a state of disbelief. Had I just been rejected as not worthy of having a pet? And was it really that unsafe to let a cat have a little freedom? I knew lots of people who let their cats out for exercise. Sure, occasionally they got into fights with other cats or brought home dead birds or rats as gifts, but that seemed like a normal cat life to me. Oh well, there were other shelters.

The next day I went to a shelter a little further away. Their website said "appointments preferred; walk-ins welcome." I would be a welcome walk-in.

The animal rescuer that greeted me was a little older than Marissa, but she had the same smiley attitude. And, like Marissa, she had a clipboard with a form attached. But this time I knew what the right answer was when asked about having enough space for a cat. I'd looked up the rules online and was prepared to ace the test.

"Name?" she asked.

"Callista Jones."

She paused and looked directly at me. After a long silence, she said, "I'm sorry, Ms. Jones. But I believe you've already been to another of our shelters and been disqualified."

I was impressed that word had spread so quickly. Impressed and irritated at the same time. "But now that I understand the reason for keeping a cat indoors, I'm fine with that."

"I'm sorry. It's our policy."

"I just said that I understand and am fine with your policy." I wanted to scream, "It's just a damn cat."

"Perhaps you should try a pet store. Or check bulletin boards in stores near you. That's where people often post when their cat has a litter." She sounded almost sympathetic. But it was clear that she wasn't about to bend, not one tiny bit.

It seemed pointless to argue further, so I walked out—without a cat.

Later that evening, I kept experiencing tiny flickers of anger. What right did those shelter volunteers have for not accepting me at my word? And was I blacklisted at *all* rescue shelters? Forever? How was that better for the huge number of abandoned animals in our country? And how many people lied about that stupid rule anyway? I had to remind myself that I was no longer in the revenge business. And I could find a cat elsewhere. But thoughts of getting even kept flickering through my brain. I imagined sneaking into the shelter at night and releasing all of the cats and dogs from their cages. Of course, I wouldn't want to endanger any of them, so I would need to leave them inside. It would only be a minor inconvenience to whoever opened up the shelter in the morning. Maybe I should simply write a letter to whoever was in charge, either protesting their policy or complaining about the fact that they didn't give a potential pet owner a second chance. Or, maybe I should just suck it up and get a cat elsewhere.

In the following few weeks, I was busy at work. Thoughts about pets and putdowns were placed on a back burner. Everything else in my life was going smoothly. My direct reports seemed to respect me and respond well to my suggestions. Upper management was appreciative of my work. Karen and I enjoyed several dinners together.

And Jay was still in the picture, although not in the center, more off to one side.

Friday evening I started by looking for a calico on Craigslist. No such luck. But I did see an ad for an 8-week-old, litter box trained black and white kitten. The picture posted with the ad showed an adorable fluffball with some interesting markings. I'd originally thought of getting a misfit, a cat no one else would love. But here was a kitten that was irresistible. The price was not bad, and the address wasn't too far away. I made an appointment to take a look.

I suppose it was inevitable. Who can resist the antics of a miniature cat? Especially one that seemed to like being picked up and petted. One that looked at me with kitten love in its eyes. And in return for soft comfort, all I needed to provide was room and board. I paid the rehoming fee and asked them to keep my new friend until I could return with a travel cage.

While I was at the pet store, I also purchased a covered litter box, some expensive cat food designed especially for her age group, a food bowl and matching water bowl decorated with cat paws, a felt cave cat bed, several cat toys, a lime green collar and some special cat treats. When I went back to pick her up, the owners suggested I take her into a vet for shots, get her a pet license and a name tag for her collar. The whole process was more complicated and expensive than I'd anticipated.

When I got her home and fed, she immediately fell asleep on the couch. She seemed a bit frightened of the expensive cave bed I'd purchased for her. Maybe I could lure her into it later with one of her toys and a couple of salmon flavored cat treats.

Feeling all domestic, I called Karen and invited her over to meet "kitty" and help me name her. While drinking a nice red wine, we googled names for black and white cats and rejected one after another. Patches? No. Morticia? No. Oreo? No. Rorschach? No. Eight Ball?

"Who names a cat Eight Ball?" Karen asked. "Or Catzilla?"

"I'm leaning toward something normal. Sweet. Soft."

We sat there watching her sleep, her tiny stomach going up and down, her paws twitching occasionally as if she was running in her dreams. "I like the way the black slides down over her eyes but leaves a white space that spreads out over the rest of her face," Karen said.

"I like her black bow tie," I said. "And her three white paws."

It wasn't until the third glass of wine that we decided to name her after me, well, after the meaning of my name, but in a different language. "Bella suites her," Karen said. "I wouldn't mind being named Bella myself."

As if on cue, Bella opened her eyes and was instantly wide awake, leaping into Karen's lap and licking her arm. I didn't care much for the licking, but maybe I could train her out of it. Or get used to it. She was incredibly cute.

We drank more wine, Bella played with a couple of her toys before falling asleep again on the couch, between Karen and me. Naming and owning a cat made me feel like I'd finally joined mainstream America. Thank you, Bella.

24

LIFE'S NEW FACE

When my expertise with numbers landed me a special assignment, I was in heaven. It was a high-profile project with lots of opportunity to shine. I was given clearance to access some company files that only a handful of employees had permission to see. For the first time I felt like I was an integral part of something big. That I had a hand on the oar that was steering the ship. Not that I was making any decisions, but I was providing the data that others would use to make decisions. That was more than enough for me. At least for now.

Although I was incredibly busy with my new position, I made time to continue having regular dinners with Karen. She was an important part of my new and improved life. She too was happy. And busier than she'd ever been. Her work with WADA was filling a void in her life that she hadn't even realized was there. Whenever we met, she would regale me with stories about the women and children they helped and how fulfilling it was to see them leave a hostile environment behind and move into a safe living situation. They also provided on-going counseling and needed follow-up services.

To top it all off, as an organization WADA was doing even better than they'd hoped. They'd received enough funding to hire several staff members and were partnering with other like-minded organizations to expand the services they provided. Karen had not only turned Brian's life around, and her own as well, but had successfully launched a much-needed organization in the community.

Although Karen was no longer in direct contact with Brian, one of his teachers was keeping her up to date on how he was doing. She was pleased to learn that even with his father back in his life, he continued to do well at school and didn't display any signs of stress. Although both of us would have liked more details about his home-life, we had to be satisfied knowing things were okay, at least on the surface.

Occasionally Karen would hear something about Clint on the local grapevine and report back to me. He was said to be extremely bitter about what had happened and resented having to be retrained to do a desk job instead of the construction work he enjoyed. From macho man to desk jockey with one shot, well, with two shots. The grapevine also reported that he was drinking too much and that he refused therapy for his leg. Personally, I wasn't concerned about how deep he dug the hole of despair for himself, as long as he didn't pull his family in with him.

In some ways, I had given Clint a second chance by limiting his ability to be physically abusive. His wife had welcomed him back into the family. He was still capable of being employed and getting around on his own. It was up to him whether he accepted the wake-up call or continued on a path of self-destruction. And if the rumors were right, he'd chosen the latter.

Jay and I also continued to get together on a fairly regular basis. Our relationship was still stuck in neutral, but I was okay with that. He seemed fine with the status quo too. There was no more talk about motorcycles or any indication that he continued to harbor suspicions about my involvement with Clint's shooting. But I remained wary.

Although I was no longer constantly looking over my shoulder or concerned that at any minute police would come knocking on my door in response to one of my many misdeeds, I still had no desire to return to my list. Instead of looking back, I was committed to focusing on the future. The need for revenge had passed. I was just thankful I hadn't ruined what remained of my life by getting caught for any of the things I had done to even the score over what others had done to me.

For me, the acts of vengeance related to my list were now a closed chapter in my life, a chapter that I hoped remained closed. The names I never got to cross off dropped back into the inkwell, like Mark Twain's description of characters that he decided to eliminate from the pages of his manuscript. However, that didn't mean I never mentally revisited the acts of retribution I'd administered. In fact, I sometimes revived the memories, relishing feelings of satisfaction derived from delivering a punishment that fit the crime.

At the same time, I harbored a few regrets for the innocent bystanders who had suffered in some way, as well as misgivings about the way in which I started on my journey with Dane and Adriana. But these were things I tried not to dwell on, especially the latter. Dane was dead; I couldn't change that. Nor could I help Adriana without destroying my own life.

As I reflected on the past, I had to admit that even before being elevated to my new position at work, there had been times when I'd enjoyed what I was doing. My graduate school research for instance. Or my early project work for Keller and Eaves. But life was much sweeter now than any time in the past. Each day I got up feeling excited and positive about what lay ahead. I could even look in the mirror without feeling *fugly,* confident in my ability to tackle whatever came my way at work and knowing I wouldn't be looked down on or ignored because of my face.

Removing a couple of unsightly moles had completed my face remodel. I don't know why I hadn't done that before, except until I'd made the other changes, it hadn't seemed worth the effort. There was even more sculpting that my cosmetic surgeon wanted to do, but I was satisfied with the way I looked. I would never be referred to as pretty or turn men's heads as I passed by. But they wouldn't be scrawling nasty nicknames on bathroom walls either. Not being "fugly" was a huge improvement.

In addition, not only did I have two friends who had liked me even before my cosmetic surgery, I had an untrainable but lovable kitten who gave as much love as she demanded in return. Life was indeed good.

The first family gathering I'd attended when my face was "complete" was both satisfying and maddening. Most family members made a big fuss about my appearance and followed their comments with questions about what else I was going to have changed. They anticipated that the ugly duckling would want to turn into a swan instead of becoming an ordinary duck. In fact, several relatives went so far as to make suggestions about what I should do next! I felt like responding by suggesting things *they* might do to improve their own appearance. But I managed to withhold any witty or biting retorts, telling myself to let it go; it wasn't important. The fact that I was satisfied with how I looked was all that mattered.

My biggest letdown was my parents' response, or lack of response. They acted as if they didn't notice the changes I'd made to my face, as if I'd been normal looking all along. As if they hadn't been embarrassed to claim me as their flesh and blood. But for me, the past was a vivid reality; it wouldn't go away by pretending it had never existed. I didn't want much from them, a simple acknowledgement of how hard it must have been for me during my childhood would have been sufficient. Or, if they had just said they were happy for me for finally altering my looks, I might have forgiven them, at least a little bit. I'm not sure. And I'll never know, because they decided to bury the past instead of discussing it.

My sister didn't acknowledge my new and improved face either, but she seemed to soften toward me, almost as if our sisterhood tensions had been two-way instead of disapproval coming from her and aimed at me. Ironically, the nicer she was to me, the more my heart hardened toward her. I was the same person inside, and by failing to recognize that, there was nothing she could say to erase how miserable she had made life for me during my early, formative years.

When I told Karen about the family gathering, she thought I should talk to my parents and sister about my feelings, but I couldn't bring myself to sit down with them for that kind of conversation. What would I say—ask why they had treated me the way they did? Vent about my miserable life growing up? Request an apology? Try to shame them? I couldn't imagine a positive outcome from such a conversation. It was way too late for any of that.

Although I no longer carried a revenge list in my mind, and family members were taboo anyway, I did fantasize about getting married and having a big wedding to which family was not invited. Realistically though, if I didn't invite family members, the turnout would be very small. And though I didn't anticipate ever marrying, if I did, it would be in front of a justice of the peace. After all, even the church had failed me when I was young.

Things were going so well. On every front it was all systems go. I was finally enjoying the life I should have been having all along. Then, eight months into my new job something happened that once again changed the trajectory of my life. And this time, it was not for the better. All the excitement and positive feelings about my future came to a sudden, earth-shaking halt.

The window to a happy life was shattered.

25

THE TABLES ARE TURNED

Totally out of the blue, two men in security uniforms came to my office and asked me to accompany them to the lobby.

"Why?" I asked. "I'm right in the middle of . . ."

"Please, we must insist." One of the two men held open the door to my office while the other stood to one side and motioned for me to leave.

"Do I need to bring anything?" I asked. Should I grab my coat? My purse? Why were they being so vague? And so stiffly formal? And a tad menacing.

The two men exchanged looks. Then the one nearest to me said, "Perhaps you should bring your purse."

I picked up my purse and looked at my desk. "What about my laptop?"

"No, leave your computer here." He said it firmly, a command. This was sounding more and more ominous.

"Can't you tell me what this is about?" I tried to keep the panic out of my voice. Had something from my past finally caught up with me? But why security guards and not the police?

"We were told to escort you to the lobby. So . . ." Both men motioned toward the open door to my office. More insistent than before.

There were two of them, and they looked and sounded official. I didn't see that I had a choice. But with so little information, I didn't know if I should be calling a lawyer or not. Maybe I should be making a break for it. Although where would I go? No, my only option was to cooperate, at least for now. At least until I learned more about what was happening.

Neither man uttered a single word while we were in the elevator. One stood on either side of me, looking straight ahead. As the floors ticked by, I tried to make sense of what this could be about, but there wasn't anything I could think of that would require an escort to the lobby. Unless the police were waiting there for me. That seemed the most likely scenario. One of my past transgressions had come to light, and I was about to pay for something I had done. But after all this time? And without any warning? Surely if it was about Dane's death, Jay would have said something.

Once we stepped into the lobby, two things happened almost simultaneously: I was served with papers that I wasn't given a chance to read by someone I didn't recognize, and a vaguely familiar Human Resources representative demanded that I turn over my ID access card and the key to my office.

"I don't understand," I said. "What is this about?"

The person who had handed me the clutch of papers didn't bother answering my question. He simply turned away and headed toward the entrance of the building. His part in my little drama was over.

The HR rep didn't offer an explanation either. She held out her hand, waiting for me to comply with her request. "Your ID," she prompted. "And your key."

The two security guards were standing off to the side, like sentinels guarding the fort. From me? What did they think I was going to do—try to force my way back inside? And where were the police?

I shoved the still unread papers into my purse so I could remove my ID and take out my key. But before relinquishing either, I repeated: "What is this about? You can't just escort me out of the building and take away my ID with no explanation." I didn't know if they had the right to do so or not, but it seemed to give the HR rep pause.

"I believe you've been served," she said. "Those papers you were given—the company has filed a lawsuit against you."

"A lawsuit? For what?" How was that possible? I hadn't done anything wrong at work. Well, not that much. A few small acts of revenge on company property. Unless you counted Dane's untimely death. But that was definitely a police matter, not something the company would sue me over.

"I can't discuss the details with you. But I'd advise you to get a good lawyer." She moved her hand closer, almost touching my chest, waiting for me to hand over my ID and keys. I hesitated, sensing that as soon as I did, our conversation was over.

"Just a minute," I said, backing up a few inches. I pulled the papers out of my purse. There wasn't time to read them properly, but what immediately caught my eye was a reference to a court appearance set for late next week. To defend myself against a civil lawsuit brought against me by Keller and Eaves. She was right—my own company was suing me. But why?

"There has to be some mistake," I said to the HR rep. "Can't I talk to . . ."

She interrupted before I could think of who I should be talking to. "I was told to get your ID and your keys. If you have any questions, I'm afraid you'll have to communicate through legal." She didn't even say an obligatory "sorry" before snatching the ID and keys from me. I didn't try to hold onto them. I know when I've lost an argument.

Without so much as a "good luck" or "goodbye," the HR rep left me standing there, confused and stunned. The guards had backed off, but they were obviously going to hang around until I left the building. I couldn't get back in without my ID anyway, so I left.

It was raining. My coat was still on a hook behind the door of my office. The one I'd been evicted from. Why hadn't they at least let me take a few personal belongings? On the other hand, I was lucky to have my purse and that I hadn't left my car keys in the pocket of my coat as I so often did. Yeah, lucky. Stranded in the rain without a coat. Dismissed from my job and a pending court appearance.

I stuffed the court documents in my purse to keep them dry and headed for the parking lot two blocks away. In the rain. In a flimsy cotton jacket. Without a coat or an umbrella. And totally baffled by what had just happened.

When my phone buzzed, I paused, then stepped into the doorway to a building so I could take a look without getting my phone wet. It was my assistant. "Yes?" I said, trying to sound normal and not succeeding.

"Is it true?" she asked, her voice higher pitched than usual.

"I'm not sure why I was asked to leave," I said. "The HR rep wouldn't give me any details. What have you heard?"

"That you stole from the company."

"What?" In spite of being served papers and having a court appearance scheduled for next week, that took me totally by surprise. "What did I supposedly steal?" It flashed crossed my mind that being accused of theft was better than being accused of murder. Not that it was much consolation. When you were being accused of a crime by the company you loved, it was more than a bitter pill to swallow, it was a surprise attack by a faceless enemy you thought was your friend.

"I don't know. The HR person who came by wouldn't tell me anything except that I'm not supposed to talk to you."

"They told you not to talk to me?" That confirmed my worst fears.

"Yes, but I'm so upset, and I know you wouldn't do anything wrong."

"Not as upset as I am." I couldn't think of anything else to say. "Look, you'd better hang up. I don't want to get you in trouble. And don't worry, I'll sort this out. There's been some terrible mistake." Although I wasn't as innocent as my assistant thought, I wasn't guilty of stealing from the company. It was definitely all a mistake.

I could hear her sobbing as she hung up. I couldn't decide if that made me feel better or worse. Better because she cared enough to cry for me; worse because it was like slamming the door shut on my work life.

Once in my car, I pulled out the papers and read them carefully. The phrase "trade secrets" leapt out at me. Next week I had to appear in court to address an accusation of theft of trade secrets. The matter had been expedited because of the nature of the complaint. There was also a cease-and-desist letter attached. What on earth were they talking about? Trade secrets? Wasn't that about patents and copyrighted materials? What had that to do with me? One thing was clear: I would definitely need a lawyer.

As soon as I got home, I changed out of my damp clothes, made some coffee, and sat down at the table to try and organize my thoughts. The hearing was set for next Thursday. Obviously, the first thing I needed to do right away was to get a lawyer. One that wasn't associated with Keller and Eaves. The only lawyers I knew were ones who worked for the company. That meant I needed to either choose one by picking a law firm I'd heard of and reading resumes and looking at pictures that may or may not be recent, or by asking someone for a recommendation.

Although I hated to do it, I called Jay. He was the only person I could think of who might know of a good lawyer who specialized in this sort of thing.

He answered right away and I gave him a brief overview of what I needed and why, leaving out the part about being escorted out of the office without my coat or personal belongings.

"What are you being charged with?" he asked, sounding confused. I thought I'd been clear, but it was a lot to get your mind around.

"The papers refer to trade secrets, but I have no idea what that means. I've been sitting here going over what I've been working on that could fall into that category. It isn't as if I'm part of the inner circle. I don't have access to anything I can think of that would be labeled a trade secret."

"You want the name of a lawyer?" He still sounded confused. As if I was asking him for the name of a clown to perform at a birthday party, something outside of his wheelhouse.

"Given your connections to the court system, I was hoping you might have a recommendation. Or know someone who might. All of the lawyers I know have done work with the company."

"Off the top of my head, I can't think of anyone; let me get back to you."

I drank two cups of coffee while waiting for Jay to return my call. I assumed he was checking out the charge as well as making a short-list of lawyers. Since at one point he'd obviously entertained the thought that I was capable of shooting someone, he might also think I was capable of theft. Our friendly meals together might not count for much when his police instincts kicked in. If he decided I was guilty, would he still be willing to help?

When the phone rang, I jumped. I really needed to get a grip. "Hello," I said tentatively, even though I knew it was Jay.

"I have two names for you." He listed them off, and I wrote them down.

"I'm still in shock," I said.

"Me too. Last time we talked, you told me how much you liked your new job."

"It's been great. I wouldn't have done anything to endanger the company or my job."

"And you have no idea what trade secrets they're talking about."

"None at all. HR wouldn't tell me anything. Zip. Nada. They

had two security guards escort me to the lobby where I was served with papers and relieved of my ID and keys." Since I'd revealed that much, I decided to tell him the rest. "They didn't even let me pack up my personal belongings. My coat is still there."

"That sounds bad."

"I know. I can't believe this is happening to me." I wanted him to understand that I was truly shocked by the accusation. At the same time, I didn't want him to see me as a criminal. Even a white-collar criminal.

"Want me to poke around?"

"No, I don't want you to get into trouble. The lawyer should be able to sort this out."

A few days later I was to remember saying that the lawyer could sort things out. How naïve I'd been. Instead of proving I'd been mistakenly accused of a crime, my lawyer advised me to admit guilt and negotiate terms before the formal hearing. "You can agree to cease and desist before the court orders you to do so. Then it's a matter of whether there's any monetary damage."

"But I'm not guilty of stealing any trade secrets," I repeated for the umpteenth time. The echo of Adriana's protestations of innocence pricked my conscience, but I was more concerned with my present situation than with what I had let happen to her.

"They have an online trail proving you've done what they claim, I'm afraid. I've reviewed all of the evidence and had one of our in-house experts take a look. The only thing they don't have yet, as far as I can tell, are bank records showing you profited from the act."

I wanted to scream that I couldn't have profited from an act I hadn't committed. My lawyer had a good reputation for getting clients off, so the fact that he was advising me to admit guilt and seek a settlement was unnerving to say the least. As calmly as I could manage, I said, "Whatever evidence they claim to have has to be faked. Can't we have someone challenge its credibility?"

"As I said, I already had an expert take a look at everything. I was hoping there was something we could question. But it looks solid."

In addition to knowing I wasn't guilty, my experience with framing people in the past made me sure there was something phony about the evidence. It was a matter of finding the right person to take a look. "I think we need to find another expert."

"We can, of course, get another opinion after the hearing next week. If it turns into a battle of experts though, you never know how that will end up. Especially since you are one person going up against a huge corporation." He didn't have to spell it out; I knew they would be well represented by a team of lawyers and legal assistants.

"I still want a second opinion. I'm telling you that whatever evidence they have can't be real. Because I didn't do anything wrong."

My earnest, middle-aged lawyer had impeccable legal credentials, a face that was all hard angles, and eyes that said he didn't believe me. He sighed, leaned forward, and said, "I repeat, as your lawyer I'm advising you to make a deal. These trade secrets cases can be tricky. At this point there's no criminal complaint involved. It would be better to get this resolved as quickly as possible."

"And as your client, I'm telling you that I will not say I'm guilty of something I didn't do."

"They state that you had access to strategic marketing and customer information that was delivered to a competitor. And they've traced the transaction to you. Unless you can prove conclusively that everything they assert is untrue, there will be a civil judgement against you. Once that happens, they could decide to also make a criminal complaint. Then you would not only have a hefty fine to pay but face time in prison. You do understand your situation, don't you?"

He was talking to me as if I wasn't capable of following his logic. As if I hadn't read the evidence against me. And because he obviously believed I was guilty, he was not willing to think outside the techno box I found myself in. I was beginning to feel desperate. But after all I'd been through to get to this point in my life, I wasn't about to roll over and give it all up without a fight. No matter how badly the cards were stacked against me.

"I need time to think about this," I said finally.

"The sooner you make up your mind, the better chance you'll have to negotiate a deal." It was a dismissive statement. I took the hint and left, not bothering to respond to his receptionist's cheery, "Have a good day" as I sprinted past her desk.

26

FAKING IT

After rushing out of the lawyer's office, I practically ran down the street, as if being chased by devils instead of by accusations of theft. When I reached the deli on the corner, I decided I needed to stop and reconnoiter. I found a seat in the corner, away from the smattering of customers all looking at their computers or talking on their phones while nursing a cup of coffee, some with sandwiches piled high with meat or meat substitutes—it's hard to tell which, unless you taste them. Then the faux is obvious. Unlike the fake evidence against me.

I got out my own phone and called Jay.

"How's it going?" he asked.

"Terrible. I just met with my lawyer. He thinks I'm guilty."

"Is that what he said or what you assume based on something he said?"

"He wants me to agree to cease and desist before they order me to do so and talk settlement terms with the company. But how can I cease and desist from something I'm not doing?"

"What did he say about the evidence against you?"

"His 'expert' says the evidence is sound. But I know it can't be real. So, I need to find a really good tech expert. As soon as possible. Someone who is willing to scrub the phony evidence until they find something. Someone who won't accept what looks like strong evidence on its face. Someone who understands what goes into putting together a convincing fake.

"That's why I've called. Sorry to bother you again, but I don't know where else to turn. If you know anyone who fits that bill or anyone who might know where I can find someone who does, I could use your help."

"You basically need a credible hacker."

"I need someone willing to dig deeper, much deeper." Actually, I knew someone who I was fairly certain could get the job done for me. Someone who had done off-the-books work for me in the past. But although it was tempting to call him, I knew using him in this instance could end up exposing past activities that wouldn't help my case.

"Won't they have to, ah, get around some of the company's security to do that?"

"You're asking if I'm willing to break the law to prove I'm innocent."

"I'm just trying to assess the kind of person you're looking for."

"You think it's futile, don't you?"

"I've been thinking about your situation, and the question that keeps coming to my mind is, if you're being framed, who has the motive and the means to frame you?"

"I've spent a lot of time asking myself that same question. And for the record, there's no *if* about it. Given the evidence they say they have, someone is definitely framing me." I forgave him the use of the word "if." It was his police training to question everything and everyone. Unfortunately, media manipulation and creating disinformation were topics I knew more than a little about, although I couldn't admit that to anyone, not even to my lawyer, and especially not to Jay.

"And . . . is there anyone in particular you suspect?"

"Yes, there's at least one person at Keller and Eaves who would love to see me take a fall. I've already asked a detective who does work for WADA to see what she can dig up on him. His name is Marcus Manning. He's the guy who thought he should have my job when they promoted me instead of him."

"Is that the only reason you suspect him? Because he thought he deserved the position they gave you?"

"No, the first day in my new office he dropped by, not to congratulate me but to let me know that he was going to be waiting in the wings for me to slip up so he could step in and save the day. I told Karen about his visit at the time and what he said. We decided that I should ignore his threat, that it was sour grapes and showmanship. Now I'm thinking I should have reported him to HR. And I should definitely have kept an eye on him after that. Anyway, I've given my situation a lot of thought, and he's the only one I can think of who has a motive, from his point of view, that is."

"You think he's capable of framing you for this kind of violation?"

"Mentally, yes. Skill-wise, I don't think so. But I either have to prove the online trail is bogus or that Marcus—or someone else—hired someone to hack into the company's system and make it look like I was the one who did it. Preferably both—that I was framed and by him. So, if you can come up with the name of a person who can help me with this, I'd be forever grateful."

Two hours later Jay called me back with a first name and a telephone number. "You didn't get this from me," he said.

"Can I ask where you came up with this guy?"

"No, it's best if we forget this conversation ever happened, okay?"

"Okay. And thank you. I owe you big time."

When I called the number, the hacker was hesitant to talk over the phone but agreed to meet me at a local Starbucks in an hour. I arrived early and checked out everyone who came in after me. The person I was waiting for was either named "Link" or that was what he went by. I knew him the instant he appeared in the entrance. He fit every stereotype I had about a techie with the ethics of a hungry dog left alone with a roast on the counter. Long, unwashed hair, clothes that looked like he'd slept in them, a hole in the knee of his jeans, stubble on his chin, and a hyped-up way of moving his hands as he walked, as if they missed being on a keyboard or clutching game controls.

He looked around and then walked directly over to me and sat down. "You're in a heap of trouble," he said.

"That's why I called you." He must have already looked me up. That was fast. But then, I wanted someone who was careful and fast. "I know it's a cliché to say I'm innocent, but I really have been framed. And I'm hoping you can prove it."

"Any idea who did it?" Unlike my lawyer, he was apparently willing to take my protestation of innocence on faith.

"I have a prime candidate. He either had direct access to the data involved or knew where to look for it, but I'm not sure he had the expertise to pull off making me look like the bad guy without some technical help."

"Tell me what you need and how soon you need it."

"Proof that the evidence against me has been faked. If possible, who faked it. And yesterday."

"I'll need some money up front."

"No problem."

"In cash."

"No problem." I had anticipated the request and had what I thought was a sufficient downpayment in a manila envelope in my purse. I pulled it out and shoved it across the table. "Will this do for a start?"

He squeezed the envelope without opening it. "Unless it's in one's," he said with the ghost of a smile. "Okay. Let's start with who you think framed you and why. Then I want details about the company and the systems they use for storing and securing information."

"The *who* is easy. Here's what I know about him." I passed him a sheet of paper listing what I'd compiled about Marcus. "The *why* is fairly straightforward—he's ambitious, resents me for getting a job he thinks should have been his, and he's a nasty individual."

Link scanned the information I gave him on Marcus. When he looked up, I continued. "I've also printed a description of my job responsibilities as they relate to the goals and finances of the company with a few comments about the limitations on accessing and manipulating the data identified in the charges against me. But I'm not sure how much I can tell you about the IT infrastructure. I just know how to access the main database as an employee and how to use their applications. I know nothing about servers and operating systems. Unfortunately, my inability to do the things they say I did apparently doesn't provide a defense."

"You could have hired it done. Just like the guy you think did."

"Are there a lot of people for hire with the skills to pull off the kind of sophisticated stuff listed on this description of charges?" I handed him copies of my job description and the indictment.

"We are not a huge community." He said it as if he was proud of being part of a small club or gang. A brotherhood of hackers. Maybe they had a logo: We Be Hackers—written in code, of course.

All along I'd been assuming there was a vast network of techies who had the skills and willingness to do what was necessary to have framed me. But if their numbers were limited, maybe that's where Link would start—by tracking the person who was responsible for creating the fake trail of evidence. Although I couldn't imagine any hacker would be willing to give up the name of a paying client, even to another hacker. That would be bad for future business. I didn't care how Link went about proving my innocence though, as long as he managed to do it before I ended up in a cell next to Adriana. Go, Link.

. . .

After meeting with my lawyer and then with Link, I became more agitated with each hour that went by. I felt so helpless. There was nothing I could think of to do for myself to prove I hadn't done what I was being accused of doing. And unlike the times I'd orchestrated discrediting someone else online, there wasn't so much as a speck of truth in the evidence against me. Nor had I deliberately harmed or humiliated someone. Still, I couldn't help but wonder if what was happening to me proved that at least some of the time "what goes around comes around." Although in an indirect, circuitous way. Not a tit for a tat or an eye for an eye. Rather, I was receiving a huge slap down for all the crimes I'd committed on my journey of revenge.

Even if I deserved punishment for past crimes, I couldn't roll over and let Marcus win. My days of giving in to bullies and tyrants were over.

When a day went by without a call from Link, I began to worry that perhaps my lawyer was right. Maybe I should take responsibility for something I hadn't done to avoid going to jail. I put off making that decision, waiting impatiently to hear back from Link.

Karen kept in constant touch to make sure I was okay. Each time she called I put on a brave front that collapsed as soon as I hung up. Instead of buoying my spirits, her calls left me deflated, acutely aware of what I could potentially lose if convicted.

Early evening on the third day when the phone rang with no caller ID identified, my heart started racing. Sure enough, this time it was Link. And he had a plan. It was a longshot, he explained, but if it worked, it would instantly clear my name. It also gave me a chance to needle Marcus in person. After hearing that, I didn't hesitate to say "count me in."

The idea was to approach Marcus when no one else was around and provoke him into saying something incriminating, or to at least make him anxious enough about what I possibly knew about the frame that he would immediately contact whoever he'd paid to do his dirty work for him. Link would be there to track the call.

Although I was disappointed that Link hadn't made more

progress on dismantling the evidence against me, I felt like we had at least a chance of succeeding with the approach he'd come up with. And if it worked, it would give me leverage, maybe even a name.

Per our plan, I waited in a doorway of an apartment building across the street from Keller and Eaves at quitting time. I was fairly certain Marcus took the light rail home, so I knew what route he would most likely take when he left the office. Unless he was with someone, I would be able to approach him on the street. If he wasn't alone, I would either have try again tomorrow or figure out another time and place to corner him in the open. Maybe on his way to work in the morning. Meanwhile, I had my cell ready to record whatever I could get him to admit.

He came out right on schedule and started down the street—by himself. I caught up with him at the streetlight. "Hello, Marcus," I said as I stepped up alongside him.

His head swiveled in my direction. "Callista." He seemed surprised but quickly recovered. "What are you doing in the neighborhood? I thought you didn't work here anymore." His smug words made me that much more determined to succeed with our plan.

"Hoping to run into you."

The streetlight changed, "Well, as much as I would like to take the time to catch up, I'm afraid I need to move along. It was nice seeing you." His abruptness was rude and demeaning, but that only added fuel to my determination. I matched him long stride for long stride as he tried to get away without actually running.

"Oh, I don't want to 'catch up,' I said, keeping my tone light and non-defensive. "I want to inform you of a few things." I smiled, but I wasn't sure he saw it. "Hang onto your hat."

"What's that supposed to mean?" Now I had his attention.

"That I know you hired someone to fake evidence against me, and that it's just a matter of time until I have the name of that person."

He slowed down. "You couldn't know something that isn't true." I could tell I'd poked a hole in his confidence by the way he refused to look at me.

"The local hacking community is a tight-knit group. You may think you paid for secrecy as well as for skill, but you may have underestimated the power of the dollar. Especially when there's a bidding war."

"I don't have any idea what you're talking about." He slowed down even more, but he still refused to look in my direction.

"I've put the word out that I'm willing to pay for information. You can probably expect whoever you hired to come to you for more money to keep quiet."

He finally glanced my way. "If that were true—and I'm not saying it is—why would you tell me?"

"Because I know I'm going to win this game, and I want you to pay in more ways than one for what you've done to me. This is the kick-off. The game is afoot." It was a mixed metaphor, but it made the point.

We were at the entrance to the light rail station. He stopped and moved off to the side onto a patch of gravel. I followed. Then he leaned toward me and said: "You didn't deserve that job—I did." His voice became low, gruff, and menacing. "Now leave me alone. Or you'll be sorry. You got that?"

"I'm afraid I can't do that." I smiled, hoping I looked confident enough to be intimidating. It must have worked, at least a little, because he turned and quickly took off down the escalator steps, two at a time. I stayed where I was. I didn't have a recorded confession, but Link was right behind him, exactly as planned. He was going to do a Bluetooth hack that would enable him to see the names in Marcus's phone contact list. If he recognized anyone on the list, that would give us a starting point from which to unravel the frame that was about to ruin my life.

Also, we were hoping Marcus would call his hacker to verify if what I'd said about a bidding war was true. That would make it even easier for Link to identify him or her quickly.

As it turned out, Link scored a double. By the time Marcus reached the light rail platform and placed a call, Link was close enough to hear the name of the person Marcus said hello to. He went ahead and transferred Marcus's contact list anyway, even though he no longer needed it. Because he was almost 100 percent certain he recognized the name of the person on the other end of the conversation. Hacker tags tended to be unique.

I don't claim to understand the world of hacking, the excitement of the challenge, the money to be made, and the lack of concern with truth or right and wrong. It's a shadowy counter-culture in which the ability to do something often overrides consideration of consequences. Well, maybe I understand it a little bit. But there's also a code not unlike the one that prevents gang members from "ratting" on each other. It was no surprise that Link refused to tell me his "associate's" identity. Nor was I surprised to learn that the "associate" was unwilling to admit what they had done or who they had done it for. To complicate matters more, Link didn't want to give up the name of the person to the authorities and assured me that neither he nor his associate would cooperate if they were subpoenaed.

At the same time, now that he had a lead, Link was eager to establish that the evidence against me was fake. It really was all a game to him. A game with high stakes for me.

BIDING TIME

Link was still working on demonstrating how someone had faked the evidence against me when my court date arrived. I had little choice but to agree to the cease-and-desist order. But I wanted it made clear in court that I had nothing to cease and desist from. My lawyer reluctantly agreed to make a statement to that effect for the record. As soon as the words were out of his mouth, the judge interrupted.

"She either agrees to cease and desist or she doesn't. Which is it, counselor?"

My lawyer turned to me with an "I told you so" look, and I nodded in the affirmative.

"She agrees to cease and desist, Your Honor."

After that exchange, the judge gave us thirty days to answer the complaint, and that was the end of my first direct encounter with the civil court system. Not a particularly unpleasant experience, but not a very satisfying one either.

. . .

Even though I felt fairly confident that Link would eventually come through, waiting around for something to happen after my hearing was tough. I was fidgety and bad-tempered. Alternately depressed and enraged. I had trouble sleeping. Ate junk food instead of healthy meals. And although I half-heartedly tried to maintain a regular exercise routine, I spent a lot of time on the couch watching reruns of shows that no longer seemed as funny as I remembered them being.

Not even Bella's kitten antics could make me smile. Although she tried her best. I needed something to do other than sit around and worry about my future.

I decided it was time to become a WADA volunteer.

Initially, the WADA board members had agreed to distinguish the organization from others by focusing on the predator rather than on the victim, and they continued to be more proactive than reactive. But to stay within the law, they had to be somewhat more circumspect about their actions than they would have liked at times. Most of their cases were referrals from other agencies, usually when an agency was made aware of a problem through a third party, and the victim or victims wouldn't speak up. Few service agencies had either the bandwidth or the authority to intervene under those circumstances. But they were happy to hand off these difficult cases to someone with more flexibility and resources.

WADA volunteers were given instruction on how to approach either the victim or abuser, depending on an assessment of the situation. Assessments were done through interviews and surveillance. The facts gathered were used as leverage when approaching either the victim or the abuser. Or, sometimes when talking to other family members or even with employers. It might be argued that they stepped over the line in offering assistance where none was requested, but so far no one had sued. Given the heated nature of some of the confrontations, they were anticipating the likelihood of facing the occasional lawsuit in the future. That was one of the reasons they carefully documented cases from start to finish.

The case they gave me allegedly involved more mental than physical abuse. Tara, a friend of the supposed victim had asked WADA to look into a situation in which she'd failed to get her friend, Wanda, to seek counseling. Wanda had married Dixon two years ago. At that time, she'd been a gregarious, fun-loving woman who wore bright colors and regularly met with friends for meals or to go places together. Since her marriage, she'd slowly become reclusive, not answering phone calls, and declining offers to go out. Her family and friends were concerned but didn't know what to do.

The first thing I did was meet with Tara. She told me basically the same story she had originally told the WADA screening volunteer. In addition, she gave me the names of several relatives of the victim to speak with. I met with Wanda's mother, her younger brother, and a cousin she'd been close to before her marriage. Their stories were all consistent: her marriage to Dixon marked the beginning of the changes they had all witnessed. Although they couldn't tell me what her situation was at present, because she no longer kept in touch with her family. Everyone except her mother had given up trying. Until recently, her mother continued to call once a week, even though the conversations were brief, stilted, and uncomfortable at times. Then one day she called to find that Wanda's phone service had been discontinued. "I don't know who she is anymore," Wanda's mother told me.

The first day I watched Wanda's house, nothing happened. The only activity was Dixon leaving in the morning and returning at the end of the work day. Apparently, there was no dog to walk or errands to run. I wanted to bump into Wanda *accidentally* rather than approaching her directly at her house because it seemed to me that would make her less apprehensive and more likely to talk. But if she didn't leave the house in the next few days, I would have to knock on her door and hope she would let me in.

The next morning right after her husband left for work, Wanda came out of the house wearing a gray jacket and jeans. She was carrying a grocery bag. She walked to a grocery store two blocks away from her house with me tailing her at a distance. Once inside, I grabbed a basket and followed Wanda down several aisles, waiting for an opportunity to say something. I finally got a chance in the produce section.

I came up alongside her and said, "I always seem to choose a bad avocado—do you have some trick for picking a good one?"

Wanda turned and took a step back. "Were you speaking to me?"

"Oh, I didn't mean to startle you. It's just that I was hoping you have some suggestions on how to pick a good avocado."

"No, I don't." She started to turn away, then paused as if she might say more.

"Sorry for putting you on the spot," I said. "I hate shopping and . . ." I left the sentence hanging.

"Me too," Wanda said. "But I just guess. About the avocados, that is."

I gave her a big smile. "Well, I hope your karma is better than mine." When she didn't say anything, I added, "Well, have a good day."

It was hard to get the timing just right, but, with a little extra fussing around, I managed to get through checkout at the same time as Wanda. "Hey, we meet again," I said cheerfully. Wanda gave me a small smile in return. "I don't know about you, but I could use a cup of coffee. Want to join me?" I motioned toward the Starbucks at the front of the store. "They have a couple of tables."

Wanda hesitated.

"My treat," I said. "You'd be doing me a favor. I need a break and hate to drink coffee alone."

"Well . . ." For a moment, I thought she was going to decline, but she didn't. "I guess it wouldn't hurt."

No, Wanda, it won't hurt. It could even help.

Once we got settled, I told Wanda that I was new to the neighborhood and didn't know anyone yet and gave her a few details about my life, mostly things that were true, except for the part about moving to the neighborhood. Then I asked where she lived and whether she was married or had children. Things were going well until I suggested we have lunch some time.

"I'm not sure I can do that." Wanda seemed suddenly deflated.

"Oh?" I waited for her to respond, letting the silence hang between us like an accusing finger.

"I . . . I . . . I'm on a budget."

"No problem. What if I make up a picnic lunch. We can eat in the park." There was a park a block in the other direction from Wanda's house. I had seen it when driving around the neighborhood. Wanda obviously wanted to say "yes." I acted as though it was a done deal and suggested the very next day for our picnic. "Should I stop by and get you?" I asked. When she didn't immediately respond, I quickly added, "Or, we could meet in the park."

"Yes, that would be better," Wanda said, her face slightly flushed. Then, "I have to get going. In case Dixon calls me."

"Oh, he calls during the day. That's sweet."

Wanda blinked. "Yes, sweet. He's, ah, sweet." Then she thanked me for the coffee and left.

I called Wanda's friend Tara and told her about the picnic. "Do you want to join us?" I asked. "Even if you're right about Dixon, I'm not sure there is anything I can say to get her to leave him. But seeing you might remind her of what she's missing. And I will be there to offer her the kind of practical support she will need to move out. Assuming Dixon is the cause of her behavioral changes. And assuming she wants to get away from him."

"Oh, I'm sure he's the reason she's changed. But what if she refuses to even talk to me?"

"If we decide she's too frightened to talk to us, then I may have to have a serious talk with Dixon." Given the mood I was in, I felt sorry for Dixon if it came to that.

The next day Wanda was late showing up at the park. We were afraid she'd changed her mind. When she finally arrived, I was reminded of a timid animal who wants to be petted but is afraid to get close. Wanda stopped in her tracks when she saw Tara. I half expected her to turn and run away. Instead, when Tara walked toward her, she rushed into to her friend's arms, collapsed against her, and started to cry.

Even intelligent people can be brainwashed, especially when they become isolated and are desperate for approval. It doesn't happen overnight; it's more like a slow acting cancer that eventually dominates reality. For Wanda, once she started opening up, it was as though she'd been hoping for a long time to tell someone the sordid details of her marriage. The picture she provided of Dixon was one of a controlling husband who didn't want to share her with anyone, including family and past friends. He kept track of her movements, didn't let her drive their car, left her without any money, reviewed every purchase she made on the credit card she used for groceries, and wouldn't allow her to invite anyone over. He had also recently removed their telephone landline and took his cell phone with him to work. She was basically a prisoner. Although he didn't lock her in the house, he'd managed to mentally imprison her by discouraging contact with anyone but him. She confessed that this was the first time she had gone anywhere except to the grocery in a long time.

I called the WADA office and asked them to arrange for a place for Wanda to stay. I knew it had to be done quickly, before Wanda lost her nerve. Together, the three of us went to Wanda's house and filled a plastic bag with a few clothes. She didn't have a suitcase. Sadly, she would be leaving her marriage with nothing. No material goods, no money, no car—nothing. But, in my opinion, that was better than remaining a prisoner in her own home.

That evening, I was waiting for Dixon in the living room of their house. When he saw me, he immediately demanded to know where Wanda was.

"She's safe," I said.

"What the hell does that mean? And who are *you*?" I was glad I had my new pistol with me, although the last thing I needed while being suspected of violating the trade secrets act was to also be accused of entering someone's home uninvited and then shooting the owner when he ordered me to leave.

"I work for WADA, Women Against Domestic Abuse. It was reported to us that Wanda was being mentally abused by you, her husband."

He wasn't a bad looking man, but the slanted sneer he gave me was off-putting. "What's it to you?" His voice was loud and suddenly got louder. "You have no right to interfere with my marriage." He took a step toward me and screamed: "I want you to bring Wanda back here, NOW." Tiny blue veins were starting to bulge on either side of his face. Maybe something would burst and I wouldn't have to shoot him.

"Do you want me to call the police?" I asked calmly. "They can inform you of Wanda's rights. As well as your own. But I assure you that she left of her own free will. If and when she wants to, she will be in touch." I stood up. "I stayed to tell you where she has gone as a courtesy. So you would know that she was alright."

I sensed that he couldn't decide whether to attack me physically or not. But as I walked to the door, keeping an eye on him as I went, he stayed where he was and shouted after me, "Get the hell out of my house!" I was only too happy to oblige.

Tara called the next day to thank me. She said that the family was relieved and had hired a therapist to help Wanda through the transition as well as a lawyer to start divorce proceedings. Everything was happening fast. Usually things like this took time, sometimes only after several false starts. And other times it ended in failure. I was pleased that I would be able to put this one success story on the positive side of my personal ledger. At least I'd had a chance to help someone salvage their life, even as mine was still in jeopardy of being torn apart.

The very next day Link called and wanted to meet. He sounded excited, like someone who had good news to deliver. I didn't want to get my hopes up, but they rose like smoke from a fire anyway. I so badly wanted my life back. I wanted to be able to go to work, have dinner with friends, play with Bella, and lead a normal life. I'd worked so hard to get to this point—setting aside my revenge list, helping other women escape from bad situations, developing friendships. It wasn't as if my original acts of retaliation weren't in some ways justified. No one could dispute that I'd been treated badly since I was a child. Now that I'd turned my life around, it seemed incredibly ironic to be punished in this way.

The minute I saw Link come into the coffee shop, I knew I'd been right to have hope. He didn't just look happy, his whole body quivered with energy, like Bella when I gave her a treat.

"I'm about to make your day," he said as he sat down across from me. "Why, you may be so pleased with the information I have for you that you might even give me a bonus." He raised his eyebrows suggestively and placed a file on the table in front of me.

After a quick run-through of his report, I knew he was right about both—he'd made my day, and he'd earned a big bonus. Based on the sunshine in his voice when he'd set up the meeting, I'd come prepared—a thick wad of bills in an unmarked envelope was poking out of my jacket pocket. Pockets in women's clothes are never big enough, not for everyday needs, let alone for cash payments for work done off the books.

The next day I walked into my lawyer's office feeling like a marathon winner at the finishing line. "Wait until you see what I've got," I said.

He held out his hand and accepted the report Link had prepared. He'd done a fantastic job of putting together the list of fake server paths, spoofed information, phony headers, and falsified addresses. Most of what was in his report was like reading a foreign language to me, but Link assured me the experts on both sides would be impressed.

My lawyer leafed through the contents of the report. "This legit?" he asked.

"It will pass every test," I assured him.

"Is your source a good witness?"

"The facts will speak for themselves."

"He won't testify?"

"Show the tech experts this evidence; that's all you need to do."

"Looks like *someone* set up an overseas bank account in your name."

"But only a couple hundred dollars was deposited," I pointed out. Link thought it was supposed to look as though I hadn't been paid yet but was ready to receive the money. Fortunately, he had been able to demonstrate that I wasn't the one who had opened the account. It was all right there in the report. I didn't know or care how he had done it, I was just relieved that he had been able to.

I could tell my lawyer was impressed. But he didn't apologize for previously acting as though he thought I was guilty. Maybe he had lingering doubts about the veracity of the new evidence. It was hard to tell. One thing was for sure—I would pay his bill, but he wasn't getting a bonus.

QUEEN OF THE NIGHT

When I reflected on my lawyer's reaction to the exculpating evidence Link had come up with, I wondered if maybe he simply didn't like being wrong about his assessment of a client. He'd seemed so certain I was guilty of trade secret theft. I could forgive him for that. But his lack of an apology or acknowledgement of what I had gone through during the past month now that he knew I was innocent didn't make him my favorite lawyer. In fact, he was lucky I didn't still have a little list.

The plaintiff's lawyer wasn't that pleased when presented with the evidence Link had compiled either. He reluctantly agreed to have his team take a look and promised to let us know what their experts thought about the new information before proceeding. No one likes to look like they did a sloppy or inadequate investigation. But they could hardly refuse to reassess their position, because if they were wrong—and they were—it was better for them if it came out before things went any further.

Nor was the competitor who'd received the trade secrets happy. They'd spent a lot of money on what was apparently mostly smoke and mirrors because the "secrets" weren't as significant as they'd been led to believe. Perhaps Marcus hadn't been able to access as much data as the complaint suggested. Or, more likely in my opinion, maybe he simply didn't want to hurt Keller and Eaves all that much just to get rid of me. His goal was, after all, to become an executive in a thriving company. Then there was the money the competitor had paid for the information. It had disappeared into the ether, probably in another account set up by Marcus. They couldn't complain too much though since the entire transaction had been illegal.

Not even my family seemed prepared to celebrate the turn of events. In part, I don't think they understood all of the techno jargon that eventually proved I wasn't guilty. Besides, when the original story first came out, they'd immediately turned their backs on me. I'd only been in their good graces because of my new face for a very short time. So, I wasn't surprised our tenuous reconciliation didn't withstand the bad publicity I received. In any event, my yo-yo relationship with my parents was once again in "stall" mode.

Finally, although the case was dropped, the fact that I'd been cleared of wrongdoing earned little more than a footnote in the media, partly because there was no real resolution; hence, no opportunity for titillating headlines. Although Marcus's name was floated as *possibly involved*, he wasn't charged with a crime. With no one to blame, the case was a dead end with no closure or lurking tragedy to interest the media. For those reasons, there was no public celebration of my innocence.

I'd been tempted to confront Marcus, but Karen talked me out of it.

"What would it accomplish?" she'd said.

"It would be a satisfying gloat."

"He didn't succeed, but he didn't really lose either."

"Right. He still has his job and the money."

"Him having the money really bothers me, I admit it."

"Maybe if I confronted him, I could get him to admit he was behind it."

"Do you really believe that?"

She was right. Marcus wasn't about to confess, the competitor didn't want to create a fuss, and Keller an Eaves had decided not to pursue the breach. They wanted to bury the story as quickly as possible to avoid any further bad publicity.

Sadly, even after the charges against me were dropped, suspicions lingered among some of my former colleagues and acquaintances who I felt should have known better. Still, they probably thought there was a reason the company declined to reinstate me. An HR rep agreed to meet me out front to give me my coat and a few other personal possessions, but that was as much as they were willing to do.

My former boss said she would be willing to write a reference letter for me, but she didn't offer to fight for reinstatement on my behalf. Not that I would have returned after the way I'd been treated. In fact, if I ever decided to return to my little list, there were a few names I would be adding. They did give me severance pay, however, which I thought of as hush money. Well-deserved hush money that would help cover my legal fees.

If I had identified Link and Link had identified his hacker friend, the connection to Marcus would have been made. But I refused to give up Link, and the techies employed by the government weren't apparently as good as Link.

I tried to move on, but I couldn't let go, forget, or forgive. The thought of Marcus continuing on his career path at Eaves and Keller while I was shunned by them was like an incurable cancer of the soul. At the very least, I wanted to make sure they understood that Marcus had both motive and opportunity to have framed me. So, I sent an anonymous email from a library computer to Keller and Eaves executives, Human Resources, and the IT department and attached some of Link's conclusions and supporting data along with a list of facts about internal processes that suggested why Marcus was the most likely employee to have been responsible for the chain of events. If they figured out the message came from me, I didn't really care. I would deny it, of course, but the main thing was to call attention to the possibility that their golden boy might be tarnished.

And it worked.

It wasn't long after I sent the anonymous information to Keller and Eaves that I got a call from my former assistant.

"Did you hear?" she asked. "Marcus resigned."

"I hadn't heard. Did he give a reason?"

"No. Someone said he got a better offer."

A better offer than being under a dark cloud of suspicion instead of a fast-track to an executive position? "He's an ambitious guy" was all I could think of to say.

"Well, I know you two weren't close, but I thought you might want to join a group of us who are getting together at Tad's Bar to say goodbye. It would be nice to see you."

"Thank you, but I'm not sure others would be happy to see me."

"We all thought you might come back." It was part statement, part question.

"I haven't been asked to return." I wasn't sure what story they were telling employees about me, but I wasn't going to sugarcoat their decision.

"Oh, I didn't realize. . . I'm sorry."

"Don't be. I have several prospects." A tiny lie seemed better than the truth under the circumstances. "I do appreciate you thinking of me." And believing in me.

Marcus had taken away my first shot at true happiness, interrupted my career, ruined any chance of reconciliation with my family, and made people question my character. Losing his job didn't seem like much payback for what he had done. On the other hand, I wasn't exactly pure either. In fact, I carried a heavy load of guilt about Dane and Adriana. No matter how hard I tried to keep what I had done to them locked away in my personal memory bank, I was never able to completely forget the unfair price they'd paid for the collective anger I felt toward everyone who had wronged me over the years. Unfortunately for them, their betrayal had been a tipping point for me. Maybe I deserved some unfair payback in return.

Still, in spite of losing my job and having my reputation damaged,

I had a number of things I was thankful for: my nose and chin, my friendships with Karen and Jay, my lovely Bella and . . . thinking about ways I might eventually get even with Marcus. Maybe the urge would go away once everything settled out, but I kept feeling spikes of anger. For him, I might have to revive my little list for one last act of retribution. After sufficient time had passed so that I would not be the primary suspect, of course.

Meanwhile, to let him know I could be coming for him some time in the future, I sent him a Queen of the Night flower. Anonymously. I just hoped the symbolism wasn't lost on him. The Queen of the Night blooms once a year, at night, and wilts before morning. Forget or forgive? NEVER.

ACKNOWLEDGMENTS

Over the years friends and colleagues have shared stories about injustices suffered at the hands of bullies or mean-spirited individuals. Childhood grievances. Workplace complaints. Neighborhood squabbles. When you're young, each slight or insult can be a nick in self-esteem. Over time, we become more wary and better equipped to deal with provocations and putdowns. At least on the surface. Often, even when we tell ourselves it isn't important, a casual comment or perceived unfair treatment can be hurtful. I suppose that's why there are so many self-help books out there on topics such as controlling anger or dealing with negativity and why advice columns remain popular.

Yes, Callista was inspired by a "real" person, not someone I knew, but someone I came in contact with professionally. The woman was extremely unattractive, and I couldn't help but wonder what it must have been like for her as a child, and later, how hard she probably had to fight to get ahead in a world that values appearance, especially for women.

The concept of inflicting modest punishments was also inspired by "real" events, including several corporate "pranks" that were not at all funny to the targeted individuals. Reaching further back in time, one of my college summer jobs was at a camp for grade school age children. Unfortunately, one of the camp counselors was disliked equally by campers and other employees. She was not a friendly or particularly nice person. So, when several campers put half a dozen garter snakes in her sleeping bag one night, there were more snickers than commiseration when she crawled inside and began screaming and flailing about. And although most of us knew who was responsible, no one pointed any fingers. Was it the right thing to do? No. Was it satisfying? I'll let you decide.

In conclusion, I would like to think that it's possible to get beyond the desire for revenge. But when faced with petty spite or outright injustice, perhaps we may be excused for at least fantasizing about ways to get even. We all know that the best advice is to "let go and move on." One other possibility, however, is to read a book about retribution! Hope you have enjoyed my fantasies.

ABOUT THE AUTHOR

Award-winning author Charlotte Stuart PhD writes mysteries that fall into a number of different sub genres: cozy mysteries, character-driven mysteries featuring a female PI, a laugh out loud comedic series, as well more traditional mysteries. She also co-authored a legal thriller with Don Stuart. In general, she favors twisty plots with a dollop of adventure. Before she started writing full time, she left a tenured faculty position to go commercial salmon fishing in Alaska, spent a year sailing in the Washington and Canadian San Juans, became a partner in a management consulting group and later a VP of HR and training. After living on boats for over a decade, boating and forays into wilderness areas often find their way into her stories.

Charlotte lives on Vashon Island in the Pacific Northwest and is the past president of the Puget Sound Sisters in Crime and a member of the Mystery Writers of America and the International Thriller Writers.

To my readers: *Thank you for giving me the excuse to live part of each day in a world of memory and make believe.*

OTHER BOOKS BY CHARLOTTE STUART INCLUDE:

The Discount Detective Mysteries

The John Smith Mysteries

Bogged Down (A Vashon Island Mystery)

Raven's Grave (*A Jonah St. Clair Mystery*)

Raven's Legacy (*A Jonah St. Clair Mystery*

Midnight for Justice, a legal thriller by Charlotte Stuart and Don Stuart

You can visit her website or contact her on social media:

Website: www.charlottestuart.com

Twitter: https://twitter.com/quirkymysteries

Facebook: https://www.facebook.com/charlotte.stuart.mysterywriter

Goodreads: https://www.goodreads.com/author/show/19305587.
Charlotte_Stuart

Instagram: https://www.instagram.com/cstuartauthor/

BookBub: https://www.bookbub.com/authors/charlotte-stuart

Amazon author page: https://www.amazon.com/stores/Charlotte-Stuart/
author/B00GMQNV5C